HONOUR
BE DAMNED

Also by Tom Connery:
A SHRED OF HONOUR
HONOUR REDEEMED

HONOUR
BE DAMNED

A Markham of the Marines Novel

Tom Connery

Since 1947
REGNERY
PUBLISHING, INC.
An Eagle Publishing Company • Washington, DC

Library of Congress Cataloging-in-Publication Data

    Connery, Tom.
      Honour be damned : a Markham of the Marines novel / Tom Connery.
        p. cm.
      ISBN 0-89526-252-5
      I. Title

      PR6053.O483 H64 2000
      823'.914—dc21   00-020090

Published in the United States by
Regnery Publishing, Inc.
An Eagle Publishing Company
One Massachusetts Avenue, NW
Washington, DC 20001

Distributed to the trade by
National Book Network
4720-A Boston Way
Lanham, MD 20706

First published in Great Britain, by The Orion Publishing Group Ltd, London

Printed on acid-free paper
Manufactured in the United States of America

10 9 8 7 6 5 4 3 2 1

Books are available in quantity for promotional or premium use. Write to Director of Special Sales, Regnery Publishing, Inc., One Massachusetts Avenue, NW, Washington, DC 20001, for information on discounts and terms or call (202) 216-0600.

Chapter one

The weeks of bombardment, under a blazing summer sun had accustomed everyone to the boom of the cannon. So when the unexpected truce was called at noon the silence seemed unnatural. Despite the daily battering the walls of Calvi, the last French fortress in Corsica had not been breached. Yet artillery seemed the only way to break the defence.

Attempts at sapping across the narrow neck of rocky ground that separated the fortress from the main island had proved fruitless. Without an open breach into the town, crossing that narrow isthmus would impose a heavy a toll on the assaulting British soldiers. But in the face of determined opposition it might have to be attempted, the point from where the attack would commence just in front of the gun emplacements.

Lieutenant George Markham was, like the rest of his marine detachment, trying to find some shade behind the high sandbagged rampart of the Royal Louis Battery. Placed on a hilltop, and with the sun so high, it wasn't easy. The defenders had suffered less than their enemy from the month-long siege, though the artillerymen at this point, French royalists from Toulon, had inflicted great damage.

Yet with a *fleur-de-lis* flag standing proudly over their heads to attract counter battery fire, they'd sustained almost as much in return. And the fear that the defenders would sortie out to remove the studied insult of that flag had led to the deployment of these Lobsters to defend the position. Yet nothing like that had occurred, leaving the battle, until an hour before, looking very much like a stalemate.

The beat of the drum made Markham stand up. Crouched in the shade it had been hot. But the strength of the Corsican sun doubled that, seeming to scorch his skin through his scarlet coat, and to add a ton weight to the black broad-brimmed hat he'd adopted for the climate. Below he could see the two parties moving towards each other, one under the Union Flag, the other under a Tricolour.

I

Did those French negotiators have any notion of how depleted the besiegers had become? General Sir Charles Stuart, with the aid of Commodore Horatio Nelson, had landed two thousand troops two months before, only to find them assailed by every known disease as the siege wore on, until they could only muster half their total strength. And that was a situation deteriorating each day, as dysentery, typhoid fever and malaria took their toll.

Appeals to the Corsicans for the kind of help they'd previously provided had foundered on the endless inter-tribal warfare that seemed such a feature of island politics. The enemy, in that near formidable fortress, even if they laboured under furious bombardment, had shade and clean water. More importantly, they'd not previously been bivouacked in the swamps around Bastia, which had exposed the British soldiers to noxious vapours and hordes of biting insects.

'It is pleasant, without risking a wound, to be able to observe some of the effect of our shot, Lieutenant.'

Markham turned to look at the Comte de Puy, the captain who commanded the Royalist artillery. He was a slim, elegant man, of a rather melancholy disposition who, even under these torrid conditions, with not a breath of cooling wind, seemed not to perspire. He went so far in his sartorial maintenance that he wore a powdered wig underneath his lace-edged hat. And the white coat was as clean as his excellent linen. George Markham tried hard to keep himself smart. But in de Puy's presence, he generally felt like some kind of vagabond.

'They've rebuilt every stone we've dislodged, monsieur, more than once.'

'Yet the scars show, Lieutenant.'

He was right, of course. New mortar and hastily laid fresh stone lined the upper parapets. The defenders of Calvi were surrounded, and each face of the fortress, barring that which looked out to the deep blue sea, looked just as bruised. The repairs would not withstand too much in the way of pounding. But they were in the wrong places; high on the ramparts that held the French cannon. The besiegers had missed the vital spot, that weakness in the defences which, once broken, could not be swiftly reconstituted, the gap that would provide the breach infantrymen needed to effect entry to the citadel.

'The truce has been accepted?'

Both men turned to face the bemused newcomer, Markham

noticing fleetingly the looks of resentment flashing across the faces of his men. Monsignor Aramon was heartily disliked by his Lobsters, first for his arrogance, and secondly for his refusal to allow them the use of the nearby church as a place of shade and shelter.

The Basilica of the Madonna stood on the highest hill over-looking Calvi, and dominated the approach to the causeway. It was thick-walled and cool inside, standing above a spring that provided sweet cold water. Aramon, in typical priestly fashion, had denied it to the soldiers, on the ground that to use a sacred place as a military billet would defile it. The notion that as British marines they were heathens might be unspoken, but the Monsignor managed to convey it nonetheless.

At the same time he denied himself nothing. Aramon exuded comfort and well being, that smoothness which comes to a man who has not, for years, suffered any kind of real discomfort. He travelled with a retinue of three strapping servants, and a young lady that everyone supposed was his mistress, even if Aramon called himself her guardian. They, and the string of mules used to carry his possessions, had occupied a manor house on the lower slopes of the hill, well away from any chance of being upset by a stray French shell.

If the Monsignor depressed Markham and his Lobsters, that was nothing to the effect he had on the French captain. De Puy was regularly invited to dine, and always returned from such repasts in a silent, introspective mood. He was gloomy now as he responded to the Monsignor's question.

'It is a little less clear than that. It seems the French suggested this meeting, not General Stuart.'

'Then it is a trick,' Aramon spat.

Dark skinned, with heavy-lidded eyes and well-defined black eyebrows, he had no trouble appearing angry. In fact that was one of the two abiding traits he seemed determined to present to a world perceived as hostile.

'Why offer to treat when they have just declined General Stuart's offer of honourable surrender.'

Markham couldn't resist a jibe, given the way Aramon was forever castigating all supporters of the French Revolution as the spawn of the devil, from Robespierre and his godless Jacobins, right down to the defenders of Calvi.

'Perhaps they've had a revelation, Monsignor Aramon. And seen the light.'

That earned Markham a hearty dose of the second of Aramon's habitual expressions, wounded piety. 'It does you no good to mock, Lieutenant. A session in the confessional might be of more benefit to such a damaged soul.'

Markham didn't hold the clergyman's gaze, since he suspected the dark brown eyes had the ability to see into his innermost self. Did he somehow know that George Markham, the illegitimate son of a Protestant general, had been raised in a Catholic household? Had he in some way betrayed a secret he never referred to by some inadvertent gesture. De Puy covered his momentary confusion by seeking to explain to the Monsignor the particular rules that governed proper warfare.

Markham listened, wondering what it was that connected this pair. De Puy was not, by trade, an artilleryman. He was from one of the best of the Bourbon cavalry regiments. Serving in Toulon, he'd been evacuated with the British fleet. These gunners, also evacuees, had lacked an officer, and de Puy had taken on that role, relying heavily on his sergeant, who knew so much more than he did, to work the guns. Aramon had arrived when the siege was under way, just before the Lobsters had taken up their posting, and Markham had the distinct impression that he had deliberately sought out de Puy.

It was while he was speaking that the horseman detached himself from General Stuart's party, and rode back towards the nearest gun position. Whatever message he imparted to the gunners produced a ragged cheer, one that was taken up as the news was passed from battery to battery. It arrived at the Royal Louis Battery in due course, the increasing sound having brought all of Markham's men to their feet.

'Fifteen days without succour,' came the cry. The rasping sound that the men on the position emitted, both French and British, owed as much to thirst as to joy.

'Explain!' barked Aramon, to a clearly delighted de Puy.

That brought a hint of blood to the Royalist officer's pallid cheeks, an acknowledgement that he was not accustomed to being addressed in such a fashion. But either out of deference to the cloth, a fear of damnation, or just good manners he responded calmly.

'It means that the enemy cannot sustain the defence.'

'Why?'

Markham could see de Puy biting his lip slightly to contain himself, and prayed that the polite veneer would crack, and that the cavalryman would give this nosy, interfering cleric a piece of his mind. Disappointingly, it didn't.

'That, Monsignor Aramon, they will not impart to us. It could be many things. A pestilence, just a lack of defenders, the consternation of being unable to repair the walls, or a shortage of food or ammunition.'

'Or it could be that God has struck fear into their hearts.'

'It could be,' de Puy replied, in a weary tone of voice that showed just how much he valued that notion. 'What is certain is this. That if in the next two weeks the defenders do not receive any outside assistance, unlikely in a sea so well patrolled by the British navy, then they will lay down their arms and evacuate Calvi.'

'Do I have your permission to leave the battery, Monsieur le Comte?' The Frenchman turned to face Markham. 'With my men, of course.'

'You will leave the place undefended,' protested Aramon. 'Might I remind you that my residence is no more than a few hundred metres from this very spot.'

That interference finally cracked de Puy's carefully controlled demeanour. He positively snapped at Aramon. 'There are certain matters that are the province of the church, Monsignor. But this is not one of them.'

'It's much cooler down by the shore, Monsieur,' Markham continued hastily, cutting off Aramon's irate response. 'And my men can get out of their uniforms and perhaps bathe in the sea.'

De Puy pointedly ignored the grunt from the priest as he surveyed the scene beneath their position. Out on the causeway, the talking continued, a civilised discussion, with the parties now seated, their conversations aided by the provision from both sides of food and wine. On the lower batteries, gunners, soldiers and sailors, who until now had never raised an eyebrow above the parapets for fear of shot, were standing on the sandbags waving and dancing.

'The enemy will not break the truce without prior notice,' Markham insisted.

'You would trust those apostates? Men with no soul who have denied God!'

De Puy, to whom this outburst was aimed, threw a quick glance

5

at Aramon, a slightly defiant look in his eye, before answering Markham.

'They will give us at least twelve hours notice before renewing hostilities. Besides, we would know well before that if any ships had got through. Therefore your request is granted.'

'Sergeant Rannoch,' Markham called. 'Get the men ready to move down to the shore.'

He turned as he said this, aware of the looks, part pleasure, part anxiety on the faces of his dozen Lobsters. Like marines everywhere, they saw any change in circumstances as some kind of threat, as well as a possible opportunity for relief.

Not Rannoch! His bright red face was creased by a huge grin that showed clearly the places where the unrelenting heat had cracked his lips. Huge of frame, with his hair bleached near white by the sun, he looked more than ever like a Viking. And even with a bone-dry throat, his voice was strong as he called on the men to fall in.

'Light order, sergeant,' Markham continued. 'We'll leave our packs here.'

'Does that mean we're coming back,' asked Corporal Halsey, in a dispirited tone.

Markham smiled at the old marine, grey haired and the daddy of his unit, normally the steadiest of men. If he moaned, it didn't take a genius to guess what the others thought of this posting. That thought nagged at him constantly, that feeling he could never quite rid himself of, that his command of these men was some mistake. The differences were less obvious now. But it surfaced occasionally that half of his men were soldiers rather than proper marines. Markham turned to salute de Puy. But the motion to raise his hat died when he noticed the look of near despair on the Frenchman's face, as he listened to the whispered lecture he was receiving from Aramon.

If anything it was hotter on the heavily wooded slopes than it had been on the top of the hill, a sticky heat that not even shade could lessen. But by the time they reached the shoreline it was late afternoon. With the intensity gone out of the sun they were blessed by the beginnings of a northerly breeze, one that was cooled by its proximity to the water. The beach was piled with stores, and littered with tents, the fascines which had been used to haul up the guns running from the edge of the water to the thick scrub that covered the lower parts of the hills. There in the shade lay butts full of lukewarm water, from which everyone drank greedily.

News of the truce had preceded them, creating a carnival atmosphere. Yet Markham was amazed at how few of the Army officers had followed his example and brought their men to the shore to cool off. Rannoch, having ensured that the men stood their muskets correctly, was quick to get his coat and boots off then wade into the water, there to join both officer and men as they splashed about wildly.

Only one marine didn't partake. Eboluh Bellamy, being a Negro, scoffed at the heat that so affected his fellow marines. And he had an abiding fear of anything other than fresh water, convinced from his Caribbean upbringing that every shark in the world would foregather as soon as he chanced a toe.

Markham swam out, away from his men. None of them would willingly venture into a depth that barred their feet from touching the bottom, even the pair that could stay afloat in water. After weeks of being mewed up in close proximity, the solitude was, in itself, welcome. Occasionally he dived as far as he could, feeling the temperature cool as he went deeper, sucking the heat from a body that seemed to have been boiling for weeks.

Returning to the surface for the fifth time, he saw the dark shape of the approaching boat through the clear water. Markham hauled sideways to take himself away from the arc of the oars. His head, bobbing out of the water, brought forth a startled cry from the thwarts and a hasty command to boat oars, that followed by a laugh as the Captain being transported ashore recognised the soaking apparition.

'Damn me, Markham, you frightened young Mr Hoste here half to death.'

Recognition of the voice helped, since Nelson had a bandage covering one half of his face. Markham knew he'd suffered a wound, hardly surprising since the man was never far from the action. But he'd heard that it was slight. The bandage made him wonder if that information had been disseminated to keep up morale. The midshipman in charge of the boat looked even worse, the yellowish tinge to his skin an indication that he was exceedingly ill.

'I trust I find you well, sir?' Markham replied, treading water until the absurd formality of the remark, more suited to a drawing room, made him duck his head under the surface.

7

'You find me alarmed, man,' Nelson replied when he resurfaced. 'I am all for a sail over the side to cool the hands, but this larking about in ten-fathom water is hazardous.'

'How is the eye?' the swimmer asked, too bored by constant repetition to explain the benefits of deep-sea swimming.

'It does nicely, Markham, and I'm obliged by your concern. Don't be fooled by this swaddling cloth. My surgeon insisted I wear it to keep out the glare from the sun on the water. I shall whip it off ashore.'

Nelson smiled, and even with his face half bandaged it had real warmth. 'Can we offer you rescue from the wiles of Neptune.'

'Thank you sir, no. I shall return the way I came.'

'Then you must have gills, sir,' Nelson replied, looking towards the shoreline and squinting through his good eye. 'And you must scarce be human. Haul away Mr Hoste, lest we be beaten to the beach by this amphibian.'

The whey-faced youngster gave the order in a weak voice, which earned him a concerned look from his captain. But Nelson said nothing as the barge began to gather speed, the swimmer trailing in its wake. Vaguely, as he swam, Markham was aware that the barge had grounded, and that Nelson had set off up the beach with a small party to escort him.

Markham stood up as his feet found the bottom, his first glance aimed towards his own men, all standing soaking wet to take full advantage of the evening breeze. Then his eye was drawn by a slight commotion near Nelson's barge, with several fingers pointing to a spot behind his head. Turning, Markham saw the flags streaming from the masthead of *Agamemnon*, obviously conveying to those on the shore an important message. Whatever it was, it was a complete mystery to a man who'd only become a Lieutenant of Marines by the merest fluke.

One of the Agamemnons waded out towards him, his request that he come by the barge jumbled in his excitement. Markham obliged, to find the midshipman called Hoste sat on the counter, bent over. The youngster roused himself, the strain on his yellowing face ample evidence of how much effort that required.

'You have seen the signal, Lieutenant Markham?'

'I have,' Markham replied, without adding that it meant nothing to him.

'Then you will appreciate the gravity of the situation, given the nature of the truce the French had agreed.'

The simplest thing would have been to say no, to admit that all flags of whatever arrangement were incomprehensible. He knew that was probably true of half the officers in the navy as well, since few he'd met sought out the duties of reading signals. But he couldn't do it, since to publicly admit his ignorance would only underline his unfitness for his post. And it would be a tale to spread, another potential insult to add to those he knew were already whispered, behind his back, by men who despised him.

'Is it so grave?' he replied, temporising.

'Of course it is, sir,' the boy gasped.

In his eye, Markham could see that look. The shame of his past was no secret to any British officer, army or navy, serving in the Mediterranean. The prominence of his actions, well received as they should have been, had only brought attention upon his chequered history. The least emotion he felt his presence engendered was resentment. But in some cases it was upped to actual hatred by officers who considered it demeaning to serve alongside a known coward.

'If those ships get unscathed into Calvi harbour, then the truce will cease to hold.'

'Ships!' Markham expostulated, managing to make it sound like a statement instead of a question.

'Without succour,' Hoste replied, trying to haul himself to his feet. In this he had to be aided by two pigtailed sailors, who made no attempt in their glares to hide how much they blamed Markham for the boy's condition. 'That is what the truce says. Those three small vessels are succour, sir, and we do not know any more about what they carry than we do about what the defenders of Calvi lack.'

No genius was required to deduce what young Hoste was implying. General Stuart had asked the French to accept terms from the weakness of his own position, not theirs. It was, in fact, a bluff. Illness was decimating his numbers daily, and if the siege continued, he would soon be forced to raise it for lack of men to even properly man his guns. Markham and his men had been lucky, posted high above the malodorous *macchia* that some of the other batteries had occupied. And even if they'd had to fetch it in cow-skin bags, they'd had access to the clean water from the church well.

'You will observe, sir, that the breeze is northerly,' Hoste

9

continued, 'so that even if our ships get under way they will have to beat up into the wind. I fear we will not close the gap in time.'

'Commodore Nelson.'

'Is right up at the siegeworks, sir,' Hoste gasped, rubbing a hand across his sweating brow. He patently thought Markham was prevaricating. 'We have no time to consult him or the officers aboard *Agamemnon*. We must seize the moment and act ourselves. You have the marines, and I have the sailors to get them to where they can have an effect.'

'A boat attack?'

Markham hadn't meant to sound surprised.

'It is a tricky notion in open water,' Hoste agreed, a weak hand rubbing his sweating brow. 'But perhaps if we can put a volley of musketry across their decks they will turn away.'

'And if they don't?'

'Then we must board them.'

'You, young sir, will do no such thing.'

'I . . .'

Hoste got no further, his feeble protest cut off by Markham's bellow to his sergeant. Rannoch didn't even move to enquire what was afoot. He merely yelled in turn at the men to get their coats on and their muskets off the stand, before leading them at a run towards a boat already floating into the water.

'Mr Hoste, try to get a message to the Commodore, but under no circumstances are you to attempt to deliver it yourself.'

'I must come with you, sir, to steer the boat.'

That was sophistry of a high order, since there were ample sailors available to man the tiller.

'I freely admit to being a nautical novice, Mr Hoste, but even I can point a boat northwards so close to the shore.' Markham didn't like saying what came next, but it was necessary to stop a brave young man who would not admit that in the boat he would be no more than a liability. 'I am giving you an order, which you will disobey at your peril.'

The weakness of the 'sir' was heartrending. But Markham couldn't indulge in sentiment, he didn't have time. His men had piled into the boat, joining an equal number of sailors, and he had to run out into the water to catch up. It was only then he realised he himself had neither coat nor weapons. And it was doubly galling to see the grin on the black gleaming face of Eboluh Bellamy as he handed them to him.

'As Patroclus armed Achilles,' the Negro said, his refined voice adding an extra degree of impertinence to the classical Homeric allusion, 'I am here to arm you.'

'Row!' he barked at the sailors, the Irish accent made strong by passion and resentment, 'as if we are faced by the hobs of hell.'

Chapter two

Rowing a boat into the increasing wind, and the choppy sea it was throwing up, was no easy matter. But at least it had the advantage of forward motion, which was more than could be said for the warships struggling to make sail. The breeze, for them, was dead foul, which would mean a long tack out to sea before they could come round the headland and cut off the northern approach to the Calvi anchorage. The officers on board must have been aware of that, but with most of their ships' boats occupied in the duties of onshore re-supply, there was precious little they could do about it.

A couple, full of sailors, had got away, a crowded jolly boat from *Agamemnon* and a cutter from the escorting frigate, *Diomede*. But they were in deeper, rougher water than Markham, and further out the headwind was even more telling. What was plain, judging by the commotion in the crosstrees, was that whatever was approaching from the north was in view. A host of flags had been run up *Agamemnon*'s mast, emphasised with a gun, that Markham half suspected were aimed at passing information to him. If that was true, they were wasting their time. Not one of the sailors aboard could read signals, and even if they could, they were too busy rowing to bother.

It was a good fifteen minutes before he could see from his elevation what they had identified from the warships' upper masts. Three sets of topsails, not square and white like those to their rear, but triangular and red, the peak of each surmounted by a tricolour pennant whipping forward on the wind. Barring the flags, there was a familiarity to the shape; a sensation that increased as Markham saw more of their sails. He had seen any number of such rigs since arriving in the Mediterranean, on the kind of small cargo ships which abounded, especially close inshore.

'Tarantines!' he exclaimed suddenly.

Markham had feared a well armed ship carrying great guns, one he'd be forced to attack because he had no option, an opponent who would blow the barge out of the water before they even got close. But a Tarantine was a different case. In a small arms duel, he would back his Lobsters against anyone, even firing from a bobbing boat.

One by one the men facing him finished checking their muskets, flints and ammunition. Not that there was much chance of the weapons being unready. Rannoch, the slow-talking Highlander, was a real stickler regarding the use and the maintenance of the Brown Bess. A crack shot himself, he had pushed at an open door when he sought to persuade Markham of the value of well aimed fire.

Both officer and NCO had gone to great lengths to drill the men in good musketry. Each stock had been adjusted in length and shape to suit the user, while Rannoch insisted on sights being fitted at all times. Reloading had been cut from nearly two minutes in the worst cases to an almost uniform twenty-five seconds. But most of all, the Scotsman carried with him a mould to cast balls that actually fitted the barrels, a rarity in the British forces. And he'd trained them with an ample supply of powder until nearly every man could keep his eyes open when, right by his cheek, the flash went off in the pan.

As they progressed, more and more of the Calvi anchorage became visible. Markham cast a wary eye over the two French frigates anchored head and stern presenting, under the fortress cannon, a formidable defence that made any notion of cutting them out akin to suicide. They were in range, if the French wanted to try a broadside, relying on weight of shot rather than any accuracy.

But he could see little activity on deck, nor any sign that either the ships or the garrison were intent on sending out any form of assistance to the approaching cargo ships. Looking back, he could also observe how far ahead he was of any assistance from his own side. He had one boat and twelve armed marines, plus any sailor who fancied joining in a boarding operation. Not much to stop three vessels, even if they could only muster a pistol between them.

'Put up your helm,' he said to the man on the tiller.

The order earned him a long enquiring look. Markham, momentarily confused, pointed with his right arm, and said, as the word 'larboard' failed to surface in his mind, 'I want to go that way, to get across their entry to the anchorage.'

The look his ignorance produced nearly earned the sailor a

rebuke, but he bit off his anger. Dressed as he was, smart of coat, with a long greased and beribboned pigtail, the man on the tiller was a member of Nelson's barge crew. That would make him a cut above the average, a handy man in a fight, given that the officer he served was never out of the action. The sailor was a man to consult, not reprimand.

'Name?'

'Brownlee, your honour.'

'Well, Mr Brownlee,' said Markham, waving airily at the Tarantines, now hull up and in plain view. 'I can't see any way to stop them on our own, lest we block the entrance and hope they shy off.'

'Makes sense, your honour,' the sailor replied. 'But they's bound to see them other boats that's on the way. Even if they's well off, they will come into play afore it be dark.'

'I'd appreciate any suggestions you might have.'

That brought forth a surprised reaction, hastily masked. Brownlee wasn't used to being consulted. But then he wasn't used to being in the presence of an officer prepared not only to demonstrate ignorance, but also to admit it.

'We'll never stop them all. One will suffice. If we can halt a second, happen by ramming or the like, it will be nowt but a bonus.' Brownlee paused for a second, before adding, 'Best head for one and try and take it, your honour. At least under sail we'd have more chance of adding a mite of extra damage.'

Markham nodded. Whatever they achieved, it would cut the supply to Calvi garrison, and that had to be a good thing. Unbidden, it came into his mind words that Nelson was fond of using, an expression he had inherited from a much-admired older sea officer.

'Then you oblige me, Mr Brownlee, by using your knowledge to select a target, then lay me alongside the enemy.'

That made Brownlee grin. No doubt heard the very same words himself from the lips of the Commodore. 'Ain't no doubt to it, your honour. Whichever one's got lead position is the one we're after.'

That was followed by a string of personal orders, to named individuals, all delivered in an even, friendly voice, as he adjusted the tiller. If the speed of the barge picked up as a result, it was not something Markham could discern. But Brownlee had clearly identified certain faults, since their progress seemed smoother.

Craning his neck round, Markham could see the lead Tarantine, easy to identify because of a recent repair to the mainsail. With a small crew, seeking maximum speed, most of the men would be employed. But there were a few in the bows, looking anxiously towards them and ready with an array of muskets and pistols.

'I want to get off a volley of musketry across their deck before we close them.'

'Then we'd best boat our oars, your honour, to make it like smoother. The question is how near do you want it to be.'

'Very close, Brownlee. One volley with just enough time to reload for a second before we board.'

'Saving your presence, lieutenant. Might it not be better if we Agamemnons were to try to board first, us being more used to ships than Lobsters, especially them who's been ashore for weeks.'

'Weapons?'

'Your lads could spare us their bayonets.'

'Boats coming out, Jack, armed cutters.'

Markham followed Brownlee's gaze, and saw the two heavily laden boats heading out from Calvi. There was something odd about them, but he lacked the clear view to see, especially since they seemed so low in the water. Then the lead cutter lifted on a wave, and the snout of the cannon protruding over the bows was silhouetted against the flannel shirts of the men in the thwarts.

'Four pounders, looks like, Jack.'

'You mind to your oar,' Brownlee snapped.

His head was turning right and forward as he calculated their rate of progress, against that of the barge and the fast approaching Tarantines. He continued that as he spoke, never once looking at the marine officer sitting in front of him.

'They would have had those rigged to ward off any cutting out capers Old Nellie might spring.'

'How much of a threat are they?'

'We can get alongside well afore they can do 'owt to stop us, your honour. But when they get close, they can sink us easy, be we in the barge or on that there Tarantines deck. A four-pounder ball will go through that kind of hull, easy as warm cheese. As for the barge, it don't need to strike too hard to have it fall apart strake by strake.'

'Then let's pray we're on the Tarantines deck, Brownlee. Because we'll be standing on the supplies they need to keep up the siege. Somehow I don't think they'll be too quick to put any shot into that.'

Markham half turned, amazed that the lead boat was now so close. Their speed across the bay had seemed lamentable, with the target they were aiming to intercept rarely appearing to come any nearer. Now the combined speed of oar and sail had closed the gap so that the men in the Tarantines bows were in plain view. They had their weapons up to take aim, the muzzles swaying in a circle that stood testimony to the unsteadiness of their platform. The other pair seemed to have slowed, spilling a little wind from the sails, content to let the lead vessel take whatever it was their British attackers had in mind.

'Sergeant Rannoch. The men will pass their bayonets into the lap of the sailor nearest to them! Brownlee here will then give the command to boat oars. As soon as they are raised, I want that deck of that ship cleared with a volley.'

Rannoch replied in that slow way of his, that lilting highland tone which so annoyed Markham when he was, himself, keyed up.

'It will not be a task simple to put in an accurate volley from a bobbing about boat, especially being sat down.'

'Then Dornan and Bellamy should do great damage.' Markham snapped.

The former, a ponderous, well-meaning dimwit, was the worst shot in his command. Eboluh Bellamy, the only black marine Markham had ever come across, was a recent addition, and one who'd failed to respond well to training. A cunning naval commander had foisted the Negro, educated and proud of it, on Markham. The officer was happy to rid himself of a man who, by merely speaking, could cause so much trouble between his decks. Bellamy hated ignorance as much as he hated firing a musket. That was something he carried out with eyes firmly shut, never even attempting to take aim.

Rannoch didn't respond to that jibe. He merely confirmed his superiority in a certain area by instructing the men to aim their weapons at the ship's rail, reminding them that the combined recoil of a dozen muskets, acting on an unstable boat, would be likely to lift every Brown Bess barrel at once.

The water around the stern suddenly showed small spurts, as musket and pistol balls sprayed the top of a wave. Markham reckoned they were as much at risk as if they had faced the best shots in the French army. With the rise and fall of the Tarantine, and being shot at, probably, by people of indifferent skill, luck would play a great part in any hit they secured. That dependence of fortune induced a very odd feeling.

Suddenly Brownlee swung the tiller and shouted his command, Rannoch's order to aim so swift as seem part of the word. The larboard side oars rose sharply and evenly, as befitted the men who rowed a senior captain. Markham felt the seawater from the nearest oar on his face as he turned to see the volley.

Those Lobsters on the starboard side had aimed their muskets through the gaps of their larboard side comrades, presenting an even row of muzzles that would have look fine on any parade ground. It certainly looked threatening to those armed opponents, who gave up any idea of reloading their own weapons and ducked below the rail as the guns went off.

Markham grabbed the side of the barge to steady himself as the boat dipped to starboard, an action halted by the rowers on that side laying their blades flat on the water. Apart from two balls which clipped the rail itself, sending up a shower of splinters, and another that went through the sail well aft, it was impossible to see the final effect of the volley. But it must have been close enough to frighten the defenders, since not one put his head or a weapon above the side of the ship as Markham's men reloaded. Brownlee, close by, was issuing a string of orders; to get some way back on the barge and close the Tarantine.

'I will go first,' Markham said, a remark which got the coxswain's undivided attention. He opened his mouth to speak, but the marine lieutenant was looking into his eyes, seeing there what he'd half suspected; that even amongst the lower deck of a ship he'd never served on, his name and reputation were common knowledge. If Brownlee had intended to protest, to point out his own superior skill in that direction, the words died on his lips in the face of Markham's cold stare.

'Aye, aye, sir.'

'Rannoch, the tars are boarding first, behind me. Detail some-one to keep the boat hooked on, then as soon as we are aboard follow us onto the deck. Shoot anyone who looks like causing us trouble, but I want every weapon loaded as quick as possible, to be pointing over the larboard rail at those armed cutters coming our way. If you think you can hit anyone yourself, to discourage them, you have my permission to try.'

Markham felt his broad-brimmed hat go at the very second that the crack of the ball passed his ear. He ducked even when he knew, as an experienced soldier, that it was too late, to be handed his hat by Brownlee, who'd caught it, expertly, on the wing before it hit the water. He threw it into the bottom of the boat, and eased out both his pistol and his sword.

The side of the ship was now close, the sinking western sun sending shards of bright light out where it caught the gaudy paintwork. Markham began to raise himself into a crouch, from which he could spring for the side, now lined with a dozen heads, which barring the man on the wheel was probably every sailor on the ship.

His pistol was inaccurate at the best of times; with him unsteady its discharge did no more than drive a few heads away from the rail. But that gave him his gap, and as the barge crashed into the side of the Tarantine he leapt for the rail, screaming hoarsely, and swung his sword in a huge arc that would decapitate anyone who decided to reconsider their earlier withdrawal. The Tarantine had a low freeboard, and the barge had hit on the rise, either through luck or Brownlee's skill. But he was wearing boots, and though he got one hand on the rail, he failed to get any purchase with his feet.

Two things saved him from either a drubbing or a pike in the chest, the most telling being the screeching Agamemnons. They first used their oars to sweep the rail, then followed that up with a mad barefoot rush, bayonets in their teeth, that took them up the ship's side like squirrels, on to the deck. Occupied with that, no one had time to despatch the struggling officer. The second factor was the man below, even more vital, who got his hands under the scrabbling boots, and heaved Markham up with such force that he flew over the Tarantine's side to land in a heap on the deck.

Markham started rolling as soon as he made contact with the planking, unaware if he was under threat, but sure that movement was safer than being stationary. His action nearly did for one of the Agamemnons, since his rolling body took the man's legs away, leaving him at the mercy of the Frenchman he'd being grappling with. Ignoring the scarlet-coated figure at his feet, the man leant forward, club in hand, to brain the boarder. Markham's sword swept up as the club swung, taking the crewman from underneath, at the point where his arm joined his breast, nearly severing the whole shoulder with the force of the blow. The club was dropped, and a British bayonet swept past Markham's ear to finish the job.

The words 'Bless you, you useless bugger,' were just an

18

accompaniment to the help he received in getting to his feet. Once up, Markham could pick his targets, jabbing forward with his sword to pin men struggling to overcome some Agamemnon. Behind him his lobsters were struggling aboard. The single gunshot came from Rannoch, and took out the man on the wheel, causing the Tarantine to suddenly jibe sideways as the way came off the rudder. The sail cracked and flapped wildly, as slowly and steadily the boarding party drove the defenders back. The deck was slippery with blood, and Markham could see that quite a few of the Agamemnons had wounds. But that did little to interfere with their relentless advance, as jabbing, punching and gouging, blood afire, they drove back their enemy.

The boom of the four-pounder cannon, if it was designed to aid the defender, had the opposite effect, driving from them any desire to sustain the fight. Their arms dropped just before their knees, as they pleaded to be allowed to live. The British sailors then performed a remarkable transformation, from blind bloodlust to jovial celebration in the twinkling of an eye, though taking care to remove any weapons from their enemies which might pose a threat. Brownlee had already taken the wheel, and got some way back on the ship, as the original crew were herded below.

Behind Markham, in strict obedience to his orders, Rannoch had lined up the Lobsters, and as his officer approached, was himself crouched down with his barrel pointing over the prow, taking careful aim on the leading cutter. In the bows of that, Markham could see three men struggling in the confined space to reload, a blue-coated officer calling instructions. At no more than a hundred yards, Rannoch's shot did not kill him, as it would have almost certainly done on dry land. But it caught him in the upper thigh of his right leg, sending him spinning in amongst his boat crew.

The Highlander didn't even linger long enough to see the effect of his shot. He was too busy reloading himself. He had his musket back over the ship's rail in twenty seconds, squinting to take aim on the men in the bows of the second cutter. This was standing a little further off, prepared to take on the boats coming in from the British warships as well as aiding the assault on the now captured Tarantine. A quick glance over the stern established that the other two cargo ships had practically halted in the water, backing and filling, unsure whether to proceed or retreat. Behind him Rannoch kept up a steady fire, each shot accompanied by a curse as he missed whatever it was he'd aimed at.

'Brownlee, can you put us about to threaten those other ships.'

'I can, your honour,' he replied, following that with another stream of concise instructions to secure the prisoners then man the sails. George Markham hadn't spent much time on ships, but he had rarely seen a man handle responsibility better. The progress of the action was now his to command. Until he got them close enough to threaten another ship, Markham and his Lobsters were playing second fiddle.

That at least allowed the luxury of time to assess the situation. The sun was going, leaving him with no more than an hour of fading light. Nelson's ships had beat out to sea, *Diomede* well ahead of *Agamemnon*. But even a totally inexperienced eye could see that they would never come round quickly enough on the other tack to close the entrance to Calvi anchorage. Their cutter and the crowded jolly boat were still pulling towards them, but faced, as they would be with at least one gunboat, he doubted that they could do much to aid him. In the French cutter that had fired the shot, the crew seemed more intent on tending to their wounded officer than continuing the action. So his task was simple, even if he was left to his own devices to undertake its execution.

'Mr Brownlee, we must drive those ships away from the shore by whatever means we possess, and allow our frigates time to close the entrance to the anchorage. With night falling, what will they do?'

'They must enter in daylight, your honour. Even with beacons well lit on the fortress, no captain would risk his ship on such a rocky shore in the dark.'

That reasoning must have made equal sense to them. Practically before Brownlee had finished speaking they brought their heads round and filled their sails on the steady northern breeze to close with the land. Markham smiled. He had possession of a third of the available re-supply, and with Brownlee at the wheel he thought he could double that. Without succour was a term to be decided by the French commander, but he doubted if one Tarantine carried enough of anything to materially alter the nature of the siege.

'How we doing, your honour?' asked Halsey, stood to close by, staring over the rail at the stationary cutters.

'I doubt you'll have to go back to the Royal Louis Battery, Halsey.'

Quinlan, the skinny Londoner spoke up, his voice full of venom. 'Does that mean we'll never have to suffer that effing priest again?'

'Stuck up sod,' added his best friend, Ettrick. 'Though the Crapaud Colonel was a proper gent.'

Markham smiled and ignored them, addressing his calls to Brownlee. 'We must make sure of one of them. If we try to take both we could fail. Get me alongside one by whatever means.'

Markham was suddenly tired and very thirsty. He lifted the ladle from the water butt by the companionway and drank greedily. But whatever else he felt, he was content. They had done well, better than he'd expected, and could look forward to completing an action that would make every naval officer jealous. It would certainly be one in the eye for those who saw fit to condescend to him.

Chapter three

The boom of the cannon, and the crack as the single mainmast split, seemed almost simultaneous. Slowly, agonisingly, it began to topple sideways, the rending of wood accompanied by the snapping of ropes through the warm evening air. It was hard to believe when Markham spun round to look, that the nearest cutter, a few seconds before intent on treating their officer's condition, could have fired the shot.

But they had, a fact that was very obvious as the smoke cleared from the muzzle, and the glee of the man who'd aimed the piece spread to his companions. The officer Rannoch had hit, was sitting up again, bloody leg bandaged, pointing his sword, and seemingly encouraging his boat crew to repeat the exercise.

Brownlee was calling out commands again, his men rushing around, looking for axes to cut the debris clear. With the sail removed, Markham had no trouble in seeing the other Tarantines, their sails aloft straining on the wind as they sought to pass by him at a safe distance.

'Yon cutter is closing in,' called Rannoch. 'They will be fashioning a shot for our hull next.'

The remark cleared Markham's thinking, mainly because he knew the sergeant to be wrong. They would not hull the ship, though they might try to make the threat look real. That wounded officer, who'd probably directed the lucky shot that had taken away the mast, must have ordered his men to fire high deliberately. The last thing he wanted to see was any of the available supplies to the garrison slipping beneath the waves, even if in doing so it took some of the British besiegers with it.

The next shot hit the water and bounced into the straking well clear of the sea. With some of the force absorbed by the deflection, the ball was too weak to pierce the side, instead embedding itself in the wood, sending a shudder through the whole frame of the vessel. The broken mast was cut free almost at the same moment, which caused the Tarantine to keel over to the opposite side, throwing several of his Lobsters onto their knees.

The next cannon boom came from the second cutter, and was aimed at the other boats still trying to close the gap with the stranded boarding party. It hit close enough to send up a huge fountain of water, which drenched the men in the jolly boat. It was admirable the way that it didn't deter them from coming on. In fact, they seemed to be increasing their efforts to come to his aid.

Markham knew that the men aboard were looking at him, awaiting clear orders. He was in an agony of indecision. On land he felt he would have acted quickly. But the sea was not his element, and the variations that were possible presented too much of a mystery. He shot down the companionway, just as much to get away from those stares, as to find out what kind of cargo the ship was carrying.

Hair awry, sword out, with blood on his face from the fighting on deck, his appearance in the *glim* from a single guttering lantern made the downcast prisoners, sat in a circle, recoil. The questions he asked fired off in rapid and fluent French, got a response before any of the speakers realised that silence would have served their country better.

The captain had been on the wheel, killed by a musket ball as the redcoats came aboard. All three ships were laden with flour and barrels of salted meats, food for the Calvi garrison. They knew nothing of negotiations to end the siege, their arrival seemingly fortuitous rather than planned. The information didn't aid George Markham's thinking very much. If anything the heat and stench in the cramped 'tween decks made it harder to draw cogent conclusions. But that changed as he hit the fresh air, and he observed the two other Tarantines had now drawn abreast, and were heading into the arc of safety created by the fortress guns.

Both cannons boomed again, the ball from the nearest flying uselessly overhead. The other was more telling, landing close enough to one of the frigate's boats to make it change to a safer course. Yet Markham knew those sailors would come on, and wondered to what purpose; to support him in an action he couldn't win. If the armed French cutter had wanted to sink the ship, they would have begun the process by now, and he would have been in no position to oppose it. Therefore it was obvious that they wanted both vessel and cargo, so his job was to deny them that.

'Brownlee, is there any way to get the boats coming to our aid to sheer off?'

That threw the coxswain, who until now had answered every request put to him with heartening speed.

'The next thing I need to know is how to sink this damned ship.'

'Sink her?'

'Yes. We'll get everybody back in the barge, and smash a hole in her hull.'

'That'll take an age your honour. If you want her destroyed, best way is to torch the bugger. And the flames would stand as the signal you want to send to our boats.'

'Lash off the wheel, Brownlee, then tell me how long you need to set your fires.'

'Don't take more'n a few minutes to torch a ship. All I need do is find a bit of turps or oil.'

'Then get on with it. Set light to some of the damaged rigging first to signal our boats to haul off. Sergeant Rannoch! Sustained volley fire on each cutter in turn if you please.'

'We will not hit much on this swell. That ball that hit the officer was luck.'

'I just want them convinced we intend to make a fight for it. Brownlee and his men are going to start a fire in the holds. We will be back in the barge and well clear before it takes hold.'

'What about the Crapaud prisoners, 'tween decks?' called one of the sailors.

'They will come with us.'

Any response was delayed by the discharge of Rannoch's first salvo, which peppered the water around the French cutter, without doing any harm at all to the occupants.

'That barge'll be a mite crowded your honour. How the hell are we going to row back to *Agamemnon* with that number on board.'

The question stopped everyone for just a second, including the Lobsters reloading the muskets, as even the most feeble brain registered that so close to those armed cutters, there was no way they would get clear, and that they were sinking this ship before surrendering themselves into captivity.

'Don't harm so much as a hair on them Crapauds' heads,' said

Brownlee to his men, as he hurried them back to their tasks. 'Or it'll be us that pays when they get us into their dungeons.'

There was nothing to go aloft on to set alight. What rigging remained was hanging loose, mostly over the side. Brownlee poured some oil onto a skein of tangled ropes, and taking the flint from the binnacle locker, set a spark to it. Dry from the high Mediterranean temperatures, it caught quickly, flaring up in seconds, brighter than expected in the gathering gloom.

'Cutter is manning his oars, your honour,' called Rannoch. That was followed immediately by a second salvo, at the tail of which came a high-pitched scream which echoed across the water, evidence that at least one ball had found it's target.

'I'll wager he is,' murmured Markham to himself. His attention was concentrated on the other British boats, and he was gratified to see the speed with which they responded to the fire, and put up their helms to head into an area of greater safety.

'I have to get the Crapaud prisoners up on deck, your honour?' said Brownlee.

'Make it so.' Markham replied, softly, before calling out to his own men. 'Sergeant Rannoch, one more salvo to keep them at bay, then get the men into the barge.'

The volley followed within a second. So did the arrival of the French prisoners. They had smelled the first hint of smoke, and had no doubt guessed what the cursed *rosbifs* were up to. Nothing scared a sailor more than a shipboard fire, and these men were no exception. The first hint of what Brownlee was doing came up the companionway behind them, a whiff of a newly lit fire, and the oily fumes that it generated. The sailor wasn't far behind.

'Be blazing end to end in ten minutes, your honour.'

'Get your men into the barge. My Lobsters will follow you.' Markham turned and stabbed with his sword, to cut away a piece of ragged white cloth from the back of the dead captain. 'And Brownlee, you will need to hoist this. I don't want our wounded friend yonder to take a shot at us, claiming it was too dark to see.'

'He won't be a happy man, an' that's no error.'

A *Sous Lieutenant*, he was not only angry, he was in great pain from the wound in his leg. That rendered his acceptance of Markham's sword far from gracious. It was, like his men's muskets, grabbed unceremoniously from his hand. This was followed by curt orders to the French sailors to take over the oars, and to keep an eye on those with whom they'd so recently traded places.

The other cutter had joined them, now that the frigate's boats were out of sight in the darkness, and both took station on either side of Nelson's barge to escort them in. Once clear of the burning wreckage, it was necessary to light torches in the bows, so that the captured *rosbifs* could be kept under observation. It was in that state that they rowed past the silent French warships, hats held firmly on to deflect the gobbets of spit that were aimed in their direction.

The party waiting for them on the quayside included more senior officers, soldiers rather than sailors. The introductions between the men of rank were formal and polite. Markham's request that his men, both sailors and lobsters be treated with gentility was acknowledged, the instruction that it be so made forcibly to the French sergeant waiting to take them to a place of confinement.

'You will accompany me, Lieutenant,' said the senior officer, a colonel. 'The general is anxious to meet you.'

Bowing acknowledgement, Markham followed the colonel along the quay, two other officers, and a file of troops bringing up his rear. They passed the two Tarantines which had evaded him, which were now tied up and in the process of being unloaded by men of the garrison. Considering that the ships had brought succour to the besieged, there seemed, to Markham's way of thinking, little joy in the task. Looking at the disgruntled faces of the French troopers, he put their dejection down to the lateness of the hour, plus the fact that they were being obliged to perform a task that could easily have been undertaken by civilians.

But his mind was working on a quite separate level, his interest in the sweating troopers extending to their physical condition, which appeared to be good. Morale was too nebulous a concept to pursue in such a short space of time, and once he was off the quay, and inside the walls of the town, he could observe little. There were few civilians about, and those he did see tended to scurry out of the way as soon as they heard the boots striking the cobbles of the narrow streets. The route was uphill from the shore all the way to the citadel, the central castillion that dominated the town.

He was received in the French headquarters with a punctilious-ness he'd not expected. Which made him think of Monsignor Aramon, and his charge that the besieged were 'Godless heathens and apostates', the implication being that neither their word nor their behaviour could be deemed civilised. Nothing was further from the truth. Could these men really be the military representatives of the Terror, with its trial of blood and innocent, headless corpses? In a long soldiering career, during which he'd mingled with the officers of several armies, French, Russian, Austrian and even Turkish, Markham knew what constituted proper conduct. He could observe no departure from that here.

The General, Pierre Francois d'Issillen, when he entered his chamber, stood to receive him, even though he was a mere marine lieutenant, introducing himself with old world courtesy. The enquiry after his well being, delivered at the same time as a glass of wine, was genuine, as was the relief on the commander's face when he confirmed he had suffered no wounds. But that was as nothing to the praise heaped upon his recent exploits.

'A most gallant affair, Lieutenant.' This was followed by a subdued agreement from the other officers in the room, all now hatless, and standing stiffly and respectfully in the presence of their general. 'I watched the whole thing from the very top of this tower. You acted with despatch and courage, and not one of my officers could fault a single decision you made. Your superiors will, I'm sure, be very proud of you.'

Markham, being dog tired, nearly blurted out 'some of them'. But he stopped himself just in time, murmuring a modest response that included a reference to the quality of the men he led.

'Do you think it would be in order for me to visit those men?' d'Issillen enquired. 'I would want them to know how much I admired their application.'

Markham was slightly startled by that, since it seemed to be carrying the bonds of polite military conduct too far. But he was quick to concede, since nothing would ensure their proper treatment more than a visit to the dungeons by such an elevated personage.

'We could perhaps do so before I invite you to dine.'

'Of course,' Markham replied, suppressing the selfish thought that had first come to mind; that he was ravenous, very thirsty, filthy, and impatient to be rid of all these encumbrances.

D'Issellin smiled, which went some way to lightening the look on his old tired face. 'I think you will require another glass of this fortifying wine to sustain you.'

Markham accepted, and it was only when they were leaving and he hit the warm evening air that he realised it was probably a mistake. With no food in his belly, the wine had gone straight to his head, making him feel fuzzy. He had to hold himself stiff to avoid any hint of a stagger, not easy on the uneven, steeply cobbled streets, and he was sweating in the humid night air, which doubled his discomfort.

At least the room in which his men had been accommodated was cool and roomy. The general asked him to interpret for him, himself having no English, so that Markham was privy to every question posed. Not that he needed to worry. D'Issellin avoided all reference to anything pertaining to the nature of the siege. He enquired about the place of birth of each individual, where it was and what kind of occupation they had pursued before taking the King's shilling.

Rannoch responded quite warmly when the general alluded to the Old Alliance, to the time when Scots and Frenchmen had been allies not enemies. Eboluh Bellamy showed off not only his command of French, but demonstrated, as usual, his endemic desire to hog any conversation that might show him in a flattering light. He was the only one to relax enough to respond to the general as a fellow human being, instead of the near-God-like presence his rank imposed. D'Issellin also enquired after each man's health with a tenderness that Markham found quite touching, and expressed some surprise that none of them had succumbed to the very noxious airs and vapours with which Corsica abounded.

Markham was about to tell him about the advantages of the Royal Louis Battery, especially its cool clean water and elevated position above the humid forests. But he stopped himself just in time, because to do so would give information that the enemy might find useful. Nor did he want to mention, as a concomitant to that, the state of health of the rest of the besiegers. The next thought sobered him up in a split second.

He tried very hard to keep the same expression on his face and he looked at the smiling, weary countenance of General d'Issellin. The cunning old bastard! The French could not be entirely unaware of the health of the British troops. They must know that sickness was a problem for General Stuart. What they didn't know was the extent of the problem, and how to apply it to the notion of extending the siege till those carrying it out were forced to retire from lack of strength.

Markham knew; that the offer of a truce from d'Issellin had come at a most fortuitous time; that Stuart had contemplated launching a premature assault just because if he waited he might lack the troops to do so at a later stage. The question buzzing about in his brain now was how to exploit this in such a way that would not raise the least suspicion in the wily old general's mind. Silently, he thanked the gods that had stopped him from fetching along the whey-faced Midshipman Hoste.

'I'm sure, sir, my men would wish to thank you most heartily for your evident concern for their well being.' He turned to face the row of Lobsters and sailors, speaking rapidly and laying on the Irish accent so that anyone capable of speaking English in the room would be confused. 'So now me boyos, we'll be after givin' the auld general here some damned huzzahs, the kind that you'd reserve for the last horse that won you a guinea. I want it in three, and I want the rafters to rattle.'

His men outdid the tars, perhaps because they knew him better, or even because they reckoned him half deranged. Their three times three bounced off the low ceiling, and it was gratifying for Markham to see just how much such evident healthy enthusiasm depressed the recipient.

'I think you need your dinner now, Lieutenant,' he growled, before turning on his heel and stomping out of the room.

Markham contemplated warning Rannoch, to say that if any-one enquired, he should tell them that the troops outside the walls of Calvi all looked the picture of rude, good health. But he decided against it. Any hint picked up by those still present would be passed on immediately to the general, who might just be desperate enough to try less benign methods of finding out what he needed to know.

The dinner d'Issellin served was plain but wholesome. And it was more than ample for the officers that sat at table. The conversation was pleasant, a discussion of past campaigns. This included an interrogation of the most gentle kind regarding Markham's service in both the Americas during the Revolution, and in the Russian army since then. There was just a hint of surprise that given the length of his service his rank was so meagre. They discussed openly the quality of the Turks he had fought on behalf of the Czarina, while showing proper amazement at the size of the forces engaged, and the sheer vastness of the territory over which they had campaigned.

Clearly, food and wine in Calvi was not a problem. Nor from what little he had been able to observe was the health of the garrison. The men unloading the Tarantines had looked unhappy certainly, but in reasonable shape. Given that, numbers should not be a problem. He knew from personal observation that the walls, while battered, were still sound, which left only one thing lacking; powder and shot.

Was that why the frigates hadn't fired when he was at long range? He recalled the two cutters. They'd used those cannon a mite sparingly, when to loose off plenty of shot might have secured a more successful outcome. A dose of grape across the deck of the captured ship might have achieved a better result than the round shot that smashed the mainmast. Having indulged in polite conversation, Markham made a sudden decision to change all that, and when he did speak, he shattered whatever genial atmosphere had existed at the table.

'Well, General, now that you have your succour, do you require an officer to inform General Stuart of the changed circumstances?'

The implication that he should send Markham was obvious, and produced a flash of annoyance on the old man's face.

'I do not lack for officers to carry messages, monsieur.'

'Or perhaps you could attach the message to a piece of round-shot, and fire it over to our encampment. Damn the expense, eh!'

'There is a convention, Lieutenant, that it is bad manners to allude to military maters in a situation such as yours. I had, until now, thought you the type to respect that.'

'There is, I am sure, no precedent for a general doing his own interrogation of mere rankers, sir, to find out the state of health of his opponent's troops.'

The rest of the officers at the table looked shocked. D'Issellin just smiled, slowly for sure, but with an open acknowledgement that he had been unmasked.

'Since you are to be our guest, Lieutenant, I may as well tell you one thing the ships did bring in, and that is the news from Paris.'

Markham suspected, by the way d'Issillen said it, that it must be good news. He had a sudden vision of peace, not really sure if he welcomed it. For a penniless rake with few prospects, war was just about the only employment he could find. Peace meant a return home, a happy prospect to some, no doubt. But not to a man who'd left Britain with the bailiffs on his heels. The vision still haunted; of him fleeing his Chatham lodgings, leaving most of his possessions behind, and racing for the safety of one of His Majesty's frigates moored at the Nore. He was so intent on this he almost missed what it was that d'Issillen was telling him.

' . . . That culminated, at the end of July, with the fall of Robespierre and St Just. They met the same fate as their predecessors, and faced Madame Guillotine. There is a new government in Paris, one less wedded, we hope, to judicial murder.'

'The war will end?'

'Unlikely. Even now the Russians, Prussians and Austrians are, with subsidies from your British, forming a new alliance to invade France. And the Comte d'Artois has been particularly insensitive in his dealings with the new regime.'

'The news must affect their decision, surely.'

'Will it?' d'Issillen demanded, quite sharply. He continued, becoming more heated as continued. 'Every prince in Europe, including our own *émigré* King wants to invade us. Why! So that they may force us to take back the Bourbons without any change in their behaviour. That we will never consent to!'

The murmur from the other officers present underlined that d'Issillen spoke for them all.

'You fail to understand all of you, that the soldiers you meet on the frontiers are Frenchmen first. Let the political clubs of Paris annihilate each other. The Revolution was not for them. It was for us all, to end a system that was rotten to the core.'

The older man had become very animated indeed, quite the firebrand. Markham, who'd seen him as the embodiment of old world charm, was forced to remind himself of one salient fact: that this was the army of the Committee of Public Safety. Not a single officer in the room, especially the general in command, could have held on to his position without the blessing of those Parisian madmen.

'Anyway, Lieutenant,' the general continued, struggling to soften his tone, 'since I must keep you here, I would want your stay to be as pleasant as possible.'

'Sure, general, if the food and drink is as good as this, and I'm allowed some shade in the daytime, I can't see that you'll hear me complain.'

'And your men?'

'As long as you feed them.'

'We'll do that all right, Lieutenant Markham. For if we do

not, it will only go, in fifteen days, to your compatriots outside the walls.'

Markham soon learned that what he'd suspected was true. The Tarantines had brought to Calvi the one thing the defenders didn't need, food. The supply of powder and shot was desperately low. He felt some sympathy for his hosts, as they searched the horizon daily for the ships that would save them from surrender. He and his party were released two weeks later, just in time to take up his position on the causeway, to salute the French as they marched out behind their general.

He was privileged enough to get a clear view of d'Issellin's face as he saw the state of the besiegers. First there were few of them, and those standing to attention as convention demanded were almost uniformly yellow of complexion. At a quick count, General Stuart had been barely able to mount a guard of some three hundred and fifty men. It wasn't a smile d'Issillen threw George Markham when he realised that he'd been duped into surrendering to a force which now numbered less than his own.

The interview in Nelson's cabin was, on the whole, a very pleasant affair, private apart from his secretary. There was his dark side of course, the continuing pain of the Commodore's wound then the list of those who had perished here at Calvi, mostly from disease. Tactfully, Markham enquired after the young midshipman who'd been in the Commodore's boat, expecting the worst.

'Young Hoste. He's a gamecock, Markham, and looks set to make a full recovery.'

'I'm pleased to hear it, sir.'

'I don't know why,' Nelson replied, a twinkle of amusement in his eye. 'His return to health bodes ill for you. He'd like to call you out for denying him a chance of distinction. He should have led that boarding party, Markham, not you.'

Markham was wondering what impression a yellow-faced Mr Hoste would have made on d'Issillen, which made his expression appear somewhat sombre.

'I was jesting, Markham!

'Yes, sir.'

'The question arises, what am I now to do with you?'

'Wherever I shift to, sir, I'd like to take my men along with me.'

Nelson shook his head slowly. 'Not easy. Especially as I have praised you so in my despatch to Admiral Hood. There's a recommendation for promotion there, Markham, fully deserved.'

'Thank you, sir.'

Nelson turned to his secretary, Scott. 'Have we anything decent that will keep this man occupied till the Admiral responds?' Scott didn't reply verbally. He merely shuffled the papers in his hand and gave one to Nelson. The Commodore examined it, then nodded.

'A happy coincidence, Scott.' Nelson fixed Markham with his good eye. 'This might just suit. It will keep you and your men together for a while, and it might even put some coin in that scarlet coat of yours.'

'That would be most welcome,' Markham responded with feeling. 'Will it keep me with my men?'

'It will for now. Whether that holds, long term, I cannot say. Perhaps if you, and they, distinguish themselves, it will be made easy.'

Chapter four

'I asked for you personally, Markham,' said the Honourable George Germain. 'Does that surprise you?'

'Should it?' asked Markham.

This was said guardedly, while accepting the invitation to sit down, a blessing since the alternative, in such a cramped, low cabin, was to stand half bent like a servant in mid bow. He wondered if that was what Nelson had meant by a happy coincidence.

Germain noticed the hesitation and that produced a half-smile. He was a good ten years younger than the marine officer, a lieutenant himself, recently appointed to command the sloop *Syilphide*. The ship had, along with the two frigates, been taken from the French as part of the surrender terms. His naval rank was superior to Markham's. But now Germain was Master and Commander of the newly captured sixth rate. He had, on his own vessel, all the power and prestige of a captain.

'Not given your actions in the Calvi approaches. I was in *Diomede*'s cutter, one of the boats trying to give you assistance. I saw everything. The Commodore has, apparently, suggested to Lord Hood that promotion is in order. That is a sentiment with which I heartily concur. But until that is approved, you are just the kind of man I want along for the task with which I have been charged.'

Germain wanted him to ask what that was. His body position, pressed forward, made it obvious. Apart from a streak of sheer stubbornness Markham wasn't sure what caused him to refuse to oblige. His new superior had some difficulty in masking his disappointment.

'*Syilphide* draws little water under her keel. That makes her perfect for inshore work. We are to head for the enemy coast to the east of Toulon, and there to try to harry the French communications as they seek to make inroads against our Piedmontese allies. Hood's reports talk of that front being

34

reinforced, with the possibility of a major incursion into Italy. That will mean more than just attacking and sinking the transports that seek to supply the French army by sea. I intend that we should go ashore, when the opportunity permits, and do our very best to interrupt their land communications as well as destroying their installations. Be assured Markham, you and your Lobsters will be well employed.'

The knock at the door obviated any need for a response. What could Markham say anyway? Young Germain was in command. He would want a bit of glory and he would grab it if chance permitted. Command of this vessel was just a stepping stone to greater things. What troubled Markham was very far removed from any fear of action, why ask personally for him?

Could that decision have something to do with Germain's surname? Was he related to that Lord George Germain, later Lord Sackville, who'd so disgraced himself at the battle of Minden, retiring with his cavalry from the battlefield before the action was joined? If so, it would make for an interesting combination; the offspring of a man rated a coward, serving cheek by jowl with a person who, to many people, carried that stigma personally.

'Boat approaching, sir,' said the senior midshipman, and now acting Lieutenant, Mr Fletcher. 'There's a Bourbon officer on board, judging by his garb, and I think some kind of cleric with a purple soutaine.'

'Well I'll be damned,' Germain exclaimed, his eyes opening wide, the voice pitched in a way that, to Markham, sounded a touch contrived. 'Pipe them aboard, Mr Fletcher, and if it is a cleric, best break out more than one flagon of the wine. We all know how men of the cloth like to imbibe.'

Germain bustled about a bit, tidying up his small desk, trying to make his cabin look respectable, while his servant, sent for, arrived with goblets and two straw-covered flagons.

'That at least should be good,' Germain exclaimed. 'It was in the captain's storeroom when we took over the ship. Jean Crapaud never stints himself in the article of wine.'

Markham was about to suggest tasting it first. But then he realised that he had an almost certain knowledge of who was coming aboard. It might not be the Comte de Puy. But with that purple soutaine it was almost certainly Monsignor Aramon. Suddenly he found himself hoping the flagons contained vinegar.

'Best go on deck to greet them, Markham. I hope your sergeant has had the wit to line up the Lobsters.'

'He will, sir.'

As they exited straight on to the absurdly small deck, Rannoch was there, walking the line, tugging at straps and belts, realigning muskets, so that his men, crowded close as they were, looked the part. Markham was pleased at the standard they'd achieved. His men looked exceedingly smart in the sunlight, which showed off their white belts to advantage against their thick red coats. The brasswork of the muskets, generously returned by General d'Issellin, gleamed, and the wooden stocks were polished to perfection.

'An excellent showing, Markham,' exclaimed Germain, patting him on the shoulder of his own scarlet coat.

That got a single raised eyebrow from Rannoch, who knew as well as his officer who was responsible for the quality of the turnout, as well as how difficult it had been to achieve. Coming aboard *Syilphide* had brought back some of the divisions that existed below the surface. His original soldiers, drafted in to make up the numbers in a country newly embarked on war, had served in frigates until now. Not exactly spacious, they were palaces compared to the sixteen-gun sloop.

The ex-members of the 65th foot, led by Rannoch, had asked if they were to be obliged to serve in a canoe. Halsey and his true marines had scoffed and named it a right good billet. It wasn't of course. It was cramped, smelly and having been tied to the shore for months, rat-infested. Bellamy, neither of one group or the other, and by far the most fastidious of the bunch, had likened it to the bowels of a West Indian slaver.

'How I wish I could fire a salute, Markham,' hissed Germain excitedly. 'I do so long to let off the great guns in a proper salvo.'

Germain was looking eagerly at the approaching boat as he spoke, giving Markham a chance to examine him. The ship's captain was like a dog at the leash in his suppressed agitation, an impression heightened by his fine aristocratic features. He had a thin angular face, lively green eyes, and a ready smile. Markham found he was cursing himself. Habit, and many years of slights, made him suspicious of any fellow officer. It had also made him, he realised, too sensitive. The young man beside him was, it appeared, entirely genuine in both his actions and his words. Yet George Markham could not accept this at face value, and had to be continually looking for extraneous reasons for perfectly normal behaviour.

'Holy Mary, mother of Christ, Georgie, you've become a bit of a bloody bore.'

'Sorry?' asked Germain.

Markham was unaware that he'd spoken. It was having identified Aramon that saved him. 'I said to watch for that cleric, sir. He's a bit of a bore.'

'Well, since he's a papist, we shall ply him with the Thirty-Nine Articles, and see how he takes a jest.'

That earned Germain another sideways look. Those were the articles of his father's faith, and they had caused him nothing but trouble all his life. But the youngster killed any suspicion by his next remark.

'Give him your sword, Markham. He ranks as a bishop, don't you know, in our church.'

Markham pulled his sword from its scabbard, and as Aramon followed de Puy up the side, he raised it till the blade stood upright between his eyes, at the same time calling his men sharply to attention. As the face appeared, he felt there was some doubt if Aramon had ever been greeted in such a manner. But his countenance betrayed no surprise. He took the compliment of a military salute as nothing more than his due.

'Welcome aboard, sir,' cried Germain, stepping forward, his hands outstretched. 'You stand as the first non-naval visitor to my ship, and therefore make the circumstance memorable.'

Aramon held out his hand to be kissed. It was either an oversight or a deliberate piece of clerical condescension. Whichever, it was wasted on the young commander. He merely grasped the outstretched hand and shook it vigorously.

'Allow me to present to you Lieutenant Markham, sir.'

'You should know that I have met the officer before.'

'Indeed! Then will you inspect his men?'

Aramon made no attempt to keep the distaste out of his voice.

'They too I have met before, Captain. And it has been my misfortune to see too much of their slovenliness. I am unlikely in any way to be impressed by a sudden dab of polish.'

Behind Aramon, Colonel le Comte de Puy was sucking hard on his teeth. He stepped forward smartly, almost brushing the Monsignor aside, and lifting his hat in salute, addressed Germain.

'The duty of inspection falls to me, Captain, as the military part of this small embassy.'

'Of course,' Germain replied, clearly somewhat confused.

De Puy stepped forward, and by acknowledging Markham's salute permitted him to lower his sword. Then, with the marine officer one pace behind, he carried out the inspection like a royal prince, addressing several men by name, and with many a jaundiced reference to the duty they suffered on the Royal Louis Battery. The Lobsters responded in kind, having taken to de Puy while serving with him, naming him a true gent.

'I have refreshments waiting in my cabin,' said Germain, as soon as he finished. 'I would be obliged if you would join us, Lieutenant Markham.'

'Is that strictly necessary?' hissed Aramon.

'Why it is essential, sir,' Germain said, his thin eyebrows rising. 'Apart from myself, Mr Markham is the only commissioned officer on the ship. I can hardly listen to your proposal, or conceive of acting on it, without both his opinion, and his active participation.'

'Proposal,' Markham thought. 'What bloody proposal.'

Aramon seemed to fill the cabin. He was a big man. But it was the way he spread himself that counted, as though no one else in the place was entitled to any consideration. Germain, behind his desk, was fine. But de Puy and Markham were pushed against the two cannon that stood either side, eventually required to sit on them to avoid standing in a half stoop. Wine was poured and tasted. That at least seemed to the cleric's satisfaction, as he grunted with approval.

'I'm curious, Monsignor, of how you came to know so much about my orders?'

'You should not be, Captain Germain.' The recipient of this preened slightly at the title. 'Even if Calvi was not a hotbed of rumour, few good sons of the church would dare to prevaricate when I tax them with a direct enquiry.'

'Which was it?' asked Markham.

That interjection earned him a look from Germain that told him, in no uncertain terms, not to interrupt. It was quite interesting to note how commanding he could be when he wished it, the green eyes narrowing and the bones of his thin cheeks becoming much more prominent. It was as well to remember that this stripling had been at sea for years, and had probably served a good few of them as someone's First Lieutenant. The fact that the Monsignor ignored the same question came as no surprise. He'd taken to ignoring Markham after only a short, awkward acquaintance.

'And what is it you seek?'

'The recovery of something extremely valuable.'

'Valuable is a very inexact term, Monsignor.'

Aramon parried him expertly. 'Extremely is not, Captain.'

'And I can be of service in this?'

'You have the means to carry the Comte de Puy and I to where we need to be, the coast of France.'

'This item of extreme value is there?'

'Not on the coast. It is some way inland.'

'You could hire a ship to take you there.'

'We may wish to be taken off again, sure that what we have recovered will get to its proper destination.' Aramon sat forward suddenly, his voice dropping an octave, as if he was imparting a secret. 'And if we succeed in our aim, it would be in your own interest as well as that of your country. We are as one in our desire to defeat the forces of Revolution, are we not?'

'Of course.'

'Quite apart from any personal gain, you will receive the gratitude of all Europe, as well as that of your own government, when you transport us to our next port of call.'

'Which is?'

Aramon sat back and smiled, waving an admonitory finger before picking up his wine. 'One thing at a time, young man.'

Germain bridled at that. He was young compared to the others in the room. But he was also Master and Commander of the *Syilphide*, newly promoted, and that made him sensitive. Aramon, his face deep in the goblet, didn't notice. De Puy did, and sought once more to cover up for the cleric's manner.

'You come to us highly recommended as a most zealous officer, Captain Germain. If you will consent to the transport of the Monsignor, myself and my men.'

'Your men?' Germain interrupted, in a quiet voice.

There was a degree of uncertainty in the way that de Puy nodded, accompanied by a quick glance at Aramon, as if what was being discussed should have already been agreed. Markham, watching carefully, was confused. If Germain was hearing their proposal for the first time, nothing should be settled. But then he'd been subjected to an odd feeling previously, in the way that his new commander had reacted to the news of the Monsignor's arrival.

'I cannot consent to take a party of soldiers aboard.'

'Even for such a short journey?'

Germain became quite animated, arms waving and eyes bright, in the way a man does when he is unsure that what he is saying deserves to be believed.

'Do not be deceived by looking at a map, sir. This is the sea. We are subject to wind and weather. A journey that, on land, would take a mere two days, could, at sea, take a week. You will have observed that the ship is not spacious, and you will also have seen, on the deck, that the crew is numerous.'

That provided another reason for suspicion in Markham's mind. Even he knew that with a reasonable wind, the coast of France was no further away than a day's sailing.

'It is scarcely possible that what we seek can be recovered without the aid of an armed escort,' said Aramon. 'First, we must land in, and traverse what to us is hostile territory. Then, having recovered what it is we seek, we must re-embark on your vessel. Can we achieve that without some news of our presence becoming known?'

'I shouldn't be concerned on that score, Monsignor.' He looked at Markham and smiled. 'We have the means to provide you with armed assistance.'

Aramon followed his gaze, his dark brown eyes ranging over the marine lieutenant in a way that made Markham bridle.

'I would need to confer with Monsieur de Puy.'

Germain was off his seat in a flash, head bent to avoid the low deckbeams. 'Please use my cabin. Mr Markham and I will take a turn around the deck.'

He had his hand on Markham's elbow, and was hustling him out before anyone could speak. On deck, it was now clear of marines, and those sailors working moved away to leeward as Germain made for the windward rail. This, on any ship, was the preserve of the captain, his to walk in peace and tranquillity whenever he chose. The fact that on *Syilphide* it measured not more than ten feet from poop to gangway did not distract from the obvious pleasure Germain took in claiming it.

'He's a rum cove that priest, don't you think, Markham.'

40

'He is more than that. He's devious and self serving, and to my mind, totally untrustworthy.'

'You know more of priests than I,' Germain replied, before adding hurriedly. 'Being Irish, of course.'

'Not just priests.' It was the tone rather than the words that stopped Germain. He looked at his marine lieutenant quizzically, before Markham added. 'It would be nice, sir, to be aware of what is going on.'

'I don't follow.'

'Yes you do,' said Markham, with some asperity. 'You knew Aramon was coming, knew he had a proposal, and for all I can tell, were well aware of the nature of it before he set foot in your cabin.'

There was a slight smile playing on the corners of Germain's lips. 'Now it's me that you make sound devious and self serving.'

'Are you?'

'I admit to a hint of deviousness. But my aim is to serve my king and country, rather than myself.' He began pacing again, somewhat faster than before, forcing Markham to follow suit. 'You are right, of course. Aramon approached me ashore. I admit that he came out here quicker than I supposed, though I ought to have guessed, him being an ardent sort. Still . . .'

Markham cut across him, ignoring the convention that stated he should remain silent while a superior officer was speaking.

'He needs de Puy for whatever it is he has planned. The Colonel wants his men. It is your job to persuade him that my Lobsters can do a better job than his own soldiers.'

Germain was looking at him quizzically, not sure whether to be pleased or angry. 'I shall have to watch you, Markham. I had you down as game, and I reckoned you sharp-witted. But not quite the stropped razor, if you get my drift.'

'Which one of the two induced you to ask for me personally?'

Germain turned away abruptly at that, leaving his marine lieutenant to speculate that it was probably neither.

'I have a job to do, orders to obey. It just so happens that Aramon's proposition accords with those. There is nothing to say that I can't land shore parties, in fact I could well be damned if I don't. You heard what he said. That which he seeks is not far inland, though he keeps the actual location close.'

'It would be better to know what it is, don't you think?'

'He won't say.'

Germain had responded ruefully, before dropping his voice to a near whisper that became more eager the more he spoke. He seemed totally unaware that by saying that he'd admitted to prior knowledge.

'But he keeps harping on about the value. I reckon it to be some kind of treasure. He was at Avignon before fleeing to save his neck, a small detail that I did wheedle out of him. That was a papal palace once, rich as Croesus, even by a Papist yardstick. You know these places, stuffed to the lintels with precious articles. Gawd, even the everyday plate they use can be worth a mint.'

'So you intend to put me ashore to find and gift to Aramon the possessions which he deems so extremely valuable, before transporting him to where he wants to go. That seems a rather commercial approach to duty, sir.'

'Find and take possession of, Markham! And if it is legitimate booty we will do so on behalf of the King of England. We might well find ourselves handing both Aramon and his treasure over to Lord Hood to decide what happens next. That will earn us both a feather for our caps. And perhaps, if what we find is big enough, a reward somewhat greater than that hinted at by the priest.'

Markham had the feeling that it mattered little what Aramon recovered. Germain would take it to Hood anyway, less concerned by the value than by the proof it would provide of his diligence. There might be advantage for him there too, a chance to produce that stroke that Nelson alluded to, one that might allow him to request a favour from Hood; that if he was promoted, he could take his men with him.

'So we are going to steal it?' he said, wickedly.

'Good God, no!' exclaimed Germain. 'I will not indulge in theft. It grieves me that you think of me in those terms, Markham. I certainly have a higher regard for you.'

'You mustn't go supposing the notion of theft bothers me, sir. Relieving that stuck up bastard of his possessions will make both my Lobsters, as well as the officer who leads them, very happy.'

Aramon had consumed half the contents of the wine flask by the time they returned to the cabin, though that induced no more than a slight flush on his dark olive cheeks. De Puy looked more unsettled. He wasn't, by nature, a happy man; Markham knew that, just as he knew that Aramon always seemed to depress him even further. But now he was more downcast than ever, the fact that he had acquiesced in what was being demanded of him fairly obvious, given the self-satisfied air of his clerical companion.

'The captain accepts that you possess too little space to transport his men. I have pointed out the obvious to him. That to take a hired vessel and his soldiers would leave us at the mercy of men unknown to us, men on whom we might not be able to rely to fully aid us. That, I am happy to say does not apply in the confines of a British warship.'

Markham clenched his jaw, but Germain, of a fairer complexion, blushed, a fact of which he was aware since he covered it with a fine outpouring of modesty. The Monsignor continued, with his head shaking and his voice carrying an air of slight disbelief.

'And it has to be said, the prospect of relying on Lieutenant Markham and his men does not seem to trouble him unduly.'

Germain responded quickly. 'I intend to sail at sunset, Monsignor, my orders demand it. I will go whether you are aboard or not.'

Markham suppressed a smile. He doubted if Germain had received any such orders, other than the general instruction from Admiral Hood to cruise off the southern French shores. He was keen to be off for two very good reasons. The first was to demonstrate his zeal, the second to be away from a gossipy shore, one that might just leak information regarding his unorthodox arrangements. That would certainly bring down on him unwelcome questions, as well as interference from his superiors. It might even lead to a strict command to desist.

'We are ready to come aboard now,' stated Aramon.

'Then we are agreed,' Germain said. 'We will transport you to France, help you recover the property you seek, then transport you to your destination.'

The Monsignor smacked his lips in approval. De Puy nodded slowly, failing to respond to the eagerness in Germain's look. Only Markham kept his head still. He had, in his mind, a nagging need to register his doubts, not least the obvious one that no actual reward had been mentioned. Clearly that was another fact that Germain and Aramon had discussed between themselves. And they had no intention of sharing the figure with anyone else. Then there was the thought of going ashore on a hostile coast, not to hit and run, but to head inland to a degree as yet unstated.

But that was being overborne by a twinge of excitement. He hated to be still, and though well aware that he could, if he wished, decline to serve with Germain, he knew he'd be forced to leave his men behind if he decided to stay in Corsica. And then there was the prospect of what duty he might be offered in place of this. Markham had enjoyed a degree of independence since coming out to the Mediterranean, both in Toulon and on Corsica, one to which his rank scarcely entitled him.

The notion of that freedom being curtailed, of his serving as a subordinate marine officer aboard a ship of the line, was not a happy prospect. What Germain was proposing to do might be hare-brained and even illegal. But it was movement, tinged with risk and adventure. And then, to a man who had enjoyed a degree of comfort and had lost it, there was always the prospect, once he'd wormed a figure out of his captain, of a little bit of profit.

Aramon was seen over the side with as much ceremony as had attended his arrival, this time, at Germain's insistence, in the *Syilphide*'s own cutter. The newly appointed commander did not wish either man to communicate with anyone they didn't have to.

'Mr Fletcher, I would ask you to shape me a course that will take us to the southwest. Once out of sight of land, we will want to box the compass for a while.'

He was aware of Markham looking at him, aware of the unstated questions that were forming in the marine officer's mind.

'I must work up the crew a bit, Markham,' he continued quietly. 'They are all seamen, I know. But they have been gathered from any number of ships. Nothing in my experience leads me to believe that those who gave them up passed on to me their best men. Some of them are bound to be right hard bargains. I would see them work as a unit before we head for the French coast. God forbid that we should turn into an enemy ship without them knowing what it is I require of them.'

'It is merely a bonus then, that a few days delay will provide a good opportunity to pump the good Monsignor about where it is he wants to go?'

'I admire you, Markham,' Germain responded, though his tone of voice made such a proposition sound doubtful, 'and for a variety of reasons. But please try to remember that I am your superior officer.'

'I can be sure, sir,' Markham replied, matching Germain's asperity, 'that if I forget, you will be there to remind me.'

Chapter five

The first shock, when the party they were to transport returned aboard, was the sheer numbers. De Puy was not to be allowed any of his soldiers, but Monsignor Aramon saw no reason why he should forego any of his own comforts. He brought his servants, three sturdy clear-eyed men, and it seemed, all of his possessions. And that included his charge, the young lady to whom he stood as 'guardian'.

She came aboard wearing a veil that hid her features, accompanied by an extensive wardrobe, a box containing a musical instrument and a young Negro maid who moved with stunning grace. Thus her face, which had only ever been glimpsed in a heavily shaded distance, remained a mystery to Markham and his men, a fact that had led to no end of speculation.

Germain hopped about from foot to foot, caught between his desire to question her presence, while at the same time seeking to appear gallant. He also had a deep need to impress this member of the opposite sex with a demonstration of his newly acquired authority, which led to a string of contradictory and useless orders. Aramon watched this with wry amusement, before condescending to offer an introduction.

'Allow me to present to you, Captain Germain, Mademoiselle Ghislane Moulins. I am responsible for both her spiritual and physical well-being. As I shall not be returning to Corsica, she must, as I'm sure you understand, travel with me.'

The response, 'Quite!' was accompanied by a deep blush.

What followed was a continuation of the comedy. Talking about Aramon, Markham had passed on to Germain what he and his men suspected regarding the cleric's domestic arrangements, which rendered the young lady in a certain light. But she was on his deck, having been introduced as a thoroughly respectable person. The young commander of the *Syilphide* didn't quite know what to do, so that the bow was only half the depth he intended, while his voice, mouthing 'charmed' sounded decidedly gruff and carnal.

'You will forgive me,' he continued, almost stuttering. 'I must be about my duties.'

'If you will permit me, sir,' said Markham. 'I will see that the young lady is properly accommodated.'

The look that received spoke volumes. It was common gossip in the fleet that Markham was a gambler and a rake, a ne'er do well who had, just before joining his ship, fought and killed the husband of one of his lovers in a Finsbury Park duel. He was the very last person who should be left to care for a woman, one who, since she was still termed Mademoiselle, must be of tender years. Germain's pinched expression at this invasion of his prerogative was matched by Aramon's sharp rejoinder.

'The lady has my own trusted servants, as well as Monsieur le Comte de Puy, to carry out that task, Lieutenant!'

'Quite!' Germain gasped, before finally scurrying away.

The master, Mr Conmorran, a portly and cheerful individual, stepped into the breach. He saw the servants and the luggage taken below and escorted Mademoiselle Moulins and her male companions to the main cabin. Then, after a long talk with Germain, they worked out a satisfactory arrangement regarding who would sleep where, a matter that involved a great deal of shifting about.

Germain was as good as his word. They were at sea before nightfall. The *Syilphide*'s crew had worked flat out during the remainder of the day to load the only thing the captured sloop was short on, powder to fire the cannon. Shot was less of a problem, its small calibre guns providing balls too light for the recent defence of the fortress.

Aramon and his charge were in one half of Germain's cabin, while de Puy had to be given a berth in the tiny wardroom. Markham, not required like the midshipmen to stand a watch, offered to shift himself to a screened off cot on the main deck. The cleric then, without protest, abrogated to himself the right to the windward side of the deck without bothering to ask for permission. The young commander put this down to ignorance, a conclusion with which Markham could not agree.

Dinner, taken late to accommodate the guests, was a cramped affair, even with only five people around the table. Aramon's servants and the Negro maid had been banished to the gunner's quarters to take their meals, which had led to a long moan on 'things not being right,' from the man so burdened. It was, according to the warrant holder, bad enough with foreign types to contend with. But the addition of a female, and a black at that, who was 'like to excite the hands' was 'coming it too high'.

Germain, not wishing to commence his commission on a sour note, had tried being emollient first. Jocularity was second and an appeal to camaraderie third. When that failed he finally lost his temper and sent the still grumbling gunner off with a flea in his ear.

It was in that harassed manner that he sat down to dinner. The night air was hot, enough to make anyone perspire, the scents Ghislane Moulins had applied filling the cabin air enough to disturb the men present. But Markham and Germain had the added burden of discovering that the young lady was, without her veil, a very pretty creature indeed.

Her skin was pale olive and flawless, with just a hint of that excess of flesh that goes with female youth, the eyes large dark brown orbs. She spoke little, revealing strong white teeth under full lips, and only really employed more than two consecutive words when Aramon addressed a question directly to her, the voice made to sound more thin and nervous by her guardian's brusque, slightly hectoring tone.

Markham knew that any hint of gallantry on his part would be squashed, so, in that department, he left the field clear for Germain. That proved unwise. The young man proved totally incapable of even the rudiments of dalliance. When not boasting, any questions he posed to her were either rhetorical and short, or so long-winded as to be abstract in the extreme. He then launched into a long and tedious explanation of what training he had in mind for the ship's crew, apologising in advance for the discomfort and the noise this would create. Designed to make the young lady feel relaxed, everything he attempted clearly had the opposite effect.

De Puy evoked greater curiosity. Markham knew about women. He liked and admired them, while well aware that his interest had often led him into trouble. He would have had a lot more if he hadn't possessed the very necessary ability to assess how other men responded to their presence. The Frenchman rarely took his eyes off the young lady. And his expression, though admiring, also carried with it that extra tinge of gloom that Markham had witnessed whenever he returned for dinner with Aramon. His position, sitting to one side of her, made it more

47

obvious to the observer than the subject. But her guardian must be aware of it too, even if the cleric showed no sign of having noticed.

Germain, finally aware that his pleasantries were falling on stony ground, instead began to interrogate the Monsignor. He had all the enthusiasm of his youth, and a hide thick enough to deflect Aramon's evident annoyance at being subjected to constant questions. It was interesting to watch the youngster's mind at work. He probed with what he considered to be deep artifice for some clue at to what it was the man was after. But he was up against a much more sophisticated opponent, who never let slip any detail that was not a deliberate leak designed to excite or tease.

But it was during that duel of wits that the young Ghislane showed the first hint of vitality. As Germain probed and Aramon fielded, her eyes darted between them, her lips occasionally pursing, he assumed at either the temerity of a question or the sharp response it received. Altogether such animation showed her in a more flattering light. It was some time before she noticed how closely the man opposite was watching her. She responded with a sniff of disapproval, and a glare, to the slight smile of interest on Markham's face.

Aramon heard the sniff and followed the direction of the look. But George Markham was too experienced to be caught out. He was already gone, engaging de Puy in a discussion of how General Stuart had humbugged his fellow countrymen; of how d'Issillen must have felt at surrendering to so few, fever-ridden troops. Engaging him fully was hard work, since his attention kept wandering towards the young lady. But Markham stuck at it until the port had done the rounds and the dinner could reasonably end. His final task, before retiring for the night, was to check on the well being of his men, and to forewarn Rannoch of a busy day on the morrow.

On deck he paused, to let the heat and fug of the small cabin clear from his head. The night was clear, the sky a mass of stars, with the ship sailing easy on a gentle but steady breeze. It was simple to imagine that this was not a posting but a cruise, a privilege to be enjoyed by a wealthy man who had hired a yacht for his own amusement. There was even the remembered smell of a woman to go with the tang of the sea. Perfect to imagine, as long as you removed Aramon, Germain and de Puy from the reverie.

The Monsignor's servants had also come up from below to

escape the 'tween-deck heat. They sat on the forepeak in shirtsleeves, talking, shadow-boxing and occasionally laughing. Their shape, a uniform height and fitness, struck Markham as odd.

Servants normally came in varying sizes, short, tall, fat and thin. It was rare that they had any physical grace whatsoever, once you took them away from the place in which they were most comfortable, the house of their master. These men were different. But then Markham reasoned that they must serve a dual function to a wealthy travelling cleric, acting perhaps as bodyguards.

Reluctantly he went below, sensing immediately the warmth and odour of packed humanity, mixed with the smell of bilge. Ducking low at the bottom of the companionway, and entering on to the mess deck, Markham had the distinct impression that he was interrupting something. All serving men, of whatever kind, were adept at avoiding too much attention from officers. But normality in an encampment, or here in the cramped area that provided both living a sleeping accommodation to seamen and marines, entailed a certain amount of bustle.

In the small quantity of light provided by the ship's lanterns, everyone appeared to be standing so still that Markham felt as if he was witnessing a tableau, as though they'd stopped dead as soon as someone had seen his legs descending the ladder.

'Sergeant Rannoch?' Markham called, peering into the gloom.

'Here.'

Rannoch stepped forward, ducking below the crossbeams because of his height. He was, like nearly everyone else, stripped to the waist, his muscled torso gleaming with sweat, the pallid white of his body in sharp contrast to the bright red of his face and neck. Markham looked past him, observing that his men were bunched on one side of the deck, while the more numerous tars filled the other. More telling than that was the clear gap in between.

'I came below to warn you that we are set for a busy day tomorrow. Mr Germain is keen to work up the crew, and I fear our exploits at Calvi so impressed him that he will certainly demand that we repeat our boarding exploits.'

'It will be warm work, right enough.'

Markham was close to Rannoch now, and able to whisper so that only he could hear. 'Is everything as it should be?'

Rannoch, when he replied, didn't look him in the eye. The

Highlander hated officers as a breed, and never failed to exchange an insolent stare with one in order that they should be aware if it. Having observed this, Markham took as a mark of respect that the man normally treated him with some deference.

He had, though, opined on more than one occasion, in a voice larded with irony, that this superior was such a poor specimen that he hardly rated the title. And Rannoch held on to certain habits so that mutual esteem was never sacrificed. For Markham to get an acknowledgement of his rank without there being present another officer, was like drawing teeth from a bad-tempered elephant.

But the Highlander brought the same passion to the care of those he led, and that, to Markham, forgave a great deal. They'd clashed on first meeting. But shared danger, and the knowledge that his superior was intent on keeping his men alive rather than getting them killed in pursuit of personal glory, had softened that to something that was more akin to friendship.

'Apart for the heat, which is no good to man nor beast in the article of slumber.'

There had been some kind of dispute going on, of that Markham was certain. The whole mess deck reeked of it, a feeling of trouble so all pervasive as to be almost tangible. And no great wit was required to see where the lines were drawn.

'Heat is not much good for short tempers, either.'

That did make Rannoch look him in the eye. But there was no deference or regard there, just a blank stare that was designed to tell him that what was happening was none of his business. Markham knew he should withdraw, turn a blind eye, to leave whatever was going on to the men concerned. But he couldn't help himself, seeing that his Lobsters were outnumbered by at least three to one, and that was without the presence of the watch on duty.

'Captain Germain strikes me as a bit of a flogger. He is also keen to see how we all perform. So he'll want to see all his men, Lobsters and tars, fit and well, ready for duty, as soon as he's downed his breakfast.'

'That is his right,' said Rannoch formally.

'Then let us not disappoint him. It would be a shame to start the opening day of his first independent cruise with some poor creature rigged to the grating.'

Markham had taken one step up the companionway as he said

this, which allowed him to look over Rannoch's shoulder. His eyes flicked to the item each man was carrying, a chain here, a mess kid there, and one or two with half-knotted ropes; innocent enough if you didn't anticipate trouble. His own men were very close to their muskets, and he had to hope they would get the message as he deliberately addressed the sailors.

'But he'll flog every man jack of you if he has to, even if the man who heads your division pleads your case. He has guests aboard and will not stand to be embarrassed.'

That pleading part only made sense if you accepted his presence. He was telling the sailors that he had seen and understood what was happening; that any mark on one of his own men would lead to an enquiry, one in which he would be bound take the side of those he led. It wasn't the commander who would see them flogged, but him. Some shoulders slumped, a release of tension that spread rapidly, and to avoid his stare men began to shuffle around. He was tempted to take Rannoch up with him, to read him the riot act and cap a stopper on any trouble. But that might undermine the man. He had no way of knowing for certain whether his sergeant had been just about to start a fight, or just about to stop one.

'Sleep,' he said loudly, 'and that is an order.'

Rannoch nodded, and then turned away. 'You heard what the good lieutenant said. Get your heads down.'

Later, lying in his cot, Markham ruminated over that, as well as the events of the day. And much as he tried to avoid it, on his past, which intruded constantly. The image of Ghislane Moulins was at the forefront of his consciousness, though it inevitably faded into a more distant vision, to that of the first girl he'd ever paid court to.

He always had to shut his eyes tight then, to blur out the way his imagination led him to her death, the flames that had consumed Flora Imrie and her family inevitably mixed with the sound on fury of the battle he'd left in an attempt to save them.

Had Germain asked for him personally because, even to someone bearing his name, George Markham had a worse reputation? The more he nagged at that thought the more annoyed he became. He'd been branded a coward at the Battle of Guilford. Lord George Germain had been called the same at the Battle of Minden, and for much the same reason; leaving the field.

Yet there was difference. George Markham had been a fifteen-year-old ensign, Germain the commander of the King's cavalry. He had faced a court martial, which had acquitted him; Germain had escaped even that, and carried on a political career, merely taking the title Lord Sackville, as if nothing untoward had happened.

There was no escaping the past though, and his own reaction to his new commander's surname proved it. The Markham name had stood proud before he'd besmirched it, with a father who'd risen from humble soldier to full general. He'd been elevated initially for his outstanding bravery at the siege of Cartagena, and from that famous siege had accumulated enough money to purchase his way up the promotion ladder.

Yet the old man had kept a firm grip on the common touch, and had never allowed neighbourly disapproval, a potent force in the Wexford military district he commanded, to stop him acknowledging his bastard son. Nor had he paid the slightest heed to the wagging tongues of the local Catholics, making a point of visiting the boy's mother on a regular basis, and acting, within the walls of her house, as if they were a normal family.

He'd been appointed Governor of New York during the American war, and it was his influence that had gained illegitimate George his commission. It was only later the youngster discovered that the Colonel of the 65th foot had owed General Markham a good deal of money. Still he was in the army, with a promising future that all went to pieces in the forests of Carolina. His father had arranged his court martial as well, which was why no one took the acquittal seriously.

So, would future Markhams carry the stigma of his name in the same way as Germain? Would there be young Markhams to worry about? That thought led to a review of the possibilities, each woman he'd made love to, and those with whom he'd failed, appearing in a whirring catalogue of faces and bodies, dressed and naked, which brought him right back to Ghislane Moulins.

'You keep your pego in your breeches, Georgie,' he said quietly to himself, one hand running across the prominent bones on his face, fingers rubbing at the numerous scars.

His thoughts were at odds with his whispered admonition. She was a pretty creature. And he, if not quite classically handsome himself, knew that he had good-enough looks and the wit to interest most women. 'Sure, she's only a bairn,' was the last thought he had, as he drifted into sleep.

Though still hot in the morning, there was at sea a breeze to keep them from frying, though it was not one, as Germain explained, to favour a swift passage to the French coast. Aramon, who had come on deck early, while it was still being swabbed, looked pointedly at the sun over the larboard rail, as if to say he new they were sailing south, not north. With a new crew on an unfamiliar ship, and plenty to keep them occupied, Germain had a good excuse to avoid further explanation by demanding that his guests stay clear of the deck. He was, he explained, a modern young officer, who believed in training his men for every eventuality.

So, as Aramon and his party sweltered below decks, there were mock alarms, with the drums beating to quarters twice in every watch. The guns were loosed, hauled out and fired in dumb show, the expense of powder to actually shoot at targets beyond the captain's means.

'One prize will see to that, Markham,' he cried, as his men piled into the cutter for the fourth time. 'A decent merchantman will provide either the means or the money. And if I can't lay alongside an enemy ship, I know the value of your Lobsters when it comes to boarding from a boat.'

Markham's men, without the presence of their officer, practised that too. An opposed boarding followed the swift entry to the cutter, with half the crew using padded capstan bars and marlin to fend off the mock attackers. Their officer watched them carefully, keeping in mind the events of last night, as well as Germain's supposition; that asked to cull the crew of one fighting ship to man the new captures, few captains would strip out their best men.

He was half convinced that some of those who fought most heartily in a rehearsal would prove the most shy in a real action. They were also the type to cause most of the 'tween decks trouble. Germain, he noticed, watched with as much care, constantly turning to the junior midshipman, Booker, requiring him to make a note in the ledger he carried.

There was animosity between the Lobsters and tars on any ship, and any given chance to clip each other round the ear without fear of punishment was never one to be passed up. But what Markham saw here was an excessive dimension to the dislike, an extra effort in each blow that stood as a determined attempt to make a point. After a few rehearsals it wasn't hard to see that Bellamy was the main target of the sailors, while his own men made great efforts to get between the Negro and those who were clearly after him.

His own ineptitude was more to blame for the blows he did receive, rather than any failure by the rest of the Lobsters. Being late in boarding, he left himself isolated. When required to re-enter the cutter for another attempt, he was always last to the rail. This, on one occasion, when the tars thought no one was looking, earned Bellamy a vicious jab from a pike that send him flying over the side. Only Rannoch's strength and speed saved him from landing headfirst. The laugh that followed, rippling across the deck, must have wounded the Negro more than anything. He was a proud individual, too much so for his own well being, and humiliation was the one thing he couldn't stand.

But he was far from being a good fighter, lacking that instinct that can turn even the most passive soul into an animal. Markham knew that self-preservation was where it started. But in a professional fighter it went on from that, to become a feeling of pride in ability for its own sake, a cold-blooded determination that in a scrap, it was the other man who would die, not you.

He couldn't interfere, but Markham was angry. He'd managed to isolate the four main culprits who made it their business to go after Bellamy, often passing up on an easier target in the process. His request that he partake of the next boarding was readily agreed to, and wrapping canvas around his sword, he dropped down into the cutter, his eyes meeting those of Rannoch as the sailors rowing the boat pulled away from the side. The Highlander gave him a slow smile, then addressed the Lobsters.

'We will be required to perform to perfection with Mr Markham aboard, lads. It would be a hellish thing to do, to let him down. So go aboard with right good intent, and let us drive those sodomitical tars from their own deck.'

Rannoch's eyes flicked along those sailors rowing the cutter, as if challenging them to disagree, before alighting on those of his officer. Then he winked.

'Look sharp this time, Bellamy,' Rannoch said.

Markham gave the order to close with the *Syilphide* then took a tight grip on his sword. The blade he would use flat, but the guard was just the thing to aid a punch. As the boat struck, he was the first up the side. The tars were shy of trying too hard to stop an officer, which allowed him get on to the deck with ease. He knew what he was about as he plunged into the sailors, shoving aside several as he made for those awaiting the arrival of Bellamy. The Negro was barely out of the boat, aware that four pairs of eyes were on him, and anticipating the blows that would be coming his way.

Markham's sword took the back marker right across the crown of his head, felling him immediately. Then he was amongst them, cursing and swearing as he slashed right and left to break up their formation. One got the guard right under the nose, he was pole-axed in a spraying cloud of blood; the third, dropping low to jab at his belly, got Markham's boot right on the chin. The last man swung his pike, and did make contact, though the officer fell more in expectation of the blow than any strength it had. As he hit the deck, Markham swung a leg that took the pikeman's feet from under him. He was upright in a flash, the canvas tipped point of his blade pressed on the sailor's neck.

'Single out one of my men again, and the next time you see this, you bastard, it will be naked steel.'

'My god, Markham, you're a scrapper,' called Germain. 'Play-acting is clearly not your forte after all. You must have a care, sir. I cannot afford to have men on the sick list.'

He held the blade where it was, as he replied, his chest heaving from his exertions. 'I have had the good fortune to mix with theatre people, sir. And they are all of the opinion that only total belief in the part will sustain a performance.'

The voice dropped as he said his parting words to the recumbent sailor. 'And I'll act on you so well, you'll be lucky to have limbs enough to warrant a berth in Greenwich Hospital.'

Markham spun away, and as he did so he saw Bellamy, well to the rear of his fellow Lobsters, dancing around disengaged, jabbing with his musket at the fresh air, pretending to look for a target while actually avoiding contact, which made him wonder if his intervention had been worthwhile.

'Belay!' shouted Germain. 'That was the best yet, all of you. But it is time for a rest. Mr Booker, you may tell the bosun to pipe the hands to dinner.'

The officer's dinner not yet being ready, de Puy was allowed on deck for fencing practice, and since that freed the poop, Germain invited the rest of Aramon's party to take the air. Given that the Monsignor was unhappy about their course, there was little actual conversation. He stood his servants around him, taking a keen interest in the techniques being displayed.

They ceased when dinner was called. Germain excused himself with the need to consult with the master, so taking his meal in Conmorran's tiny deck cabin. The following day it was his midshipmen. Clearly he had no intention of engaging in more communal dinners where he would be bound to face questions about his intentions.

And he kept everyone alert. He did this by creating alarms, pretending either the threat of an attack or a sudden change of course and sail. His aim seemed to be to exhaust everyone aboard, sailors and passengers, since, with half of these taking place during the hours of darkness, no one could sleep through the noise and commotion of the ship clearing for action.

But it had to be said he did not spare himself. Finally, after four days, a red-eyed Master and Commander pronounced himself satisfied, tinkered with the watches to balance his crew, then called Aramon on deck. There the cleric was required to witness his turn to the north, the prow set for the coast of France, his yards almost fore and aft to take advantage of the quartering west wind.

'She's a handsome sailer. Don't you reckon, Markham?'

'Very good on a bowline,' Markham replied, using an expression he'd heard aboard another vessel.

'Well spotted, sir,' Germain cried. 'It's not often a Lobster appreciates how close a ship can carry the wind. My *Syilphide* will still hold it eleven points free. What do you say to that, sir!'

Markham had very little idea of what the youngster was talking about. But he knew how naval officers felt about their ships. They spoke of them as a man might talk of a chaste and beautiful wife, even if the creature in question was a toothless, whey-faced wanton. Germain was no different. He would be blind to any fault in his new command. At least he seemed to be satisfied with the single word Markham employed.

'Amazing!'

'We will be well to the north of Cap Corse before the first dog watch. Then we must keep our eyes peeled, for it is there, between Marseilles and the Italian states that we might pick up a prize.'

'I think a day's rest might be in order, sir.'

'I daresay you have the right of it, Markham. I am puffed myself from our exertions. We shall have a capital dinner tonight, and an uninterrupted night's sleep.'

The voice, sounding disembodied, floated down from aloft. 'Sail, capt'n, fine on the larboard bow.'

Chapter six

Germain was taking no chances. These were hostile waters and he beat to quarters immediately. Suddenly the deck was, once again, full of running sailors. And from below decks came the crashing sound as the ship was cleared fore and aft. In the main cabin, the officers' servants were busy breaking down the furniture so that it could be struck down into the hold, while the carpenter and his mates hammered out the wedges that held the walls in place. These too were struck down below, and the crews assigned the cabin guns were at last free to cast them off from the tight breechings that held them to the hull.

'Mr Fletcher, we will have a French pennant at the masthead if you please. They may well know this ship. What they will not know is the fact that she has been taken.'

Markham wasn't aware that he'd pulled a face. But he must have, since Germain addressed something that was to a professional soldier, anathema.

'It is a legitimate ruse of war, Markham, but only in the approach. As long as I haul down that pennant before we open fire, I will have acted properly.'

'I give way to your greater experience in these matters,' Markham replied.

'Boarding nets, sir?' asked Fletcher.

'Not yet! Let's see what we have first.'

On the lower deck the gunner shooed his enforced guests out of the way, sending them to make out as best they could in the sail room, while he made sure the blankets covering his private domain were good and wet, so that the risk of a spark was minimised. Then he set to making up the charges necessary to fire the guns. Men were busy in the shot locker, passing out the freshly chipped six-pounder balls which were manhandled on to the deck, there to be laid in the rope garlands which would hold them against the pitch and roll of the ship. The youngsters, powder monkeys, ran from below in a constant stream, laying the canvas charges where the loader could get at them.

In the galley the one-legged cook dowsed the fire under his coppers, then joined with the armourer, working to ensure that cutlass blades were razor sharp, and that pike points were fine enough to penetrate human flesh. Rannoch was checking on the muskets, Markham's men lined up between the mainmast and the waist, awaiting instructions. The person who would give them, the Honourable George Germain, stood by the rail, telescope in hand, waiting to pick up a sight of what the man aloft had spotted. Midshipman Booker had joined him at the crosstrees and he was calling down a stream of information, first identifying the approaching vessel as a merchantman, then sending a *frisson* of anticipation and excitement through the ship by pronouncing it to be French.

'Is he coming on, Mr Booker?'

'He is, sir. If he's spied the tricolour pennant, you have completely fooled him.'

'We are going to have a chance to test the guns, Mr Markham,' cried Germain excitedly, a red flush tingeing his high cheekbones. 'Not much of a battle, of course, but even a merchant vessel will not strike to us without a broadside. This is just what the ship's company needs. That is prize money you are staring at, sir. So let the men know it. They'll ply more hearty if they know they're lining their pockets.'

There was an air of excitability about Germain that troubled Markham. He'd been in too many fights to get passionate himself, long ago realising that cool objective appraisal was worth ten tons of *élan*. The sound of gunfire was not, to him, a new experience. He wondered if it was for Germain. He knew the ship's captain had seen service, he could not have achieved his present rank without it. But the state he was in now led him to question how much action he'd been through. There was, Markham knew, a difference between talk of battle and the actuality.

He could not, of course, ask. Besides, what they were engaged in looked simple enough. For a second Germain looked at Aramon and de Puy, who came on deck and, with the trio of servants, now stood a few paces behind the captain. But he said nothing, instead he spun round and lifted his glass again, that followed by a shout to tell everyone he had 'the enemy topsails in sight.'

'Can you tell yet what she is, Mr Booker.'

'Two-masted and square-rigged. Broad in the beam. A merchant vessel for certain. Might be a Levant trader.'

'Would that you were a warship,' Germain murmured to himself.

'You sound disappointed,' said Aramon, who had moved close enough to Germain to hear.

'There's not much glory in taking a merchant vessel, Monsignor. I would want a rated French ship before this cruise is over, that is if I can have one. But I will not shy from a fat and easy merchant capture that will provide us all with some income. Especially one that seems intent on sailing into my pocket without so much as a fluff of her sail.'

'That might not last when they see the guns run out,' said Markham, quietly.

Under normal circumstances, given his ignorance of matters nautical, he would have held his tongue. He was still unhappy about sailing under a false flag. But he also knew that with little coin in his purse, he was as eager as anyone aboard to acquire a bit of prize money. The flag and the guns were sending two contradictory messages and that could not be right.

Germain didn't respond for nearly a minute, long enough not only to absorb the import of Markham's words, but to make the reaction sound like an idea of his own.

'Mr Fletcher. Before they get a clear view of our deck, re-house the guns and get the crews hidden behind the bulwarks. Shot and charges to be left in place, but take the match amidships so that the smoke looks as though it is coming from the galley chimney.'

He looked over the stern, to where the boats lay, towed and full of the animals from the manger. 'Boats in the water, in such hot weather, will excite no comment. The animals will just have to stay. But you, Mr Markham, will oblige me by taking your men below out of sight. Their red coats will certainly give the game away.'

'Sergeant Rannoch,' called Markham. 'Do as the captain asks, but be ready to return to the deck at a moment's notice.'

He took his own scarlet coat off and dropped it and the round black hat by the rail, throwing his sword on top. Germain didn't object, he just continued to study the merchantman.

'He's certainly a complacent fellow. He hasn't changed his course by a point since he spotted us.'

'Why should he, if he rates us friendly.'

'There is no love lost between warships and merchantmen, Mr Markham, in any language. No English trader would sail so close to a King's ship, for fear of losing half his crew. It can only be because he has the wind that he acts so.'

That was true. While *Syilphide*'s yards were braced hard round, the merchantman's sails were nearly square, the mizzen set angled just enough to allow main course and topsail to draw. He was making good speed, certainly better than the sloop. As in all actions at sea, time seemed to stand still, the vessels approaching each other at what could only be called a snail's pace. But eventually the merchant ship was hull up, and as she rose on a swell, Germain spotted something that made him move suddenly forward.

'How many guns does she carry?' he barked.

Booker answered in his thin reedy voice. 'She has ports for ten, sir, five on each side, though they are closed.'

'I can see that for myself.'

'There are guns housed behind them, with the same number on the starboard side.'

'But no merchant vessel carries so much. Is there any activity on the deck?'

'None but the usual, sir. There are men by the wheel, and a few working on deck. The rest are just staring over the rail at us, calm as you like.'

'Keep a sharp eye out.'

Germain was clearly nervous. And so he should be in this, his first independent action. It was a lonely life, being a ship's captain, and this was the pinnacle of that isolation. He was responsible for the ship and all that happened to her. Taking prizes was all very well, but the navy would want to account for any powder and shot expended. And the cost of repairing any damage, should the merchantman retaliate successfully, could easily fall at Germain's door.

'Pray God she's not carrying anything too heavy.'

'Which will force a retirement?' asked Aramon.

He said that in a tone that implied he would not be disappointed if that was the case. Clearly he saw this as a mere diversion, another delay to a matter which he held to be much more important.

Germain glared at him. 'I would not retire in the face of a hundred gun ship, sir. I merely allude to the fact that though merchant ships generally carry few cannon, they are often of a size to inflict damage on a thin-hulled ship like *Syilphide*.'

'Indeed?'

'I shall therefore not underestimate the threat they might pose, and act accordingly. Mr Fletcher, we will pass by within hailing distance. At the point at which we would be expected to trade pleasantries, strike that damned tricolour, and get our proper pennant up on the masthead.'

'And man the guns, sir?' the acting lieutenant asked.

'Yes,' Germain grinned. 'Let them see our teeth. The first broadside to be fired high, to scare them, then we will luff up to cross her stern, and with the wind so placed have all the advantage. At that point Mr Markham, you may don your coat and reassemble your men. I will need them to take possession of the prize.'

It was as the bowsprits came level that the merchantman suddenly began to edge away. The master had charge of *Syilphide*'s wheel. By instinct and without orders, he trimmed his own rudder, until a barked order from Germain ordered him back on course. As ordered, the flag came down, to be replaced by *Syilphide*'s own pennant. Almost simultaneously, those five ports across the water flew open, and a row of black snouts protruded, that followed by a rippling broadside from guns that must have been, like those on the sloop, pre-loaded.

Germain was issuing orders before the shots struck home; to man the guns and respond; to change course and wear away from their assailant. Markham had grabbed his coat, hat and sword, and was running for the companionway, yelling for Rannoch as the salvo struck home. Not well aimed, it was a ragged affair. But the cannon were of large calibre, and what shot did strike, all of it before the mainmast, inflicted significant damage.

The sloop shuddered as though slapped by a great hand, some shot striking the hull. Other cannonballs wrecked the forward bulwarks. One gun was dismounted, the breechings parting so that the carriage slewed across the sloping deck. Wood flew across the forecastle, great splinters dislodged, shaped like spears. Blocks fell from above to add to the mayhem, and before they'd hit deck or exposed head, the enemy had got off another salvo.

It was only the quality of the crew that got them clear. Hard bargains they might be, but they were King's Navy, proper seamen by trade, who'd been serving for over a year in the Mediterranean.

They went about their tasks with a deliberation that was admirable. There was no panic; just clear orders from petty officers, competently obeyed. The men on the guns, while their pieces bore, fired at will, and once they no longer had a target they housed them and immediately went to help with the sails and rigging. The yards were hauled round to take the wind, and being a swift sailer, *Syilphide* was soon out of the zone of maximum danger.

Germain had stood rigid in position, while all around him men struggled to effect emergency repairs, the bones on his face standing out because of the way he was clenching his jaw. His voice, when he spoke, had that same tightly drawn quality. But it was calm, a very necessary trait at a time like this.

'Mr Booker, please oblige me by returning to the deck. Mr Fletcher, I will be coming about to pursue. Please make sure that all the guns are fully manned.'

'You intend to continue the action?' asked Aramon, who hadn't moved from the spot where he stood. His dark complexioned face looked more outraged than surprised.

'You, sir, should have gone below deck. This is no place for a man of the cloth.'

Germain glared at Aramon, to very little effect. He then issued the orders that brought the sloop round into the other vessel's wake. Immediately the gap began to close. The enemy ship was making no attempt to put on speed. Indeed she was busy taking in her maincourse and mizzen gaff, reducing to topsails only. This was, Markham knew, the proper thing to do in a sea fight, fire being a huge risk with the lower sails still loose. Germain was ignoring that danger, setting sails one after the other, and with the wind now astern, coming up hand over fist.

'Can she be a merchantman, sir,' said Booker, fresh from the masthead. 'The guns were fully manned and as they fired their first salvo more came up from below.'

'A privateer, I should think,' Germain barked, so loud the youngster recoiled. 'And, what's more, Mr Booker, one who knew very well that Calvi has fallen.'

'I would be happier if you tell me what you plan to do, Captain,' said Aramon.

Germain gritted his teeth, and hissed his reply. 'Not that it is any of your concern, Monsignor. But it is my intention to lay alongside that damned vessel, give her several broadsides, and board in the smoke.'

'I am no warrior,' Aramon said, in a smooth, infuriating way. 'But it seems they have heavier guns that you, and they certainly have a more numerous crew.'

'I have faith in my country, and the God that protects it.'

Aramon snorted. 'I think you will find some of that same sentiment over yonder, young man, on that other ship. Which means at the very least God is neutral.'

'Your God may be, sir.'

'Is there any place that I can be of use?' asked de Puy.

Germain blinked, almost as if he didn't recognise the speaker, before responding. 'As a soldier, sir, I would say you would be best placed assisting Lieutenant Markham.'

Aramon's voice thundered out. 'You will stay clear of any danger de Puy, do you hear me. You are too valuable to be taking risks. Markham must manage without you.'

The object of this remark was amidships, which on the *Syilphide* was not too far away. But his thoughts were, and he wondered, as he saw a dispirited de Puy turn away, if Germain shared them. Markham was operating in a strange environment. But certain things applied to military affairs whether they were carried out on land or sea. Numbers and weight of firepower respected no individual location. And if Germain was right, and the enemy ship was a privateer instead of a proper rated vessel, then there were certain conclusions that could be drawn.

The first was that no such vessel was in the game of engaging in long drawn out fights, especially against proper warships. If *Syilphide* had been anything bigger than a sloop, then it was almost certain they would have put their helm over the minute they'd sighted her. But they'd come on, which must mean that they were prepared to do battle. That in itself was singular. The aim of a privateer was to capture, intact, both the ship and cargoes of her nation's enemies, then to sell both for the highest sum they could command. To this end they carried numerous crew, bloodthirsty rogues in the main, who worked for profit rather than any patriotic feelings. What could they possibly want with a sloop of war?

He'd heard Germain's reply to Aramon, and that too had given him cause for concern. Germain had gone on enough about the manoeuvrability of his new ship. Yet here he was proposing to throw that advantage aside and seek to engage the enemy on what could only be his terms. Why not lay off her stern as he'd originally proposed, out of the arc of her guns, and try and reduce the odds by bombardment. Clearly he was angry, smarting from having been outwitted by what looked like an easy capture. But was he letting his temper get in the way of his better judgement?

'If you will forgive me,' he said, as de Puy approached the companionway. Markham smiled reassuringly at the Frenchman, before slipping past him to approach Germain's back. 'May I have a private word, sir?'

'What!'

Markham touched his arm, causing Germain to jerk it a way in response. He'd also leant close, so that the words he spoke would not be overheard.

'I can understand your desire to pay them out in kind, but boarding against superior odds is hardly a wise idea.'

'You as well, Markham?' Germain responded loudly, green eyes flashing and cheekbones covered with taut skin. 'Am I to be plagued by unwanted advice all day? Neither you nor the Monsignor has the faintest notion of naval tactics, yet you both see fit to lecture me.'

'I have no desire to do anything of the sort, sir. But since it is my men who will lead the assault, I would be happier if the numbers on the enemy deck could be reduced somewhat by firepower.'

'Is this the same man I watched at Calvi?'

'Exactly the same, sir. The man at Calvi knew just as well the difference between an unarmed ship and that vessel we are pursuing. We have the ability to lay off and use our cannon.'

'I intend to take that ship, Markham, and send her to Lord Hood in a condition that will guarantee she fetches a decent price. That will no be got for something whose stern I have reduced to matchstick. No Frenchman can hold a candle to us in rate of fire. And as for the numbers you so fear, by the time I have swept their deck with grapeshot a couple of times, I daresay they will have evened out somewhat. Now be so good as to take up your proper station.'

'Can I put men in the tops as sharpshooters?'

'No. We are carrying too much sail. They will do more to start a fire with their damned powder flash than the enemy.'

Markham had to agree with that, and was slightly annoyed with himself for not realising it before asking. He went back to his men, the thought of grapeshot uppermost in his mind. Firing that was a two-way street, a tactic just as available to the French captain, if he had the means aboard, as it was to Germain. A group of red-coated marines, lined up neat and ready to board, would provide a tempting target to anyone planning to employ it.

Standing before them, his mind went back to the first action he had seen as their commander. That had been a fiasco, one in which they'd demonstrated fully their contempt for him. Many things had changed since then, but looking at what was happening now, he could not avoid the feeling that though the circumstances might be different, and his Lobsters willing to support him, the end result might just be the same.

'Sergeant Rannoch, I want to disperse the men. Split them into three sections. You take one to the bows, Corporal Halsey will man the poop, and I will keep the others here. You may threaten with your muskets, but don't fire them unless you're absolutely certain of hitting someone. Mr Germain intends at some point to close with the enemy and attempt to board. I want us concentrated at whatever seems to be the salient point, at the moment of contact, and I want a proper fusillade that will clear our way on to the enemy deck.'

'He is never going to send us amongst that crowd, is he?' asked Rannoch.

'Be thankful, sergeant. The mood he's in, and the way he sees us, I'm surprised he hasn't dropped us into a boat.'

'He is in a passion right enough,' Rannoch responded bitterly. 'How many men have I seen die for an officer's loss of temper.'

There was no time to ask Rannoch what he meant by that. Nor would asking have done any good. The Highlander had been a soldier a long time, and a damned good one. He also had, on his thumb, an 'M' that had been put there with a branding iron, the sign that he'd been found guilty of manslaughter. But he was cagey about discussing it, and could get very belligerent if quizzed. One thing was certain. He hated that breed of officers, of which Germain it seemed was one, who cared more for glory than for the men they killed in pursuit of it.

'What are you about, Mr Markham,' called Germain, as he saw the marines divide.

'If they cannot lay down musketry from the tops sir, they may be able to do something from both ends of the deck, as long as they are clear of the gunners.'

'May God rest your soul.'

The voice was Bellamy's, and had his usual tone of deep irony.

It came as no surprise that his two NCOs had left the Negro with him, though it did anger him.

'I wish he would rest your tongue. And you should pray so too, considering the trouble it gets you into.'

'Should I, sir, faced with pig-like ignorance, say nothing.'

'What caused that near riot below decks?' demanded Markham, wondering where the sudden inspiration had come from to make him ask now.

Bellamy wasn't Rannoch. He had no notion that officers, as a separate breed, should be kept in the dark about certain matters. He was only too keen to tell his side of the story.

'They were saying the most lewd things about the Mademoiselle's maid, just because she was a Negro. They do not see beauty or grace in the way she moves.'

'You sound a bit struck yourself, Bellamy.'

'I admit to an attraction as great as that which you harbour for her mistress.' Bellamy, if he heard the sharp intake of breath at such damned cheek, ignored it. Nor did his expression betray any hint that he might have said anything untoward. 'It was natural then, that I should make every effort to ensure her comfort and well being. I took every opportunity, when my duties permitted, to deepen the acquaintance.'

'A fact which would hardly be a secret from the crew.'

'All they saw was an outlet for their lowlife libidinous ways. They were laying bets, in my hearing, as to how many of them she could service in one watch. Some of them, it seemed, had been to the gunner's quarters and tried to ask her price. That was bad enough, but one fellow went so far as to make an approach while I was actually talking with her.'

'What's her name?' asked Markham, his eyes firmly fixed on the approaching ship.

'Renate, and she is a Coptic Christian from Abyssinia, of good family, and can read and write. And there she was being treated like a harlot. I could hardly be expected to remain silent in the face of such behaviour. I pointed out to several of them, when I got back to the mess deck, that just because their own mothers had probably been whores of the most brutish variety, it gave them no right to so judge other people.'

'That sounds like a recipe for harmony,' said Markham, with deep irony. Bellamy could have the right of it, but it was more than likely that, observing his interest, the sailors had set out to guy him. The Negro had taken seriously what had probably been intended as a rather cruel joke.

'I will not see any women traduced, sir, especially those of my own colour.'

'Bellamy. I hope you never end up in a prison.'

'May I wish you the same, sir.' the Negro replied, in a voice that was as sarcastic as it was solicitous.

Germain had nearly overhauled the chase, and was now shortening sail while at the same time calling for the guns to be trained forward to give the enemy a taste of powder. They in turn had their cannon levered towards their stern, and were just waiting for *Syilphide* to come in range before serving her out once more. Markham was more concerned about the relative sizes. The sloop was low in the water compared to the merchant ship; normally he assumed no cause for alarm when boarding due to the relative disparity in numbers.

But now it was the wrong way round. He faced superior numbers and he and his men would have to clamber up the side of the ship to engage them, this while both vessels rocked on the swell. And that would have to be undertaken when they'd already been exposed to concentrated musket fire, or even worse, cannon. It seemed like a recipe for disaster in his book, and he sought desperately for a solution. The only one that presented itself was the idea that he could get aboard where they didn't expect him. How to achieve that, when overlooked, seemed impossible.

These ruminations were shattered by the first salvo from both sets of cannon, which wreathed the fighting ships in great clouds of grey and black smoke. Blown forward, that was more of an advantage to Germain than his opposite number, and he made full use of it, edging in closer to the enemy wake so that their second salvo missed completely, churning up the water off the larboard mainchains.

Against that, the increased angle meant that for a while Germain's guns couldn't bear, and the wind had whipped his protective smokescreen away by the time they did. But he had gained on his foe, with his bows now beginning to overhaul the broad stern, so that his forward cannon, even though only of six-pound weight, could inflict real damage on the merchant vessel. One shot went straight through the rear port, and the satisfying clang of metal on metal, accompanied by loud screams, was enough to establish that they had dismounted a gun.

The reply killed any euphoria, as a swathe of bar shot swept across the prow, high enough to spare Rannoch and the men Markham had sent there, but deadly enough to remove every forward sail, half the bowsprit, and the top portion of the foremast. *Syilphide's* speed dropped immediately, and her head yawed away despite the best efforts of the master to hold it steady.

That brought every gun on the deck to bear and they used the opportunity well, catching their opponents reloading and doing telling damage. But Germain must have known what was coming, a full broadside from the enemy, since he yelled to Conmorran to let go and let the ship fall away from its course. At the same time, the marlin spikes holding the falls were pulled, releasing the clove hitch knots and the pressure on the yards, which spun sideways as the wind took them, to leave the sails flapping uselessly.

The sloop lost most of its forward motion, which saved Germain from the drubbing he'd anticipated. The water forward seemed to boil as thousands of rounds of grapeshot peppered the sea right at the point where *Syilphide* should have been. Germain was still yelling, calling men from the guns to reset the yards, screaming at the master to down his helm so that the sloop would yaw across the merchantman's stern. And his marine officer was not excluded.

'I intend to remove those deadlights, Mr Markham,' he bellowed, pointing to the thick, carved sheets of timber that had been rigged to protect the vulnerable casement windows that covered the enemy's stern. 'And when they are shattered, I want you to lead your marines though the gap.'

'Holy Mary, mother of Christ,' Markham said to himself.

'Man the larboard cannon and fire as you bear,' shouted Germain to the crew, his voice mixing with that of his marine lieutenant, as he called his men to form up amidships with him.

Chapter seven

Converting a merchant ship to fight proved to have one major drawback. It was not equipped to defend itself either to the front or the rear, an obvious vulnerability that Germain should have exploited from the very first. His anger at that opening broadside had obviously blinded him. But the enemy had, inadvertently, forced him into taking a second chance. There were no stern chaser cannon and the square construction of the hull made it impossible for the deck guns to bear.

Faced with only inaccurate musket fire over the taffrail, *Syilphide* could edge right in so that the cannon did maximum damage. Markham, no longer exposed to a full broadside with grapeshot, had gathered his marines amidships and had them firing volleys to clear the defenders from the taffrail. All they needed now was a point of entry, which had to be through the cabin area, the casements of which were covered by sections of heavy oak, elaborately carved with smiling cupids and dancing nymphs. It also told them the ship's name was *Massime* and that its home port was Marseilles.

Germain was firing at near point-blank range. Even so the deadlights cracked but didn't shatter. It took three full salvoes to effect the first breech. Then every gun had to be aimed into that spot to finally open up an avenue which Markham and his Lobsters could exploit.

That was still something easier to contemplate than to achieve. There were bound to be defenders waiting on the lower deck to stop them. They would move into position as soon as Germain stopped plying his guns. Markham yelled to him for another salvo as he moved his men into position, crammed in two groups between a pair of six-pounder cannon. The request produced no more than a blank stare of incomprehension. But the gun captains nearby had carried out the reloading procedure without orders, so that they were ready to oblige.

No one waited for orders from the quarterdeck. They took the command straight from the marine officer, and though grape would have been better, they put half-a-dozen balls into the cabin, that followed by a heart-warming sound of splintering wood, shattering glass and several human screams.

Markham was first through the narrow gap, losing his hat right away, with his coat snagged on the sharp-edged timbers. Coming out of searing sunlight into near darkness, he felt utterly helpless, so he fired off his pistol as a precaution before he finally manoeuvred his body into the shattered cabin. This was another feature different on a merchant vessel. In a warship there would have been no impediments to stop either defender or attacker, nothing but a clean sweep fore and aft.

That, once the deadlights had been breached, would have exposed those on the lower deck to a murderous fire, as the cannonballs ripped from one end of the ship to the other. But here, as well as broken window frames and a carpet of glass, there was furniture, though it had been pulped by the gunfire. Also, on the far side, stood the remains of the bulkhead that had separated the captain's day cabin from his sleeping quarters and those of his servants.

There were bodies too, the crumpled forms of men who had been sent into the cabin when they should have stayed outside. Perhaps they had been caught by that last, extra salvo that Markham had called for. It made no difference, he was just grateful, since it gave him a chance to form up his men in some kind of order before they became engaged. Rannoch was hauling the last of them through the gap, cursing at them roundly in a mixture of English and his Highland Gaelic, ordering those already through to fix bayonets and form a proper line.

Markham knew his job. There would be no rushing forward. Instead they must advance steadily, and hold off any challenge, so that Germain and his sailors could follow them through and provide sufficient numbers for an assault on the upper deck. On *Syilphide* they'd aim the guns high, to fire up through the stern-deck planking and keep it clear.

Musketry, with precious little time to reload, might consist of one salvo, which would need to be timed to perfection to achieve the maximum result. The Syilphides were still outnumbered. The only hope they had of success was sheer brio: to inflict such casualties on their enemy with the bayonet, cutlass and pike that the remainder would give way for fear of their lives.

A lack of discipline in the defence helped considerably. A commander in proper control of his men would have avoided close action, and instead set up a line of muskets to keep a clear space between the attackers and his crew, decimating the British assault every time they tried to advance. Clearly they lacked a file of marines to employ the method Markham would have used if the positions had been reversed.

Close-quarter fighting in a confined space favoured Markham's men, as was proved as soon as the defenders tried to engage. They couldn't bring their superior numbers to bear. The line of marines, with Markham at one end and Rannoch at the other, formed a solid wall of advancing bayonets. And the enemy, even if they had much longer pikes and boat hooks, were up against men well trained in mutual support, as well as the art of parry and thrust with Brown Bess and bayonet.

The first impediment to this steady forward progress was the shattered bulkhead that stood between the cabins and the main-deck. Some of the panelling remained intact, while other sections had been blown apart. The French stood on one side, and his marines on the other. Markham accepted a halt, content to hold the cabin till the Syilphides could build up their strength. They, with Germain and young Fletcher at their head, were crowding in behind him, over thirty determined sailors, with their blood up, aching to be at the enemy, frustrated by the marines standing foursquare in their path.

Some form of order was a priority; otherwise his own men would be jostled forward. But to assert control in a crowded cabin, with everyone shouting at once, was impossible. The two naval officers were trying in vain to hold their men back, each one they stopped matched by another who slipped through, every shout they delivered answered by an angry curse. Even that collective bellowing was drowned by a salvo from *Syilphide*, not only the crash of the guns, but the wrenching of timbers being torn apart by metal right above their heads. Only by furious pushing and shoving could Markham split his men, trying to get them to form some sort of funnel through which the sailors pressing at their backs could advance.

He shouted his order without any sure knowledge that they would hear. Led by Rannoch, they fired across each other, an untidy salvo that was no more than follow my leader. The first batch of some fifteen boarders rushed through the belching smoke to reach the gaps in the bulkhead. Markham took a chance on them holding at least, and gave his men time to reload, something that few of them managed in the allotted twenty seconds. Bellamy and Dornan, the two least useful pair, were still ramming home their cartridges when the enemy put in an extra effort that pressed the Syilphides back. The rest of the Lobsters reacted well, jamming their muskets through the throng, either between bodies or over shoulders, and just letting fly to ease the pressure.

It worked, even if they could not be sure they hadn't hit their own. The French suddenly fell back enough to let the attack get past the bulkhead on to the open deck behind. Germain and the other half of his boarding party followed, yelling like banshees. When the marines got through, Markham could see only a frenzy of wild activity, in which it was near impossible to tell friend from foe.

Germain and Fletcher were visible because of the blue coats and the officer's swords. They were trying to employ them in regulation fashion, as if they were still practising on their own deck. But for the rest there was no line as such, just a melee of swinging clubs, jabbing sabres, of punching, gouging and biting, as the two evenly matched groups fought to gain a degree of supremacy.

Markham concentrated his men on the larboard side of the ship, and forming them into a phalanx pushed forward, his left marker brushing the bulkhead. They had to use their butts to clear a path through the battling Syilphides. Only then could they employ their bayonets on the French. The collective discipline was rewarded by an immediate withdrawal. That swept clear a space from which he could push back towards the centre of the deck, taking the bulk of the enemy in flank until he was shoulder to shoulder with the captain, the result a clear gain of some ten feet.

'We have them, Markham,' Germain shouted, eyes blazing.

As he said that Fletcher went down, the point of the pike that had caught him with such force protruding from the top half of his back. Germain stepped forward, sword extended, his front knee bending to increase his range, the tip taking Fletcher's killer in the throat. Markham, temporarily not engaged, stooped down and pulled the young midshipman clear. Looking down into his startled eyes, and at the blood pumping out through his gaping mouth, it was obvious he was dying.

The attack was going well. After his rush, the Syilphides were still making steady if unspectacular progress, pressing the enemy back to the companionways that ran up on to the deck. Any hope of repeating his previous manoeuvre was rendered impossible by the way his men had become entangled with the fight, clubbing and stabbing where they were allowed the space to do so.

The planking beneath their feet was running with blood, and one of the greatest dangers faced by the advancing men was to trip over a recumbent body, friend or foe, an act which opened them up to a blow from the enemy. Markham, using his height, was slashing forward with his sword. Vaguely he became aware that Rannoch, as cool and professional as ever, was dragging from the fight two men at a time so that they could reload their muskets.

Nothing is more exhausting than the continual exertions of battle. And in the heat of a Mediterranean summer, here between crowded decks, that was magnified tenfold. Markham was sweating buckets, his tongue feeling like a piece of leather in his parched mouth. And he knew that he was tiring, his right arm aching from swinging and stabbing with his blade. His marines would be the same, and it was only a matter of time before the Syilphides, with half-a-dozen men already down, began to relax an onward drive so ferocious that would be impossible to sustain.

Perhaps the French had calculated for that, since the pair of companionways that straddled the mainmast, which they were struggling to reach, now so tantalisingly close, were suddenly full of reinforcements. Here was a body of fresh defenders, led by men in light blue uniform coats, rushing to the relief of their wilting comrades, in sufficient quantity to outnumber the attackers.

Markham stopped at fifty. He had anyway, no need to count them. Anyone with an ounce of sense could see the game was up as soon as they appeared; that up against fresh arms and over-whelming superiority, the boarding party would have to give ground. And he also suspected, seeing those uniforms, that this was no privateer, but a ship converted by the French Navy, quite possibly for the very task of surprising British warships. Any lack of a disciplined response changed with proper officers in control, and that alone swiftly altered the nature of the conflict.

The Syilphides didn't surrender ground immediately. They seemed, at Germain's behest, to redouble their efforts in the face of this magnified threat, enforcing a temporary stalemate. That, at least, gave him time to disengage and think. If they fell back piecemeal, they would lose men and cohesion. That could, if properly pressed home, take the French back through the

73

shattered cabin, and right on to the deck of *Syilphide*. If they managed to maintain their momentum, and get aboard in enough numbers, they would achieve their ultimate aim and take the ship. That had to be avoided, even if in the process he would be forced to sacrifice some of the men fighting alongside him.

The only people who could hold a disciplined line were his marines, and for that they needed space to bring their superior skills to bear. There was no time to consult Germain, still in the thick of things, still calling for greater efforts. Markham yelled for his Lobsters to disengage, grabbing at several to haul them clear, since they could barely hear him.

Rannoch, even taller than his officer, must have drawn the same conclusion. Markham had the distinct impression that he'd started jerking men back before the order was actually given. They didn't all get clear. Yelland, Dymock and Tully were still in there, trapped in the heaving mass of bodies, unaware of their mates lining up all the way back by the shattered bulkheads, raising their weapons to fire a volley.

'Steady,' Markham shouted.

His voice was rasping due to his previous exertions, leaving him wondering how many of his men actually understood the command. He had to physically raise the nearest bayonets, fearing that the retreating Syilphides would impale themselves. Luckily those out of his reach copied their mates, and aimed their points at the overhead deck beams. There was neither time nor sufficient silence for complicated commands. He had to trust that they'd be ready to drop and fire on the fall of his up-raised sword. They would need to obey, even if some of their own men, including the captain, were still out front. Rannoch, on the other end of the line, was talking to those closest to him, quite possibly saying the very same. Even in dumb show the movement of his lips seemed slow and even, an oasis of calm in a hot, noise-filled and bloody arena.

The Syilphides begin to give ground, hardly surprising given the numbers they faced. Germain was doing his best to rally them, but it was in vain. Worse than that, it was the wrong tactic in the situation. Markham, lubricating his throat with what little saliva he could muster, waited until the movement spread, till the back markers were taking consecutive paces to the rear, pushing to try and hold their mates in front. The noise abated just a fraction, as contact was broken, so he filled his lungs and yelled.

'Syilphides to me!'

The deck remained full of shouting cursing men, with the clang of striking metal and wood still very audible. He could not expect them all to hear, even less to react. Germain did, stepping back and turning his head, the pointed sword keeping him safe, the surprise in his eyes total. Markham leant forward to yell in his ear.

'We must retreat, sir, or risk the ship.'

Even if it was only a few seconds, the captain seemed to take an age to comprehend what was at risk. Fortunately the men falling back swept him along till any choice in the matter was removed. Germain, at least, could step back smartly. But for those at the very front it was no easy matter to completely disengage in a fight, especially with no clear route to your rear. But the men nearest the line of marines reacted swiftly, which increased the pressure on those in front. Speed of retreat aided quite a few, Germain included, though Markham saw several go down under a rain of blows that now came from all angles.

'What are you about man?' Germain screamed, sweat streaking the filth that had covered his face. 'We had them beat!'

'You have been humbugged again, sir. Your opponent practically invited you to board so that he could trap you.'

It was an unpleasant thing to say, and definitely not what Germain wanted to hear. But it had to be done, in an attempt to make the captain see sense. And he knew there was no perfect time for the action he proposed to take. It was just a case of personal judgement, allied to a determination that the ship would not be taken.

'Get back aboard *Syilphide* sir, and do what you have to do to get us clear.'

Men were slipping through and under the Lobsters' bayonets, including Tully and Yelland. Only the later still had his musket. But Dymock was caught in the back, falling forward at the feet of his mates, who had to leave him be as they concentrated on what needed to be done.

There were still half-a-dozen British sailors in there when Markham yelled the order to fire, the salvo filling the intervening space with a huge cloud of smoke. Bellamy's rammer was still in his musket, and it impaled two Frenchman standing so close to each other they were like one torso. The enemy recoiled, taken totally by surprise, so most of the attackers got clear. But Markham could just see one of the men who'd baited Bellamy writhing on the deck, clutching at his gut.

Markham's throat now felt as though it was lined with sand, but he managed enough of a shout to relay his orders. 'Bellamy, Dornan, drag that damned tar out of there. Then try to aid Dymock.'

Dornan, as bovine as ever, was too slow to react. But Tully, since he had no musket, was there with the Negro as he moved forward on the command. Markham knew that Bellamy had only acted out of pure instinct. Had the Negro paused, to give a second's thought to what he was being told to do, he would have stayed rock still. But he moved, dropping on one knee to clutch at the armpit of the screaming sailor. Tully had the other, and under the frisson of pointing bayonets and reloaded muskets, they hauled him clear, handing him over to two waiting sailors. Then they looked to help Dymock, now writhing between his comrades' legs.

'Keep going,' Markham shouted, when he saw they had him.

The second salvo went off above the two Samaritans' heads, the flaming wads from the cartridges landing on their coats and singing them. The French were halted, though. Even better, the men to the fore who were still standing were trying to hide, trying to find succour in the body mass of their mates who stood behind them.

All they could see was the line of red coats before them, half-a-dozen men reloading with parade ground precision. The officers who'd come down the companionway were trapped at the rear, their superior numbers now an impediment instead of an asset. There was no one amongst the original defenders with either the wit or the stature to state the obvious. That if they charged immediately after a salvo, they might have risked a bayonet, but they would easily overwhelm this meagre line of defence. Finally, one of the officers managed to make himself heard, cursing at his men to advance.

'Behind the bulkhead,' he rasped.

Lobsters, instead of firing, stepped back. That did cause the enemy to try a rush, a foolish move against loaded muskets. The next volley sent those still on their feet scurrying back, slipping and tripping on the blood and the bodies that littered the deck. By the time they reformed, the guns were loaded again. There was little shouting now from the rank and file, more a discontented murmuring above which their officers were calling for action.

'Corporal Halsey, see how matters are progressing on the ship.

We must have it clear and able to haul off, but not so far that they can leave us behind.'

The old man slipped back to the casement windows, through the now empty cabin, to peer through the shattered deadlights. The scream that followed was totally out of character.

'They've cut loose your honour, and are polling off.'

'Get yourself aboard, Halsey. The rest of you fall back at the double, two at a time.'

He could do no more. To rush for safety would jeopardise them all, since there was no room to get everyone out at once.

'Sergeant Rannoch, get over by those deadlights and supervise the retreat.'

'One more volley, sir.'

The 'sir' was rare, and engendered in Markham, exhausted as he was, a good feeling. But he also knew the word volley was gilding in, with so few men left.

'As you wish, then go.'

The muskets crashed out, and before the sound had faded Rannoch was tallying off the men to go, smallest first, all the while reloading his own weapon.

'Ettrick and Quinlan move! Yelland and Gibbons follow. Dornan, you slow arse, with me.'

Markham felt the musket pressed into his hand as Rannoch departed, and he threw his sword to the sergeant just as he reached the point of exit. The retreat had not gone unnoticed by the enemy, some of whom had already started forward.

'Come now, man,' shouted Rannoch, who was halfway through the deadlights. 'I am having to jump.'

Which he did, his body disappearing to reveal a patch of bright sunlight, and some of *Syilphide*'s departing rigging. Time assumed another dimension. Before him the French were breaking into a run, behind there was nothing but the jagged hole made by Germain's cannon. Was there time?

He was barely aware of pulling the trigger, and had no idea where the ball went. Then he was running, what only seemed a few steps, but which felt like a lifetime. Behind him his pursuers were yelling, a mixture of triumph and calls for revenge, the sound of their slithering feet strange on the blood-soaked deck.

He threw the musket through the hole, just as he would a spear, hard enough for it to land on *Syilphide*'s deck and jammed himself through, scrabbling in near panic to get his legs to follow his trunk. One foot got purchase and he was able to lever himself out, throwing his body to one side so that the thick oak would protect his vital parts.

The man who came through behind him, waving a deadly cleaver died before he could swing it, his body slumping to close that gap. Markham was vaguely aware of Rannoch, standing feet apart on the deck not ten feet away. He was also aware that ten feet was too far for him to jump without taking a decent run. Above him the enemy had reclaimed the taffrail, and it was only a matter of time before pikes would be jabbing down to impale him, despite the gunfire being aimed at them by his Lobsters. Behind him, hands were hauling the dead man out of the way.

'Mister Markham can swim,' yelled Rannoch. 'Throw a line into the water.'

Putting his hands together above his head, Markham executed a perfect dive into the cooling sea, deliberately going deep to avoid the hail of missiles that were sure to follow. Coming up, he could see the musket balls that entered the water, there to die in silver streaks as the sea took away their velocity. Surfacing so close to the French ship was a chance he had to take, though he struck out at his fastest swim to fool anyone just taking aim.

The ropes thrown from the deck straddled him, and Markham, in his panic, grabbed and missed the first one. But he got the second, twisting it round his wrist. The men on *Syilphide* began to haul just as the next round of musket fire came from the stern of the converted merchantman. Most missed, but one caught him in the leg that had come out of the water, searing across his breeches, and he was sure, drawing blood.

Germain was firing his cannon now, smashing the deadlights again, as well as the taffrail, driving the enemy from the positions they'd occupied. And he was setting as much sail as he could, heading into the wind, which took him clear slowly. But could he be certain, with the damage he'd suffered, that he could sail closer to the wind that his opponent? Could they get clear, or would his first task on getting on board be to prepare for another battle?

Markham observed all this from the sea, hauled in like a caught fish to the side. Some of the Syilphides had dropped a line from the yards, and he took hold of that so that when they hauled him aboard, he was not scrapped bloodily up the rough planking, nor dragged across the barnacle-encrusted copper that showed as the ship heeled over. Finally he was on deck, able to look down and see the slash across his calf, just above his left boot, and the blood streaming from the wound to run into the pool of seawater gathering around his feet.

He could also see the tally of dead and wounded, which did not include those they'd left aboard the enemy ship. Germain took refuge in his toil, the need to get the ship back to some semblance of its former self. He did not even look in Markham's direction, though there was no doubt he had a sight of him firmly in the corner of his eye, as the marine officer removed his soaking coat.

'Might I suggest you go below, Lieutenant Markham,' said the Comte de Puy. 'Mademoiselle Moulins and her maid have set up a sick bay, and will attend to your wounds.'

He was just about to reply that there might still be work to do, but the Frenchman's doleful expression changed the words on his lips. 'Where is Monsignor Aramon?'

De Puy gestured to the hunched figure, bent over an inert body of a sailor by the shattered bulwark. 'The man, it seems, is a Catholic.'

'Then God rest his soul,' Markham replied softly.

But he stopped himself from making the sign of the cross, something no commissioned officer in the British forces would do. Instead he hobbled across the deck.

'Sergeant, how many of the men are fit for duty?'

'Dymock is bad, with a cutlass wound in his back that you could put your hand in. The young French lady and her black maid have bandaged him up. For the rest, there is many a cut and bruise, though nothing that will see them unfit for another bout.'

'We got off light just now.'

Rannoch glared at Germain's back. 'If that man had been given his way, we would not have got off at all. You had best go below, and get that wound of your own seen to.' Markham jerked his head to indicate the enemy, a factor that the Highlander acknowledged with a nod.

'There will be time.'

'You're right. Can you get someone to fetch me a drink.'

'Water?' asked Rannoch, smiling.

'That first, sergeant. Then I'd like a flagon of that stuff Germain purloined when he took over the ship.'

'Enemy coming about,' came the shout from the masthead.

Markham raised himself just enough to see the truth of that. But he could see that the manoeuvre was slow, that the merchant ship

79

seemed a poor sailor. But given his endemic nautical ignorance he needed to have the fact confirmed by the bosun, close by him supervising repairs.

'Catch us, your honour? That barky! Never in life, 'cepting he sprouts wings.'

'We have suffered some damage.'

The sailor grinned. 'Why, we could outrun him wi' no more'n your stock on a yard.'

The whole of the lower deck had been turned into a sickbay, with recumbent bodies everywhere. The most serious wounds were laying flat on the planking, some still, others softly moaning. Those less badly hurt were sitting against the side, patiently waiting for attention. Mademoiselle Moulins and her maid moved amongst them, the Negro girl dispensing much needed water while her mistress distributed bandages, requesting those who could manage to attend to those who could not.

Markham found a chest to sit on, and, removing his boot and stocking, he rolled up his breeches to reveal a deep gash. The ball had gouged out a goodly section of flesh, which was stinging from the seawater that ran into it. But it was a surface wound, and not one for which he needed much in the way of treatment. Still probing at his calf to try and ease the pain, he was suddenly aware of the bloodstained apron in front of him.

'If you oblige me with a clean bandage, Mademoiselle Moulins, I can tend to the article myself.'

She dropped down on her knees, the musky smell of her perspiration filling his nostrils, that mixed with whatever scented preparation she used to set her hair. Her fingers, as they brushed gently across the back of his leg were cool and gentle, the combined effect of all three making George Markham decidedly uncomfortable. Gratefully, he took the ladle the Negro girl offered him, and drank deeply.

'I have some salve that will ease the pain, Lieutenant,' she said.

A quick word to her maid sent the girl scurrying off. Markham saw Bellamy in the gloom, laying a solicitous hand on Renate as she slipped past him. Was he one of the walking wounded? That was a fleeting thought. His attention was taken with the girl close by.

'The mere fact of your presence does that,' Markham replied gently.

She looked up at his, a slight smile playing on the corners of her lips. 'But I am only with you for a second. You will need something that lasts longer than that.'

'Sure, that is a pity. But I thank the gods that I am blessed with a good memory.'

'Good enough to know what kind of behaviour my present situation demands?'

'Had I ever been told, I'm sure I would remember. We have all been left to make assumptions.'

She turned away to bathe the face of one of the sailors lying on the deck. 'And which were yours.'

'I try not to make them,' he lied. 'But were I prone to, seeing you like this could not render them anything but flattering. The word angelic springs to mind.'

'That is too great a credit. Having been raised by nuns, tending to wounds was part of my schooling. So how you now see me at this moment has no special significance.'

Markham suddenly felt she was toying with him. Not that the notion offended him. All his experience pointed to that as a good sign. Women didn't bait men in whom they had no interest. The thought that she might set his imagination racing. It was fortunate that the Negro girl returned, carrying a stone jar with some pungent green liniment inside. Ghislane Moulins turned back, wafting that same mixture of odours up into his nose. She dipped her fingers in, then rubbed the unction back and forth across Markham's wound. The stinging, as it penetrated his flesh, made him suck in his breath.

'A little pain is a good sign, Lieutenant.'

'Sure,' Markham replied, shifting uneasily, 'that depends on where the pain is.'

As soon as he returned to the deck, still a hive of activity, he looked aft, only to observe that the bosun's confidence had not been misplaced. *Syilphide* was labouring, but still the *Massime* was falling behind at an almost visible rate, ploughing along, yards braced round, seeming to make little headway. Germain was no longer on the quarterdeck, and the ship was under the control of Conmorran, the master, with Midshipman Booker as officer of the watch.

'Why does he bother to pursue when he can't catch us.'

The master was an old grey-haired fellow, with grizzled ruddy features. Having spent his entire life at sea, he had little time for what he would no doubt term daft questions. His tone of voice, when he replied certainly created that impression.

'Happen he has nowt better to do, it being such a fine sunny afternoon.'

'He'll stay on the chase till nightfall, sir,' said Booker, excitedly eager to share his superior knowledge, 'hoping that he might carry something away. He cannot know the extent of the damage we have suffered.'

'Thank you, Mister Booker,' said Markham, giving the irascible master a glare as he turned away, a look that was meant to register and did. The voice behind his back, just loud enough for him to hear, made him wish he hadn't bothered.

'You don't want to be so free lad with your explainings, certainly not to the likes of a Lobster officer. Jumped up nobodies the lot of 'em I say. And that one would be better minded explaining hisself than posing questions, especially about certain events which took place when he was no more 'n your age.'

Markham forced himself to stand still by the rail, watching the rapidly diminishing French ship. But underneath he was seething, wondering why he had bothered to do anything to save the ship. He should have just let the French come on board and skewer the lot of them.

Chapter eight

It didn't take much in the way of brainpower to work out that Germain was in trouble. In his first engagement in command of his own ship he'd received a drubbing, and that from a Frenchman who'd double bluffed him. No amount of gilding would make the ship's log read any better. Every manoeuvre had to be detailed from the first sighting; times, courses and intentions, the amount of shot expended, as well as the damage listed. Then there was the fruitless attempt to board and the tally of dead and wounded that action had produced.

In a service that thrived on a constant diet of success, that would not be pleasant reading. Not that reading was necessary. Any interested party just had to look at the state to which *Syilphide* had been reduced to realise that had they faced an enemy any more speedy than a converted merchantman, they could hardly have avoided capture. The pumps were clanking away, trying to reduce the amount of water in the well. The carpenter had gloomily reported how often she'd been struck below the water-line, and his opinion of how long it would take to get at some of the shattered hull timbers. The knowledge that he was a confirmed pessimist did nothing to help.

Above there was even more damage, especially forward. Great swathes of bulwark ripped out, with only the ropes they'd rigged to stop a man falling into the sea. The dismounted cannon could not be replaced for the lack of anything with which to affix the breechings. In the sickbay there were dozens of wounded men, and they'd already had the service that had seen four canvas coffins slip over the side. A quick check on the muster roll showed that they had left a dozen men on the French ship, almost certainly dead by now if they'd not been when abandoned. The French captain would look to his own casualties before he attended to any British sailor.

Everything pointed to a return to Corsica, to the anchorage off San Fiorenzo, where repairs could be carried out and the crew numbers made up to something like their complement. Everything, that is, but Aramon's pleading. And this was allied to Germain's own inclination to put off the day of reckoning.

In some ways Markham could sympathise. Given Germain's name and position in the navy, a bold stroke, a success of some kind seemed very necessary. His rank of Master and Commander was honorary. He was still a lieutenant, still a long way from that grail of naval advancement; the need to be made a post captain. Nothing was more vital than that, since it opened a route to promotion. Such a prize presented many opportunities, for both glory and profit, and in time, as those above him died, Germain could be sure, if he himself survived, of being made an admiral. No doubt he'd dreamed that an opportunity would present itself to make the name Germain mean something other than a standard of cowardice.

To return with his ship in its present condition would certainly put a blight on that rosy prospect. He might find himself beached at his present rank. Markham had no idea how much influence it had taken to get Germain to sea in the first place. But after such a comprehensive failure, it might be that no amount of that commodity would see him re-employed. So Aramon, insisting that they continue, was pushing at an open door. But it turned out that the Monsignor was taking no chances, as Markham found out when Germain, in the middle of the night, lantern in hand, crept into his screened off quarters.

Markham was halfway out of his cot, a hand reaching for his sword, when he realised who it was. In the low light from the tallow in the lantern, the young man looked a touch fevered, especially about the eyes. The finger he put to his lips stopped Markham from speaking, and the ship's captain was sat on his cot before the owner could ask him what he thought he was about.

'I would have asked you to come to my cabin,' he whispered, 'but that, for what I have to impart, is the least secure part of the ship.'

The wave of the arm indicated that Markham should come even closer, a difficult thing to achieve, since, as it was, Germain was practically sitting on top of him.

'The old Papist has told me what it is we are after ashore. Only he, de Puy and now I, are in on the secret. He made me swear that I wouldn't tell a soul, but I cannot avoid telling you. Believe me Markham, when you hear the details, you will be astounded.'

Markham had a sudden feeling that he didn't want to know, didn't want to share the secret. Money was tempting, but dying was not, and after today his faith in the captain was severely dented. There was also his own position to consider, which would not be enhanced by Germain's failure. Care had to be taken not to compound a less than perfect situation.

If his superior officer ordered him ashore, he would be bound to obey, and in ignorance he could at least plead the excuse of duty. But once part of this conspiracy, he would have the right to accept or reject any command he was given. And that, if things went wrong, would do nothing to aid his situation. Germain didn't seem to realise that he wasn't the only one with a reputation to worry about.

Probably, if he was sent home for what happened to the *Syilphide*, Germain would return to a family and some form of stability. All that waited for George Markham back in England was a bailiff seeking money he didn't have, with quite possibly a Bow Street Runner on hand to take him up for killing his fellow duellist. And in Ireland it was even worse. His half-sister Hannah hated him for the stain his birth had placed on the family name. Worse, she had demanded back from him every penny gifted to him by his late father, and he lacked the means to fight an action in court. He needed to stay in military employment more than the man sat on his cot. But the hand he held up was ignored.

'I was right about Avignon. But not even I, in my wildest imaginings, guessed what was at stake.'

'Sir,' Markham said firmly. 'Please accede to the Monsignor's wishes, and keep whatever it is he told you to yourself.'

'Keep your voice down, man.' Germain hissed, 'do you want us to be overheard.'

Saying yes to that was as absurd as saying no. And faced with the anger in Germain's voice he had no choice but to drop his voice to a whisper.

'I would not want you to break your word.'

'It was given to a Papist, man, and has no value.' Germain must have seen the sudden danger in Markham's eyes, since he continued hurriedly. 'The man is French!'

'Aramon is a Royalist if he is anything. And they, sir, might I remind you, are on our side.'

Germain wasn't about to be deflected by inconvenient facts.

'You may make a distinction, I will not. It matters little who rules France. They are all against Britannia. But the men we have aboard have access to untold wealth, the treasure of the papal state at Avignon, removed before the Revolutionaries took it over in '92. Imagine, Markham, what that papal enclave accumulated as an independent fief. The plate, the crucifixes, the jewels and the sheer amount of coin.'

Germain was right, and even reluctantly, Markham couldn't keep out of his mind a vision of such ecclesiastical riches. Avignon was in one of the most fertile parts of France, a wholly owned fiefdom of St Peter's, exempt from any form of levy from Parisian kings. It had been rich for hundreds of years, a place where Papal Nuncios ruled, and wealthy individuals, seeking a guaranteed entry into heaven, had paid handsomely to have prayers said for their souls.

The priests who ruled there must have had forewarning that their fate was sealed when the monarchy lost power. The threat of excommunication, so feared by a succession of kings, held no terrors for the commoners who took over the government. The Assembly had voted to confiscate church property and French soldiers marched in to claim a piece of land that had been an independent state since the Middle Ages.

Markham decided on a last throw, a final effort to bring Germain to his senses. 'You do not fear exceeding your orders, sir?'

'What do you mean, man. I will be obeying them. My orders are to confound the enemy on land and sea, you know that.'

'Where is it?' asked Markham wearily.

'That Aramon has not told me.'

'There's a surprise,' Markham responded, but the irony was wasted on Germain.

'De Puy was the man tasked with escorting it to Rome. But, as you know, the French annexed Savoy as well. He had, quite naturally, avoided going over the high mountain passes, and elected to head for the coast west of the town of Nice. He stayed off the main roads to Italy, using obscure trails through the hills. By the time he was ready to come down into what was Piedmontese territory, the French army was in his way. In danger, he had no option but to secrete it in a safe place, and wait. When that became intolerable he then made for Toulon, hoping to take ship to Rome and inform Aramon. As you know, he was trapped there by the siege. So all that treasure is still where he left it.'

'The location of which you don't know.'

'That's not strictly true, Markham,' said Germain triumphantly. 'The old goat may think he's sharp, but I have ears. He let slip that it is in close proximity to the shore where he wants to land, in a bay by the name of Golfe Juan.'

'But not how close?'

'It can be no more than a few leagues.'

That, to Markham's way of thinking, was not close.

'You have explained de Puy. Where does Monsignor Aramon fit in all this?'

There was a note of impatience in the captain's voice, as though the answer was so obvious it had no need to be stated.

'He's the man who arranged the transfer in the first place, who went to Rome and waited. Nothing came, of course, so he set out to find de Puy, and, of course, the treasure.'

If Germain hadn't caught his breath then, Markham would not have heard the soft sound of a foot scraping on the deck planking. Hurriedly stopping the youngster from saying any more, he moved gingerly towards the curtain. The next sound made him move quicker; a dull but quiet thud, like a heel being dug in, which was speedily followed by another. The deck outside was in near darkness, and he could not be sure of anything other than a vague impression of the departing shape. It seemed too small to be Aramon, but Markham didn't doubt it was he. Who else on the ship wore a long black cassock?

'Do you think he heard us?'

'How can I say. We were whispering, so it wouldn't have been easy. But then, he must have had his suspicions when he followed you.'

'How do you know he followed me?'

'Because you were in here when he was outside. You don't make a habit of coming to my berth in the middle of the night, do you? And what purpose could you have in coming tonight, just after he has told you the secret of what it is he wants to recover.'

'So he will know I've told you.'

'I doubt that will affect his ultimate course of action.'

Germain was looking at him intently again, seeking an explanation of Markham's certainty. But the man in question was too tired to explain. All he wanted to do was to get back to sleep. How could the youngster not deduce that Aramon was teasing him, letting him have snips of information just before the need to impart it became essential?

He would have had to tell the ship's captain something to get the ship inshore at the right spot. Given the damage they'd sustained, with the risk that Germain might head back to Corsica, Aramon had opened up just a little earlier than he'd originally planned. But he'd told him something pretty useless, it being information Germain would have demanded to know before even approaching the shore.

'The real, question, sir, is what effect it has on you?'

'I don't follow?'

'You are still determined to proceed?'

'Of course, man. Don't you see how a stroke like this will elevate us in the admiral's estimation? I must say I can't comprehend your reluctance, Markham. I had you down as just the fellow I needed for this task.'

Markham was too bored to protest again. It was clear that Germain was obsessed to the point that no amount of cautionary advice or pessimism would sway him. He needed to shine, and whatever danger that put other people into was secondary.

'So you're ordering me to escort Monsignor Aramon and his party ashore?'

'That sounds damned formal, Markham.'

'It is so formal, sir, that I would like those orders in writing.'

Germain stiffened. 'That will not be necessary. I will lead the shore party personally, with you as my second in command.'

'You?'

'Yes.'

'What about the ship!' demanded Markham.

Germain put his fingers to his lips again, and insisted on silence, though he couldn't look his marine lieutenant in the eye, lest the man in the cot observe the captain's desperation. He wanted any success for himself, a factor which had changed since leaving Corsica. Sharing it, after what had happened during the recent action, was no longer possible.

'Mr Booker and the master will look after the ship.'

'He's no more than a boy.'

'She is barely fit for action, Markham, so their main task will be to effect decent repairs. I will require Conmorran to stand off the shore, once we are on our way, then send in the cutter at an agreed time every night from three days hence. We will arrange a signal with blue lights that will tell them to take us off at dawn.'

'And if danger threatens, like a bloody great ship of the line hoving into view.'

'Don't judge us by the standards of the army. Booker has been at sea long enough to know what action to take. The master, Mr Conmorran, is even better equipped.'

Germain followed that with a heavy sniff designed to tell Markham the matter was closed. 'Anyway, I have requested the master to shape us a course for this Golfe Juan. The place is dotted with fishing villages, but looking at his charts, there seem to be some islands in the bay. Les Lerins, they're called. We can anchor near those just this once to avoid observation. I expect to have them in view at first light.'

'Then we will need to be alert, will we not?'

'Of course.'

'Then sir, if you have no objection, I will bid you good night.'

'How can you sleep at a time like this?'

'I can easily, Mr Germain,' hissed Markham angrily, 'because I have had years of practice. That is something you learn young in the army. I have also learned that soldiers, even Lobsters, are often obliged to go without for long periods. Therefore, I tend to take, gratefully, whatever opportunities are gifted to me.'

'I shan't sleep,' Germain replied, dolefully. But then he saw the look bordering on hate that the marine officer was giving him, so he stood up, nodded and exited through the curtain.

Hard as he tried, Markham couldn't sleep. But it wasn't the notion of untold wealth that kept him awake, it was the idea that Germain was intent on leading the thing personally. Had he formed that notion before Aramon opened up to him about the treasure or afterwards? Was his desire to be there prompted by the need to impress his superiors, a distrust of his inferiors and accomplices, or even worse, personal greed?

Then there were the risks inherent in landing on a very hostile shore. He'd looked at maps of the southern coast since coming aboard, noting that the terrain became mountainous very quickly, rising towards the not too distant Alps. That forced all traffic onto the narrow flat strip of coastline. There was a road from Toulon to what had been the Piedmontese border, connecting France to city-states like Genoa. With a war in progress that would be a main supply route for the forward elements of the French army. He, and

89

his men, were being asked to move through country that might well be swarming with enemy troops.

Could he refuse? There were certainly good grounds. But Markham knew that the navy was not very different from the army when it came to dealing with officers who declined a command. A man once damned a coward for his desertion could expect little understanding from his superiors. Never mind promotion, he'd be lucky to remain a marine. Hood had gifted him that after Toulon, and the admiral could just as easily remove it. Worse, Germain would go ahead without him. And he would take, as was his right, the ship's marine detachment. That was scarcely something the men would thank him for.

There was deep and distant rumble, which given the way he was thinking, sounded like a far off battle, a huge cannonade by a large army. But it was only thunder, a sound that grew louder as the storm approached, until, over an hour later, it was right over the ship. The noise of that, and the clatter of torrential rain beating on the planking above his head, made any notion of further slumber impossible, so he rose from his cot and slipped into his breeches.

It was a delicious feeling, on the deserted forepeak, to stand under the teeming downpour, letting the lukewarm rain wash off the exertions of the last twenty-four hours. Fanciful as it was, it even seemed to cleanse his memory of some of the less pleasant things that had happened in his life, and inducing, once he had returned to his cot, a deep and refreshing slumber.

Markham was on deck with the morning watch, side-stepping their swabbing and flogging of the planking to keep his eye on the shore. It looked peaceful enough in the clear dawn light, a string of sleepy fishing villages nestling in a thin line of trees. Each was named after some saint, with the largest at both ends of the long sweeping bay. Behind, the hills stood blue-grey, with the odd granite bluff protruding from the thick vegetation. There would be tracks in that, steep, climbing affairs that would lead into the communities of the interior.

Far away to the east lay a line of thick black clouds, a curtain hanging from them that promised another heavy downpour. Sweeping with his glass again, Markham was alarmed by the clarity of vision that it afforded, one that would also apply to anyone on the shore. Certainly the overnight rain had cleared whatever mist may have obscured that view. But with a line of mountains behind, observation of shipping was easy in anything but the most inclement weather. A lookout would be able to see anything on the water many miles from shore. Even hiding behind the Isles de Lerins, there was no way a party could boat to the long open strand of beach without being seen, no way that *Syilphide* could come and go to this location without being under constant observation.

He disliked the idea of going ashore at night. There might be a moon, which in this seascape would obviate any advantage. And on a strange shore, with a limited view of what lay in front of them, his men, who could not be asked to move quietly, would be at an even greater disadvantage than they would be in daylight. But if that storm on the horizon swept over them, it would obscure the view of any observers, and send those on shore scurrying for shelter.

'Mr Booker.'

'Sir.'

'You had the watch last night.' Markham paused, wonder if the boy had seen him, half-naked on the forepeak, rain pouring through his hair. The innocent look in the eyes reassured him.

'I did, sir.'

'Which direction did that thunderstorm come from?'

'There were two, sir, both from the east, which sir, you will notice, is the direction of the wind.'

'And that on the horizon?'

'Looks like another. It will be on us in couple of hours.'

'Would you oblige me, Mr Booker, by sending someone to fetch my sergeant.' As the boy acknowledged and agreed, Markham turned towards the quarterdeck. 'Mr Germain, a word if you please?'

His conversation with Rannoch had to be brief and succinct. Rations for a week, with ample powder and shot, plus one man to carry flares, while another was given the task of transporting the tube that would fire them. He could see, in the highlander's eyes, the desire to ask questions. But Markham didn't have time to answer them if he was going to have any chance of achieving what he wanted.

He had to insist that Aramon be roused out to listen, and once they were gathered in Germain's cramped cabin, with de Puy once more obliged to sit on a cannon, Markham made no attempt to be polite to the cleric. He told him quite plainly that if they were to go ashore, it had to be under the cover of a storm.

'I insist, sir, that you cease to be obtuse, and tell us quite plainly what it is you are after, where it is located, and some notion of what route by which we can get there. And since we need to get back it would also be of some use to know what these valuables consist of.'

'And if I don't?' asked Aramon, producing an infuriating smile.

'Then I, for one,' Markham snapped, 'will refuse to go ashore.'

'What!' exclaimed Germain.

'Your presence is not a prerequisite of success, Lieutenant.'

'And neither will my men.'

'They will have to if I order them,' growled Germain.

Markham glared at him, as much for his stupidity as anything else. There was only one way to get anything out of Aramon, and that was by out-bluffing him. Germain was right, but the Monsignor didn't know that. He tried, in his stare, to get the captain to either shut up or agree, as he continued on the same tack.

'Rest assured they would obey me. I am their officer, and I expect, at any subsequent court-martial, that both their actions, and mine, will be fully vindicated.'

Germain was frowning, like a man trying, and failing to deal with two irreconcilable facts. Had he spoken then, nothing would have been achieved, but he didn't. Aramon's smile, which had never wavered, now deepened.

'I asked about you, when I entertained some of the officers who served around Calvi. From what they told me, a court of any kind is something you would be keen to avoid. Certain past difficulties might surface.'

The captain went pale. If Markham had reason to fear a court, he had even more, a fact that the Monsignor would have realised if he'd had any knowledge of recent British history. Markham pressed home the advantage.

'You misunderstand, sir. Mr Germain would have to ask for the court, and he would have to be quite specific about what orders I'd declined to carry out. At present, we are being asked to partake of a wild goose chase, which is of far more importance to you than it is to the success of the British forces in the region.'

Aramon made a steeple of his fingers then pressed his lips to the points, as if in deep contemplation. To Markham this was sheer nonsense, prevarication for no other reason than the need to retain control. Surely he didn't expect to lead them personally once they were on dry land. Then his eyes drifted to the silent de Puy, who refused to meet his eye, and he understood. He wanted the marines, and he'd probably tolerate Germain, feeling that he was easy to dominate. But he, Markham, was surplus to requirements, not least because he was prone to ask too many awkward questions. Besides, de Puy was on hand for military advice.

'My men are on attachment to this ship, obliged to obey any legitimate command. I will make it my business to point out that this escapade is anything but that.'

'You have a point there, Markham,' said Germain, finally assisting, even if, judging by his expression, he had no idea why.

'Our destination is the church of Notre Dame de Vacluse,' said Aramon suddenly, making a gesture towards de Puy that immediately brought forth a map from inside his immaculate white coat. The parchment, once spread, was very detailed and on a very small scale, showing numerous tracks, as well as a well-defined road that twisted up through the hills, each gradient penned in. 'It is situated in the hills behind the bay, some way to the west of the town of Grasse.'

'Distance?'

'Ten miles as the crow flies.'

'Twice that, probably,' said de Puy, 'We cannot get there in a straight line.'

'And what do you expect to find there?'

'Expect?' said Aramon, with a quick look at de Puy, clearly nonplussed. 'We know what we will find.'

'Then would you mind sharing it with us?'

'Captain Germain already knows.'

'Loot from Avignon, Markham,' Germain blurted out, in a silly attempt to cover the indiscretions of the previous night.

'Hardly loot, captain,' snapped Aramon, holding up a hand to still a shocked de Puy, the cleric himself roused for once out of his studied languor.

'Forgive me, Monsignor,' blurted Germain, 'a slip of the tongue.'

'It would be best to know in detail,' said Markham. 'Whether it is loot or not, the description is too vague.'

Aramon refused to be drawn. 'I have told you it is valuable, extremely so, and was transported to Notre Dame de Vacluse by

93

men carrying packs. Thus, it can be brought out by the same method. I do not see that an inventory would help.'

Markham turned abruptly to the other Frenchman. 'Captain de Puy. You recently served in King Louis' army. I daresay there were plans then to take over the land now occupied by troops of the revolution.' De Puy nodded, as Markham continued. 'So how close will we be to the supply route for the men fighting the Piedmontese?'

'We will have to cross it. It is but a thin strip of road, unless we come across a depot or an encampment.'

Markham had studied maps of the area, and the road was typical of coastal routes in mountainous terrain. Flat, easy stretches in the bays and marshlands, precipitous climbs and descents where it wound round the numerous rocky headlands. Any army dragging itself and supplies round those would use the bays, where they must land, as places of rest.

'There is no doubt that it will be well used, but once we ascend into the interior, I would anticipate little danger.'

'And can I ask you, do you approve of this operation?'

'Wholeheartedly,' de Puy replied. It hardly sounded like a complete endorsement, but that could be attributed to his being such a gloomy soul.

Again Markham heard that distant rumble of thunder. It was time to decide. The destination was some two leagues inland, nearly twelve miles, all uphill. They would have to rendezvous with *Syilphide* and bring off whatever it was they found, which might prove to be a more difficult task than getting ashore. He looked at Germain, to make sure that the captain was still determined to proceed, and was left in no doubt by the stubborn cast of the man's jaw of his intentions. There was no way he could entrust his Lobsters to such a commander.

'Then, sir, if we are going, I would like to go now.'

'Without a reconnaissance?'

'What good would that do, sir. It would only tell the enemy why *Syilphide* is here.'

'If I'm not mistaken,' Germain said, cocking an ear to the dull, far away thud, 'we are in for some pretty foul weather.'

'I hope so sir. That is when I want to get on to that beach. I have no notion to cross in sunlight, even less to take someone like the Monsignor ashore in darkness. Might I suggest you issue both he and Captain de Puy with oilskins.'

Germain thought for a moment, before he grinned, clearly comprehending his marine officer's idea. 'That's damned sharp, Markham, damned sharp. The rain will blind those on shore.'

'Will the sea not be rough?' asked de Puy.

'No, Monsieur, it will not. There might be a bit of a squall before the storm arrives. But if we have anything like the torrent we had last night, it will be beaten as flat as melted cheese.'

'There was a great deal of lightning, too, Captain.'

Markham cut in. 'I daresay you have time for a quick prayer, Monsignor Aramon, one that will keep us safe, even if it does not keep us dry.'

The sour look that earned him almost made the whole stupid enterprise worthwhile.

'How long do you need to get your men ready, Markham?' asked Germain.

'They are ready now, sir. I took the liberty of asking them to prepare before you convened this gathering. All we are waiting for is the people they have to escort.'

Aramon nodded. 'Then I will gather my possessions. Monsieur de Puy, perhaps you would oblige me by rousing out my servants. Tell them to wrap my possessions in oilskin, using the cases we brought aboard. They will know what you mean.'

'Surely you don't intend to take your valets?' Germain said, his face clearly intending the remark as a joke.

'Of course. Mademoiselle Moulins and her maid will also accompany us.'

'I'm not sure I understand that,' Germain growled, sitting forward.

The reply was harsh. 'It is not necessary for you to understand, Captain. It is what I wish, and you I'm sure would be the first to tell me that I am master of my own fate. If I am forced to leave the young lady behind, I will know little in the way of peace. I will worry about her. Better, for my sake, that she come along.'

Markham wasn't surprised at the blatant lie, nor the clear-eye gaze and deliberate tone with which it was delivered. Priests everywhere, to his mind were masters of the art. The trick was to stare hard at the person you were lying to, substitute insistence for sincerity, daring them to contradict the statement you were making. He glanced at de Puy, who was concentrating on the deckbeams above his head. Then he looked at Germain, expecting to see deep discomfort, only to observe that the captain was trying very hard to keep a smile off his face.

'That would be the last thing we would want, Monsignor,' he said, the gravity of his voice at variance with his expression. 'Why, it could distract you from our purpose and jeopardise the whole endeavour.'

Markham nearly laughed himself, and might have done if the situation had not been so serious. He was thinking that when it came to mendacity the cleric and the naval officer were evenly matched. Aramon had issued his challenge to avoid exposing his truth, which was simple. Should he recover what they sought, he wanted the freedom to choose his route to Rome, something he could not do with half his party still aboard.

Germain had responded in a like manner, well aware that what the Monsignor proposed actually suited him. It wasn't hard to imagine the trouble that would be caused when Aramon realised that, treasure in the hold, he was sailing in the wrong direction, towards Admiral Hood rather than the Pope. Yet if the women were left aboard, he could not avoid bringing the cleric back. No wonder he was struggling to hide his smile. He might as well have said, out loud, to Aramon, that as soon as success was achieved, he was planning to dump them.

And such an air of untruth was being espoused, that both men were content to accept their mutual lies, rather than to state, honestly, their individual positions. Indeed Aramon felt the need to gild the lily.

'If you can guarantee me, captain, that we will be able to return to your ship, I will leave them. But I suspect that even Lieutenant Markham here, who has little time for me or what I represent, will tell you that getting to Notre Dame de Vacluse might be simpler than getting back.'

'You make it sound as if we are expected,' Germain replied, his brow creasing with concern.

'Who knows what we will find? A subtle approach may be called for. In such circumstances a young lady with her maid can approach the church without arousing any suspicion. My servants, should trouble occur, are all capable of firing a pistol.'

'It makes me wonder why you need us,' said Markham, making no attempt to hide the sarcasm.

'He needs us!' said Germain hurriedly.

Aramon produced one of his superior smiles. 'I do not know

what we face, and neither does le Comte de Puy. I'm sure even you, Lieutenant Markham, would agree that it is best not to take anything for granted.'

Markham decided to bait them both. 'Especially the idea that you might actually be trusted.'

'What possible grounds could I have for mistrust?' asked Aramon, wickedly.

The look in his eye, aimed at Markham under a raised eyebrow, proved beyond any doubt that he had accurately read Germain's thoughts. Indeed, the young captain blushed. Perhaps Aramon had known from the first what he had in mind, content to rely on his own superior intelligence to outwit him. It made little difference. There was a task at hand, and, regardless of how unpalatable the whole affair sounded, now was the time to do it.

'I think it might be an idea for us to have a meeting with your officers, sir, Mr Booker and Conmorran, to work out how we are going to get back on board.'

'Quite!' said Germain, after a lengthy pause, during which he stared at the unconcerned cleric with barely disguised loathing.

Chapter nine

The trip ashore, without Germain and his compass, could have turned into a disaster. The rain came down in torrents, flattening the sea just as he'd forecast, but reducing visibility to an unknown quantity of yards. The shore-line, including the headlands of Theroule and Cap d'Antibes, which enclosed the bay, had vanished.

Every flash of lightning was timed with the accompanying thunder, and as half a minute reduced itself to half a second, they had a fair idea of how close they were to receiving a strike. One bolt seemed to enter the water right ahead of the boat, illuminating the rain-filled air around them in a golden glow. The thunder was so loud, a sudden crack that split the air, that even the most stout hearted cowered from nature.

The sailors were rowing hard, water running of their noses, chins and greased pigtails, though warm enough to be pleasant. The passengers cocooned in oilskins or heavy greatcoats were less exposed. But they were also a lot less comfortable, since the rain did little to take the heat out of the air. Indeed it set up a slight mist which enveloped them, so that when they ground on the shore it came as something of a surprise.

It was still raining by the time they'd unloaded the cutter and crossed the steep strand of beach, some shelter provided by the thin layer of trees that stood between the sand and the road. Markham was out ahead, his Lobsters, packs on their backs lined up in a screen, inching forward through the trees. In their greatcoats, they looked like ghosts in the mist, the main blessing being that their red uniform jackets were hidden. Behind him the cutter was hauling out to sea, to be as far away as possible from the land when the rain finally lifted.

They heard the scrunch of hundreds of boots long before they came to the road, the steady tread of a column marching across their route, this accompanied by the grinding of metal-hooped wheels, a sound which denoted the presence of carts. The rain was beginning to ease, the increasing amount of light obvious even in the mist-filled greenery. With sunlight, in these trees, Markham reckoned they would be visible as soon as the sun reappeared through. And the arrival of that would necessitate the removal of the greatcoats that disguised their nationality.

The light broke through suddenly, a shaft of gold filled with thin drizzle. The road emerged like some chimera, first the ghostly movement of hunched bodies, the eye drawn to the rumbling wheels of the indistinct carts. Then there were the colours, uniform coats green and blue soaked through and steaming from the body heat of their owners; hats of all shapes dripping water, the tricolour cockades limp and damp. Markham had seen soldiers like these outside Toulon, part of the *levee en masse* that Lazare Carnot, the commissioner responsible for the conduct of the war, had called upon to save the revolution. They had weapons and powder but few complete uniforms. And from what he could recall, little discipline. He scanned the column for officers, but could see none, either mounted or on foot.

Markham knew he had to get to the other side of that road, and into the gnarled forests and olive groves that rose up into the mountains. That meant moving right now, or waiting until nightfall, an unpleasant prospect given the nature of the cover, as well as the proximity of so many soldiers. The fishermen were another worry. They would have stayed out in the bay while the rain poured down, ready to resume their toil once it lifted. Stranded on the beach, or even in the sparse pines, the party would be visible to them. Matters could only get worse as the greatcoats, near black because of the rain, dried out to their more normal grey.

'Captain Germain. I would want all of our party to remove their oilskins.'

'The rain hasn't yet ceased, Markham.'

'No. But we must get across that road. I want to pretend that you are prisoners, the Monsignor, de Puy, the ladies and servants, plus you, being escorted by a disciplined body of men. If we can get amongst them while it's still raining, we can march in their midst till an exit presents itself.'

'The risk is too great,' said Aramon.

'Monsignor, the risk of staying still is even greater. What you see before you is an army marching towards the enemy. This could be the very tail of that, or the very tip. At some point they will call a halt, and the men on the road will disperse into the trees to take their ease and perhaps dry their clothes. You can see for yourself there is no place to readily hide.'

'I'm not sure, Markham,' murmured Germain.

There was no time for his finer feelings.

'And I am. This is land. I will defer readily to you at sea, sir, but not now. I insist that you do as I ask.'

Rannoch, following this exchange had already began to place the Lobsters in position, though not before he'd thrown a questioning glance at his officer, one that demanded to know what the hell they were playing at. But there was no time for any enquiry. Another bright shaft of sunlight burst through the trees as if to highlight the urgency. Markham was looking at Bellamy, whose black face was glistening as much from sweat as from rainfall. That skin would attract attention in a greatcoat. There were Negroes a'plenty in France, some of them in uniform, for certain. Yet they must remain an oddity, and he had to do all he could to minimise the risk of too close attention. The order was received badly.

'I have no time to ease your feelings, Bellamy, nor to explain my motives. Just do as I ask. You may mingle with Monsignor Aramon's attendants.'

The huge brown eyes, normally so passive, now flashed with anger. 'I am not a servant!'

'We all know that!' Markham snapped, making a futile gesture to indicate that the rain had nearly stopped. He motioned to Rannoch to move out, then pushed Bellamy out of his position and into the throng of supposed prisoners.

'But those men on the road will doubt you are a soldier, and may, because of you, look too closely at us. Here, take my pistol and my cloak, then give me your musket and greatcoat. You will then look like an officer. Perhaps you and Mademoiselle Moulins' maid can act as a couple.'

The offer of that didn't only mollify Bellamy somewhat, it clearly excited him. He was by the ladies' side in a flash and Markham heard him suggest that the charade they were engaged in might not be helped by her continuing to carry some of her mistress's possessions on her head.

He did not get away without a great deal of chivvying from his fellow Lobsters. They did it to allay their own fears of course; they were men who felt very exposed as they were, and probably had a vision of ending up in some festering French goal. The sun was on the water now, racing towards them as the clouds drifted away. Even Dornan, stupid as he was, knew they had little time. If anything, it was his plea that swung the argument. Bellamy was shot of his outer garments and in amongst the prisoners before they'd moved ten paces. Markham held back for a second or two, examining the group to see if it looked right.

It was an odd assembly; a British naval officer, a high church-man, de Puy's Bourbon uniform, a young lady in a good quality cloak and the two Negroes. Aramon's servants were carrying his squat oilskin packages on their backs. Even though they seemed to manage their loads with surprising ease, they looked the most incongruous, and he nearly called for the possessions to be abandoned. Then he realised that it didn't matter. They were committed; too close to the enemy to effect any changes, so he ran to the front where his knowledge of French would be necessary.

'Make way, make way,' Markham called, adopting a guttural accent, which owed more to sounds he'd heard in the Dublin fish market than anything he'd picked up in France.

The soldiers, listless from marching, looked up with scant interest at the approaching party. They saw only the dark great-coats and tricorne hats of the men at the front marching towards them, muskets sloped, as if on parade. What they didn't do was provide an opening. Markham cursed under his breath, now sure that he'd been too impetuous. If they halted by the roadside they might never get in amongst the column. They would thus become an object of curiosity to every passing eye. And it could only be a matter of time till an officer appeared, and stopped to demand of them their business.

'Move aside, damn you,' he yelled in desperation, as he came abreast of the column, poking forward with Bellamy's musket.

The reply, even delivered in a foreign tongue, left no one in no doubt where to stick both his anger and the weapon. But he was not going to be deflected, and suddenly inspiration struck. He used, with a dramatic flourish, the one name he suspected, in this part of the world, might just have an effect.

'Then you will have to deal with Citizen Commissioner Fouquert.'

The reaction was immediate, but wrong. There were men in this column that might struggle to recall the name of the king the regicides had beheaded two years previously. But the most bloodthirsty tyrants of the revolution should be famous, their names whispered with a mixture of fear and admiration. Robespierre and St Just, even if they were dead, consumed by the guillotine which had brought death to so many of their victims. Fouche, who'd cleaned out Nantes to help quell the revolt in the Vendee and then went on to help Fouquier-Tinville in the butchery of Lyon. The pair claimed to have taken more lives in one day than any other commissioners.

These were the Representatives on Mission from the Committee of Public Safety, whose power exceeded that of the generals who led the armies. Indeed those very senior officers were frequently their victims, forced either to flee to save their necks, or dragged to the guillotine to be executed in front of the troops they'd led.

Here, in the very far south, Fouquert had been that representative. He'd engendered the same level of fear as his fellow murderers, first for his actions in Marseilles, then for what he'd done in Toulon once the British had abandoned it. Innocent people, trying to flee, had been pushed into the harbour to drown. At the same time Fouquert had set up the guillotine in the main square, and there presided over a drunken orgy of formal, quasi-judicial killings.

To Markham the man was scum, typical of the type thrown up by the turmoil of the Revolution. Initially, he had applauded the way the French had thrown of the yoke of absolute monarchy, and despaired when they'd fallen victim to an even more despotic regime. The fact that the whole of Europe was ranged against them was due to men like Fouquert, who'd risen only by their blind attachment to dubious dogma, added to an ability to inspire fear. He was a killer. And Markham knew from personal experience he was not just that. No political convictions shaped his actions; he was a man who took great personal pleasure in the act. He would decimate this regiment without a qualm. So why were these French soldiers laughing?

At least that flash of humour created a small break in the column, which allowed him, Rannoch and Tully to muscle in, then hold the position until the whole party was on the road, with that same trio now bringing up the rear.

'What you got, there, friend?' a still-amused voice called from behind them.

'*Émigrés*, brother, and a couple of foreigners they're in league with. They're all traitors. Take a look at the heads on the swine.

Next time you see them, Fouquert will have them raised on a pike.'

Was it a sudden flash of fear that made Ghislane Moulins stumble, so that Bellamy, and her maid, on either side, had to grab her to keep her upright? It looked like it. And the way that de Puy and Aramon squared their backs added even more verisimilitude to the scene. Tense himself, he was at least in communication with the men behind him. They were not, and would be racked with all the fears that their imaginations could provide.

'That black pair'll look a treat. Happen we should polish them up a bit.'

Markham had to jab Bellamy with his own musket then, to stop him from spinning round. Rannoch, in an act that could only be pure guesswork, since he spoke no French, laughed out loud.

'You could pass us the womenfolk, citizen, both colours. Seeing as they're going to meet their maker, anyhow, they might as well expire from pleasures.'

'I heard they'd stopped all that game with the chopper,' came another voice, the call mixed in with raucous laughter. 'Ceptin' for the Jacobins, of course. They got theirs on Thermidor.'

'Not Fouquert, though. Mind, he's shitting himself after what they done to those bastards in Paris. He's a'feart, with good cause, that he might go the same route himself.'

'Would you to tell him that to his face?' asked Markham, with a feeling of uncertainty.

'I would have done if the bastard had hung around to look me in the eye.'

'Had?' asked Markham

A third voice called out, louder, carrying more authority. 'Where have you been, you arse in a greatcoat. Fouquert has been had up, like all the others.'

That produced more laughter, and a question from Markham.

'He was in Frejus, under arrest, when we passed through there. Now you might not know where the sun rises and falls mate, but I do, and that is behind us. As far behind us as you are behind the times.'

'Thick ain't in it mate, they ain't even got the sense to get out of them coats.'

The sun was high now, beating down on their shoulders, raising steam that had that strange, stale smell which emanated from damp cloth. They'd have to take them off soon, since to wear them now, in bright sunlight, was madness. And Markham's mind was whirring for another reason. He had used Fouquert's name to frighten the marching soldiers, and that had backfired, though the news that he was at risk of losing his own head was welcome. But he had to get away from these men, as originally planned, because another wrong answer could be fatal. There was a gate on the left, a broken affair that led to a muddy yard.

'We'd best get back to Frejus and find out what is goin' on. Up ahead there, get off the road.'

Naturally, without any knowledge of French, nothing happened. Markham began to swear, and made such a poor fist of pushing to the front of his party that he provoked even more amusement. But he got there just as Halsey, on point, came abreast of the hanging gate. The old man was marching, head down and slowly, having opened up enough of a gap between him and the French in front to avoid conversation. It needed a shove to move him sideways.

'Into the yard, Halsey, and don't turn round.'

The whole party swung to the left, ignoring the catcalls of the passing soldiers who'd talked to Markham. As soon as they passed, he shut the gate, to avoid the prying eyes of those who followed. Looking around, he saw the devastation that had been visited on what was once a reasonable manor house. It wasn't fresh, the damage to this once thriving property. But it was obvious; the heraldic device that had once decorated the lintel above the gaping main door was chipped away. Smoke stains blacked the stonework above the windows, which were without glass, consumed in the flames that had gutted the interior.

The farmyard itself was littered with the detritus of a passing army, proof that when the columns did halt, this was a space they occupied. Even destroyed the building provided shelter, and perhaps enough remaining wood to make a fire.

'Into the house,' he ordered.

The smell that hit them was overpowering. This place had been used as a latrine as well as a protective roof, and it was necessary to wade through the pile of human waste that stood as testimony to an army too lazy to dig or even walk very far. With the roof gone, as well as all the intervening floors, the heavy downpour had come straight through to the ground, to mingle and spread the ordure.

That eased as they went further in, moving silently in single file through spaces that had once been doorways, Markham searching for an exit to the rear. There had to be one, and if they could get out through it and move without being seen they had every chance of getting well away from danger. He found it, another gaping hole that led onto what had once been a formal garden and was now just a mass of weeds. At least here, in the rear portions of the property, the floors were clear of human filth, if you excluded discarded clothing and the remains of their meals.

'I think we should stop for a moment.' said Germain, solicitously. 'The lady must be fatigued.'

'I'd like to get these greatcoats off,' said Rannoch, 'and to do something about fresh flints and dry powder.'

Stopping so close to a marching army was not a notion that appealed to Markham much. But he had no real idea if there were more ahead of him than behind, and after his most recent experiences he felt he had ridden his luck more than enough for one day. It was a question of balancing risks and advantages, yet his assent had more to do with Rannoch's request than Germain's. Without weapons that could fire they were toothless. Besides any threats they might face, with time precious, they needed to establish exactly which way they were going.

'Red coats off as well, Sergeant,' Markham replied. 'Roll them inside your greatcoats. Put a man to the front of the house to keep an eye on those Frenchmen.' Then he called over to de Puy. 'Monsieur le Comte, a look at your map, if you please.'

Germain joined them, while Aramon fussed over his chests, berated his servants, and said a few kind words to his charge. Not that de Puy's map would tell them much, since in its detail it didn't include the coastal strip. And here, at the rear of the manor house, the trees hid the hills from view.

'This place will not remain secure,' said de Puy, pulling the parchment from his coat pocket.

It was reassuring to see de Puy behaving like the soldier he was, instead of some doleful lackey to Aramon. He knew as well as Markham that as soon as the marching column halted, men would use the front part of the building in a like manner to their predecessors. But some would wander further, in the hope that the men who'd already stripped the place of all its valuables had missed something.

'We have a piquet out front,' Markham replied. 'And anyone

coming in will do so at a walk. But I do agree one of our first tasks is to find a safe exit.'

He called to Rannoch, now busy supervising the return to usefulness of the marine muskets. One he'd finished, the Highlander split his men into two and sent them down either side of the ruined garden, stepping round the smashed statuary that littered the pathways.

'We know we're in the arc of the Golfe Juan,' said Markham, pointing at the now open map. 'What we don't want is to be scrabbling about looking for a route. We need a decent view of the landmarks to fix our position. We also need a reconnaissance to make sure we don't walk into more enemy forces.'

'It is true that it is a habit I have no wish to acquire.'

'Once enough for you?'

'Most certainly. Might I suggest, Lieutenant, that I too discard my uniform coat, and go out to where I can get a clear view of the highlands to the north.' He looked over Markham's shoulder, his eyes narrowing as Aramon approached.

'I'm sure, given the outline, I can tell you were we are.'

'Make sure you take a weapon with you, a pistol or a musket.'

'A sword would suit me better if I need to kill anyone.'

'It would do little to alert us, however, monsieur. I will need to get out of here very quickly if there's trouble.'

'What is proposed?' Aramon demanded.

'Someone else must go!'

The cleric insisted on this before the explanation was finished, reinforcing a suspicion that had first occurred to Markham in Germain's cabin. Aramon had tried to hold out on the captain, doling out information bit by bit. But he was a victim himself. Only de Puy knew exactly where to look for whatever it was he'd escorted from Avignon.

The thought didn't please Markham, since it hinted at some kind of bargain. Which begged the obvious question as to why any arrangement was necessary. It was too much to consider, too many questions to resolve, and he had a decision to make.

'We are not overburdened with map readers,' he said.

'I cannot see why we just do not head straight inland. That is where we must go to find the church of Notre Dame, is it not?'

Markham was angry, and his voice was loaded with sarcasm. 'Of course, let's blunder right up the hillside. If we get lost we can stop a local peasant and ask for directions. He will say nothing about the presence of a high church dignitary, not to his wife or his own priest. Nor will he think it curious that eighteen souls, a dozen of them armed and British, are seeking Notre Dame de Vacluse.'

'If he is a son of the church, I can command his silence.'

'You may be prepared to trust your life to that, Monsignor Aramon, I am not. I have seen too many men swear fidelity on the Holy Cross, only to go on and betray everything they profess to believe in. The Comte is French, and without his uniform coat, his hat and his wig, not a person to be remarked on. And he knows better than any one of us in which direction we must go, need I add, unobserved.'

'I shall say farewell to you when this is over, Lieutenant, without a qualm. Though it shames me to admit it, I cannot imagine I will even bring myself to pray for your soul.'

Markham grinned, which he was happy to see upset the Monsignor. 'Sure that's a relief. With the benefit of your good offices I'd be confined to hell, for certain.'

'You do not require any assistance from me,' Aramon snapped.

'I could go,' said Germain.

'No, Captain,' said de Puy, pulling off his hat and wig, to reveal the dark, sweat soaked hair underneath. 'It only makes sense if I go. Only I have any hope of recognising the landmarks.'

'Then if I may be permitted a word alone,' said Aramon.

His voice, for the first time that Markham could remember, carried a hint of desperation. That brought forth a grin. He couldn't help himself, confirmed in his impression that whatever de Puy had brought from Avignon, he'd kept the location to himself. That was only odd if you had no knowledge of the cleric's personality. Presumably, de Puy was just as interested in recognition as Germain, and did not want his own efforts to safeguard the valuables of Avignon to suffer from Aramon's overweening vanity. It would be just like the Monsignor to claim all the credit himself, reducing de Puy's role to that of mere helper. In fact, if he'd been open, Markham suspected the French officer would not be here now.

They were alone for some time, talking quietly, with many a hand gesture. Aramon gave some evidence of impatience, while de Puy stiffened once or twice, probably because the insensitive cleric had delivered some crass insult. Finally they concluded, though it seemed neither man was happy, returning to the main group with faces set stiff. De Puy went to talk to Ghislane Moulins, while Aramon demanded writing materials from his servants.

'What were they about, Markham,' whispered Germain.

'Sure, they were formulating a plan, sir, to slit our throats and make off with the treasure.'

It was a cheap jibe to play on Germain. He was gullible enough, and made even more so by necessity. The blood drained from his thin face, and Markham had to make amends quickly by uttering soothing words, moving away to talk to Rannoch, who had just returned from his search. Germain moved over towards Aramon, who promptly turned his back on the naval officer so that he could not see what the cleric was writing.

'There is a walled garden, with some outbuildings,' said Rannoch. 'They too have been smashed and looted, with scarce a single article unbroken. But they are roofed, and, better still, have windows that open on to a track that runs up the side of the property. It is much safer than this. We can get out that way if we are threatened.'

'Good.'

He followed that with a quick explanation of what he'd heard on the road about Fouquert, slightly non-plussed at the lack of reaction. Rannoch, if anything, hated the Frenchman more than Markham. The news that the murderous bastard had fallen victim to his own excess should have produced a huge grin instead of the enquiring look he was receiving now.

'I take it you've left the men in the outbuildings?'

'I have,' Rannoch replied, his voice as slow as measured as his officer had ever heard it. 'I thought it best, since, some of them are getting a touch excited.'

'Why?' asked Markham, trying to sound nonchalant.

'Men left in ignorance are likely to speculate. That can lead to some very fanciful notions.'

'For instance?'

'There was talk aboard ship of gold and silver and of jewels the size of an eagle's egg. I paid no heed myself.'

He was hardly surprised that what should have been a secret was open speculation. Ships were not good places to try and retain a confidence. Sailors had the ability to hear any conversation through solid planking. And with servants aboard, including the Negro maid, hiding anything of value, be it an object or an idea, became near impossible. The mere presence of such a party aboard would have set every man to questioning, the whole pieced together by patchwork gossip. It might not be the whole truth, but it would be close enough.

'I've never known a fighting man who wasn't forever dreaming of untold wealth, Sergeant. Sometimes it's the only thing that keeps them going.'

Markham was stalling and Rannoch knew it. 'I might, like you, have to order them to die. My mind would be eased if you were to tell me what we are about.'

That made Markham feel guilty. He knew he could trust this man, yet he had chosen not to confide in him. To his credit, the information was not his to share. And his men, including Rannoch, should go without question to where they were ordered. But in the eighteen months they'd been together, he'd made a habit of explaining his intentions to them, not something most officers cared to do. More than that, he'd discussed most of his actions with Rannoch before implementing them, many of his decisions influenced by the Highlander's experience and good sense. In return, when he had made a sudden choice in the heat of battle, he'd been rewarded with unquestioning obedience.

And there was another nagging suspicion; that Rannoch would think he'd not taken him into his confidence lest that good sense he so prized was used to dissuade him from participating in the whole enterprise. The Highlander could have no idea how hard he'd tried to change Germain's mind. And was there a grain of truth in that? Was he, deep down, just feigning reluctance? Try as he might, with his memory full of bailiffs and avaricious relatives, he'd been unable to avoid his own dreams.

'The Comte de Puy,' he said softly, 'was forced to abandon something very valuable in the hills behind here. Captain Germain has ordered us ashore to recover it.'

'With half the French army here to stop us. It was not wise to land with all those troops nearby.'

Markham was annoyed. Rannoch had a point. But what really stung was the way the Highlander's slow, gentle tone seemed to deepen the rebuke.

'I expected traffic, Rannoch, but not that much.'

'I always had you as one to avoid surprises.' Markham opened his mouth to remind Rannoch who was the officer, but his sergeant continued without pause. 'This valuable property we are after, it is not the French gentleman's?'

'No.'

'That goat of a priest?'

'Not him either. It was en route to Rome, which is where he wants to take it.'

'And Captain Germain decided to aid him.'

'Partly,' Markham replied, dropping his voice even lower. 'It is the captain's intention, once the goods are recovered, to deliver them up to Admiral Hood, and to let him decide where they go.'

'Does the priest know this?'

'He might suspect, but that matters little. If he has any choice but to try and get it aboard *Syilphide*, I can't think of it. He can hardly take a land route to Italy with a whole French army in the way.'

'He and the count did not seem friendly when I came back.'

'My guess is that only de Puy knows precisely where it is, and he is not willing to tell Aramon.'

'So we have two Frenchmen who don't trust each other. They are being aided in their quest by a naval captain and all his marines. And they have good reason not to trust us.' Markham couldn't really say anything, since the analysis was as faultless as the conclusion. 'Something tells me that even with a glory-hungry fool like Captain Germain, we would be safer aboard the ship.'

'Which is why I came along, Rannoch. It is my intention to keep you alive.'

'Your pistol, if you please?' said de Puy, from just behind the sergeant.

Hidden by Rannoch's bulk, Markham had no idea how long he'd been standing there. He searched the Frenchman's face for a clue, only to be struck, once more, by how gloomy he looked.

'I shall fire it only if I am compromised with no hope of escape.'

Chapter ten

There was scant light in the outhouses, only that which came through the gaps in the overhead tiles and the cracks in the shutters. Markham had been afforded a good look when de Puy exited and light flooded the place, noticing that his men as always had set about turning it into a temporary billet. The coats they'd rolled up in the main house were open again, draped and hung out to dry. Broken equipment and straw had been arranged to create places to sleep, and a space cleared against one wall to light a fire, should their officer permit. Halsey had found a well at the other end of the kitchen garden and filled everything he could with water. Dornan was asleep, his snores rising to an occasional crescendo.

They'd seen to their comforts. That didn't bother Markham, who knew that each musket was now fully working. Rannoch had made them worm their pieces to remove any damp from the downpour. Each barrel would have been oiled, the flints changed and checked for spark before reloading. God help any Lobster whose sights did not flick up at the touch. The Highland sergeant would have their guts. Casting his own balls, he hated to see them wasted, and had trained his men to use equipment that in other units never left their knapsacks. Lookouts were placed to keep an eye on the track outside, as well as the weed-filled garden to their rear.

It was amusing to see the others, in the gloomy light, take their revenge on Aramon. He and Captain Germain had been given hastily contrived seating. Mademoiselle Moulins, along with her maid, was invited to take her ease next to them, in the most comfortable part of the interior, a wheel-less cart raised off the ground to discourage vermin. They'd lined it with straw so that they would not suffer from the hardness of sitting on bare wood. Bellamy brought water to her, gabbling away in his fluent French to both women. And some of the men offered part of their rations. Aramon, along with his servants, had been hustled into the corner where everything unwanted had been chucked. Every time one of his men tried to get hold of one of the pitchers Halsey had filled, it was whipped away by a Lobster, with some acid remark designed to remind the cleric of his behaviour regarding the church at Calvi.

There was a moment when it appeared the Monsignor was about to appeal to Markham for an intervention. His body was tensed forward, but in the gloom the marine officer could not see his eyes. But he heard a sigh that seemed to denote despondency, with Aramon instead directing a question to Germain.

'Will we be lighting a fire, captain?'

It was Markham who replied. 'No, Monsignor, we will not.'

'My clothing, and that of my servants, is damp, and so is this outhouse.'

Aramon was right. The gaps in the tiles, which had let in a small amount of light, had previously let in a great deal of water. The air was sticky rather than warm, the earthen floor damp. His Lobsters had claimed any dry straw or sacking. The same men had taken some pleasure in leaving a pile of wet stuff for the Monsignor.

'The care you demonstrate for your attendants is most impressive,' said Markham with deep irony.

Aramon shifted his ground quickly, to include Ghislane Moulins. She had removed her cloak and appeared quite comfortable. 'I daresay, you, my dear, are damp too?'

'We must not let the lady get a chill, Markham,' added Germain, unhelpfully.

'Her youth, and no doubt her enormous charm, will protect her from that.'

That earned Markham a winning smile from the lady and a deep scowl from her guardian. 'I find your attempt at gallantry offensive.'

Markham made no attempt to keep the amused tone out of his voice. 'I merely meant that my men will look after her. They generally take great care of people they admire.'

'Soldiers, your honour, at the back of the house,' called Tully, softly. Rannoch had put him in the loft, a position that gave him a limited view of the main garden.

'How many?'

'Just two, I reckon, though there a chance there could be more hidden by the trees.'

'Coming this way?'

'No.'

'They would be if they saw smoke,' Markham replied.

He hauled himself upright, at the same time glaring at the priest. Their presence hinted at the fact that the column on the road had halted for one of their periodic stops. There might only be two now, but that could turn into dozens if they were curious enough.

'No noise from anyone, if you please.'

Dornan's snores stopped abruptly, as one of the others pinched his nose. Every man had his musket ready by the time Markham and Rannoch moved to the door, which, broken off at its hinges, had been propped across the entrance. Outside, it was invisible from the house, hidden by the wall of the kitchen garden, and both men eased themselves in to the open air, immediately aware of the stifling heat that raised swirls of steam from the damp earth.

Peering round the corner of the wall, they could see that Tully had been right. There were only the two soldiers, moving slowly through the debris, idly kicking at pieces of masonry or jabbing at something with their muskets, occasionally stooping to pick up a shard that took their fancy, before throwing it away. The whole way they held themselves reeked of a degree of certainty: that if there had been anything of value in this property, it had long been taken by those who'd preceded them. A voice called from just inside the building, the face hidden by the shade. One of the men they were watching shouted back, whatever he said greeted by laughter. Both soldiers turned back to head indoors to the shade, just at the moment when de Puy, returning from his reconnaissance, banged on the shutter of the outhouse.

In truth, the Frenchman hadn't hit it hard, and had the exchanges between those in the main house and the soldiers in the garden continued they could not have heard it. But they'd fallen silent, and in the still, warm air the sound carried just enough to make the duo stop, turn and look. The pair exchanged glances for a second. Neither Markham or Rannoch could hear what words they spoke, but one of them shrugged and nodded in their direction, before they both started, slowly, seemingly aimlessly, down the path.

'If they get into this garden,' whispered Rannoch, 'they will be bound to look in the sheds.'

'We can't get everyone out without making even more noise,' Markham replied, 'and if they look in the sheds they are going to peer out through the shutters too, which means they will likely spot us on the track.'

'Their comrades will surely be watching them from the back of the house.'

'Not closely. Which is why they are coming so slowly. If there's anything to find they don't want to share it.'

'Do we take them here or indoors?'

Markham was about to say indoors, but he'd looked down to see the trail their earlier progress had made across the deep garden earth made soft by the heavy rain. Their progress through the formal part had been by the remains of the stone paths, and left no trace. But here there was a prominent fresh trail through the damp weeds, as well as the odd footprints where a marine boot had dug in. If the pair saw that, and had any sense, they'd probably shout for their mates before coming on.

'It will have to be here.'

Rannoch looked doubtful, and Markham could understand why. The entrance was no more than a gap in the wall. And they were on the side that contained the outhouses. The Frenchmen would turn towards that as soon as they spied it, coming face to face with whatever threat was going to be necessary to subdue them. Both he and his officer were on the wrong side of the gap to effect any surprise by taking them from behind, and the bramble bushes that lined the stone wall were too shallow to provide any real cover. At all costs a commotion had to be avoided. It was impossible to know how many men were in the main house. But on a hot day, the prospect of a place in the shade could have attracted a whole regiment.

'Stay here,' said Markham, as he shot back towards the outhouse doorway.

He pushed the door open as gently as haste would allow, and called softly to Ghislane Moulins and Renate. With Tully in the loft space, looking through the trees, everyone in the building was aware of what was happening. And they knew why, judging by the sheepish expression on de Puy's face. His request was understood by more than those at whom it was aimed.

'You cannot do that!' snapped Aramon.

'I agree,' said de Puy.

'Shut up,' growled Markham, rudely, vaguely aware that Bellamy had made a move as well to protest.

That died, as everyone became aware that the lady herself had stood up and was advancing, with Renate trailing behind her, towards the door. De Puy stepped forward to bar her passage, only to be cruelly informed by an impatient Markham, who was busy relieving Dornan of his bayonet, that he'd done enough damage for one day.

'Do we have a clear exit, monsieur?' he demanded.

'Only onto the track. There are soldiers on the Grasse Road. Not many, but enough.'

'Then we must use the forest?'

'We can get clear now, without endangering either the Mademoiselle or Renate.'

'There is no time.' He turned away and shepherded the two women out.

'Over by the far wall,' Markham whispered. 'Start picking brambles off those bushes. On no account turn round, no matter what you hear.'

Rannoch had already pressed his own back into the bushes to the left of the gap in the wall, and Markham soon joined him. They could hear their quarry now, talking to each other in a desultory sort of way, the scrape of their trailed muskets audible evidence of the fact that they apprehended no danger. That stopped abruptly as they entered the gap in the wall, and caught sight of the two young women intent on picking berries from the bushes.

The slight sound that one of them made was quickly hushed by his companion, and both French soldiers slipped though, muskets up and grinning, exchanging excited jabs as they tiptoed towards Ghislane and Renate. The noise they made, as they swished through the high weeds, should have alerted and alarmed the women. But they didn't react. That same sound covered the movement of Rannoch and Markham. Careful to ensure that they were not observed by those at their back, they came up behind the enemy soldiers.

Ghislane didn't turn round even when she heard the sounds of death, the grunt as the covered mouths were pulled back on to the eighteen-inch bayonets, the muffled sounds of dying men rising from two throats. But her maid, Renate, was less disciplined. She did see what happened, her dark huge eyes fixed on the blood-stained steel tips that came through the front of the victims' tunics, to slice up and out as the blades tore through their vital organs. She was looking right into a pair of startled eyes, and would have screamed if Ghislane had not slapped her. Slowly, the two men let the bodies down, till they lay at their feet, twitching as the last vestiges of life were extinguished.

Markham still had his hand firmly over the mouth of the man he'd killed.

'Mademoiselle. Please ask my men to come out and assist, then request Monsieur de Puy to get you and your maid, plus, Monsignor Aramon, out through the shutters.'

'Come, Renate,' said Ghislane gently, as she dragged her still transfixed maid towards the outhouse door.

'These two have to go out through those shutters with us,' said Markham, as the kitchen garden filled with his men, Germain at their head. 'We'll hide them in the bushes over on the other side of the track. Try to keep the spilt blood to a minimum. I want their officer, and their mates, to think they've taken a chance to desert.'

'That will not survive a search,' hissed Germain.

'No. But it will buy us some time. And if that army is wanted on the border with Piedmont, and always assuming they find them, they won't have time to hang around and hunt for the folk who knifed their men.'

Germain and Markham went back in through the door to consult with de Puy about the route, while the sergeant, having set two men to get the Lobsters' packs out through the window, oversaw the transport of the bodies.

'We will have to be quick now, lads. Dymock, keep an eye on the back of that house, and make sure no other nosy swine comes this way.'

It was impossible, given the wounds Rannoch and Markham had inflicted, to avoid blood pumping out of the dead pair, as muscles in spasm continued to operate. But most of it was gone by the time they reached the outhouse, and a bit of earth turning was enough to disguise the passage. Speed saved the earthen floor from too much, but the sills were covered as the cadavers were dragged over the stone. Halsey's pitchers of water came into use to wash them down.

There was no time for careful disposal. Fifteen-minute halts every two hours were the norm for a marching army, and by Markham's reckoning they'd already exceeded that. The state of discipline might be lax, but it was not something he could calculate for, so the two bodies were thrown into a thick hedge-row and the broken branches quickly rearranged. Then the party grabbed their packs and ran to catch up with the others.

Short of breath because of the steep climb, de Puy was busy explaining the topography to Germain and Markham. They were within a few hundred yards of the winding road that ran up into the hills towards the town of Grasse. With soldiers in evidence they must avoid it, taking a wide arc to the west to avoid the need to cross it as it snaked up the mountainside. The track they were on petered out just before the farmhouse it served, and they were forced on to a narrower even steeper route to circumvent buildings that were clearly inhabited.

To call it a trail was a misnomer. It was part animal tracks, part small gullies worn away where the rain had dribbled down the mountain, the whole once turned into a route for mules. Obviously it was hardly used now, and in full summer the vegetation had run riot. Sometimes it disappeared altogether, leaving them to hack their way through the undergrowth. Under a canopy of trees, the heat of the day was trapped. Added to the torrential rain that had already fallen in the last twenty-four hours, this made the atmosphere something infernal. The ground underfoot was slippery, a mixture of damp earth and leaves that sapped the strength of everyone, male and female.

Progress was desperately slow, which had Markham harrying the stragglers. Aramon's servants, still saddled with their master's possessions, coped remarkably well. Renate had a degree of natural grace that diminished the appearance of struggle, and a very attentive Bellamy was assisting her through every difficult stretch.

But their garments, especially Mademoiselle Moulins', hampered both females. If proof were needed of the folly of bringing them along, regardless of plots and stratagems, then this was it. The Monsignor himself had hitched up his cassock in such a way as to leave his stockinged legs free to move, though he often found it necessary to use both hands and feet to make any upward progress.

Markham at least had the sense to remove his scarlet coat. De Puy hadn't even attempted to put his own back on. Not Germain! His naval uniform, even if it was made of thick broadcloth, was his badge of distinction, and he was damned if he was going to forfeit it for what he termed a minor discomfort. His neck linen was soaked with perspiration, some of that dripping from his chin onto his waistcoat. Naturally, he had not seen fit to bring any water of his own, nor even a container to carry it, and was annoyed when his marine officer restricted that which the captain could demand from his men.

Frequent halts for rest were necessary, and frustrating. But as the day wore on this lessened, and to some extent the vegetation thinned. Well clear now of the coastal strip, Markham felt he could relax. He was reasonably sure that the soldiers, even if they'd found the bodies of their comrades and picked up their trail, hadn't pursued them. And by the time they reached Nice, the next largish town, he and his party would be too far ahead of any search party that could be mounted from the permanent garrison. So, when reconnoitring ahead in the late afternoon, he and Rannoch heard the crashing sound of a body of men moving through the undergrowth, it came as quite a shock.

'They are ahead of us,' whispered Rannoch, as both men fell forward on to the ground.

'That's not possible,' Markham replied, his mind racing to confirm the validity of what he had said.

Certainly they'd halted often enough, and a mounted party sent in pursuit of them could have used the Grasse road to get in front, then cut across on another track to bar their way. But that argued they knew their route and destination, and something about the composition of the party. Or it was a sheer fluke?

Rannoch had his head cocked, his ears straining to make something of the noises coming from up ahead. There wasn't much in the way of speaking, excepting the odd curse. But there was ample sound, as bodies pushed through bushes, accompanied by the swish of the swords and bayonets that were being used to slash at the undergrowth.

'They are moving across our path, not towards us, but slowly.'

'Searching?'

'Definitely that.'

'Fetch the Comte de Puy up here, will you, Sergeant, and ask him to make sure to bring his map. Get him to this spot and keep him here till I return.'

'Shall I alert the others to be prepared to run.'

'No! Tell Halsey to be ready to retreat, but make sure no one else hears you say it. He's not to make any dispositions until you and the Monsieur de Puy are out of sight.'

Rannoch looked at him, his blue eyes boring into those of his officer. Markham had no need to speak. The Highlander could make the same deductions as he had; that if the men ahead of them were searching for their party, then someone had to have told them where to look. The only person who'd been out of contact with the rest of the group, free to arrange such a thing, had been de Puy. With a sharp nod, he slithered downhill over the covering of wet leaves.

Markham, using the undergrowth in front of him, crept forward, pistol extended, heading for the source. Aware that the searchers had moved on, he tended slightly to the right, and was soon on the edge of the area already covered, a swathe some twenty feet wide though which the evidence of human passing was plain. Bushes and plants had been cut down or trampled. In the distance he could now hear other parties, also searching, perhaps half a dozen, certainly two or tree groups. That argued a substantial body of men, some of whom were acting like beaters on a hunt.

How could they have got so organised and so placed at such speed? It was easy to imagine that with the encumbrances he and his men had, they could easily have walked smack into this search party. But that thought negated the notion of any prior knowledge. And why indulge in this elaborate search, when all they had to do was wait for their quarry to arrive, and close in on them as they unsuspectingly, and noisily, walked into a trap?'

The sight of de Puy, lying beside Rannoch, was a relief. He half-feared that the Frenchman would be gone, having slipped away from the others, well aware of what lay up ahead. On reflection of course, that didn't make sense. The Comte could stay with the party until they were taken, and he was still the only person, who, since coming ashore, had had the time to arrange matters.

But as Markham crawled closer he was struck with another obvious thought; why bother? He had been thinking through a set of ideas that applied to him, Aramon and Germain, not de Puy. He had in his mind the treasure they were after, and an individual attempt to get hold of it. Why should the man who left it behind, the only person who could take them to it, go to all this trouble to have them taken up? De Puy, once he was out on his reconnaissance, could have left them all in that outhouse, and simply not returned. As soon as he was alongside him, the Comte, in a whisper, bombarded Markham with the same set of questions with which he had taxed himself.

'I have no idea, monsieur,' Markham insisted. 'All I know is they are there, and that they represent an almost insurmountable threat to us.'

'Perhaps we would be better to stay where we are until dawn.'

'If we can't get ahead of them,' Markham said, 'I'd rather we fell back and put some distance between us. If we have to withdraw in a hurry, with women in tow, we will be hampered if they get close.'

The noise had been fading, as the distance between them and the search parties grew. But a sudden shouted order changed all that. Faint though it was, Markham was sure it was an instruction to retire. But that notion evaporated when he heard the first blades striking on wood. The group nearest to their position had come round in an arc. They were now making their way back towards the road, but lower down the slope, heading right for the place where the remainder of the party was resting.

Added to that came the unmistakable thud of hooves pounding on earth, as what sounded like a squadron of cavalry passed by, heading up towards Grasse. No horse could enter the forest, of course, it was too dense and the slope was too steep. But it was clear evidence of a mobility that Germain's party lacked. They couldn't stay in this wild woodland and survive. Remaining still invited discovery, moving up and on, sticking to their original route with its attendant noise even more so. He had no idea in which direction the searchers would move next, the only certainty being that while they were so engaged they would not be on the Grasse road. And if there were piquets there, they would be visible and perhaps avoidable, while the noise of cavalry would so precede them that avoiding action could be taken.

'Rannoch, ask Captain Germain to get everybody on their feet and heading due east. He must proceed with care. When they come to a road, request that they stay out of sight and wait by the edge of that for me. On no account are they to cross it. Keep our Lobsters in their present position and send the rest on ahead. We will form a rearguard. We have about ten minutes I reckon before they chance on this spot. They may come on and they may not. If they do, and if we can get across to the other side of the road, we will be out of their search area, and we might be safe.

'The women can't run.'

'Then carry them,' Markham snapped. 'And tell Aramon to hide his damned boxes in some bush.'

Markham grabbed de Puy as Rannoch departed, and they

moved crabwise across the hillside, the noise of the men beating through the undergrowth increasing with each step they took. Occasionally a voice floated through the trees, giving an order that kept the men in some kind of formation. He tried to calculate their pace, and to relate that to the ground his own party would have to cover. But it was a futile exercise. There was a risk and it had to be taken. To move was safer than staying still. He tugged at de Puy's shirt, to haul him back again, afraid that what remained of the startling whiteness of his linen would show up, even through this dense foliage.

He got back just as his party had begun to make their way, sending every bird and animal off in a noisy escape. Only the fact that the French were doing the same, and making so much noise of their own in the process, saved them. Ordering Rannoch to fall back in good order, he went ahead to see if he could quieten them as they approached the Grasse road.

Aramon was red-faced and gasping for breath, clearly angry, as though Markham had arranged this for his personal discomfort. Ghislane Moulins had not been carried, judging by the way her breasts were heaving, a sight that drew Markham's eye, and for a second distracted his attention. But he forced himself to concentrate, and went ahead, setting a slower, quieter pace as he tried to ease through the vegetation, rather than brush it aside.

Rannoch, meanwhile, was cursing officers in general and Markham in particular. Moving across the hill, in this way he'd been ordered to, was difficult. It seemed as if every root or obstruction had been placed especially to trip the marine rear-guard up, especially since they had to keep their muskets trained, prepared to give the French a volley should the two groups get too close to each other.

Markham had come to the edge of the road, easing himself out through the thinning trees. The light wasn't good, though there was still at least an hour of daylight left. But the angle of the sun, given the canopy of trees, cast the road into deep shadow, and it was only the small movements of men fidgeting that drew his eye. He watched for a full minute, his thoughts deeply troubled, before easing himself back in to the thicker undergrowth.

'I can't see what's over the other side. But there are soldiers up ahead on the road. There's a coach there too.'

'How many soldiers?'

'One about every fifty feet, all facing these woods which their comrades are searching.'

Markham paused, examining each face in turn for some sign that such a statement registered. It was bad enough that the enemy was looking for them. But that they should concentrate their search only on the western side of the Grasse road was singular. But no one reacted, except to keep staring at him, waiting for a decision.

'There don't appear to be any on the other side.'

'We might be able to go round them,' said Germain.

'By crossing the road,' added de Puy.

'It would be safer surely,' Germain continued. 'Once it begins to get dark, they will have to give up anyway. But they might just come close enough to us in their last cast to smoke us out.'

'Can I have a private word, sir?' asked Markham.

Germain was reluctant, perhaps guessing what he was going to be asked to do. But he had no choice but to accede, the look in his marine officer's eye leaving the captain in no doubt that he would speak out publicly if he had to.

'What is it,' he whispered, once they were alone.

'I think we should turn back.'

'No!'

'We are trapped in these woods by a superior force, and we are making slow progress anyway. You might have had what you thought were good reasons to agree to let Aramon bring his servants, let alone Mademoiselle Moulins and her maid. But that has backfired now.'

'You heard what he said. He would not move without them.'

Markham hated to be thought stupid, and that was reflected in the tone of his voice. 'I also saw what you were thinking, and how much it suited your purpose to get them all off the ship.'

'You've lost me Markham.'

'No I've not. And if you think I've read your mind, you can be certain Aramon has too. He wants that treasure in Rome.'

'That is not going to be up to him to decide. I am a naval officer, Markham, and I intend to remain so. I have already confided in you what my intentions are.'

'And I am asking you if the game is worth the candle.'

'Think of the reward,' Germain insisted.

Markham hissed his reply. 'I'm afraid, sir, if I do I will become as blind as you.'

'If you wish to return to the beach, and wait for us there, you may do so.'

The same dilemma! The odds were stacked against success, perhaps even against survival. But Markham was arrogant enough to believe that if he went that could only get worse. Germain was even less of a man to trust on land than he was at sea. He would carry on regardless. And now it wasn't just his Lobsters to worry about. Abandoning Aramon held no terrors. But there was also de Puy and Ghislane Moulins.

'I think my place is here, sir.'

'Then what I need to know, Markham, is what we do now?'

'I seem to remember that you are in command.'

Germain blinked at that, and Markham was aware that what he'd just done was deliberately cruel. He'd made all the decisions since coming ashore. Germain had acquiesced in this, no doubt because all those he'd made at sea had been uniformly disastrous. That high degree of confidence he'd displayed in Corsica had quite evaporated.

'I would appreciate your advice, Markham.'

'You will not withdraw?'

'No!'

'There is a dense thicket some fifty yards back. I suggest we pull back to that, sir, and remain there.'

'Will we not cross the road?'

'That is an operation fraught with risk, only to be considered if it becomes obvious that it is necessary. It is not one I image can be undertaken without casualties. In that regard, I think your command has suffered quite enough.'

The eyes locked, and the unspoken rebuke, that they would not be in this predicament if it weren't for Germain whoring after glory was sent and accepted.

'As you wish, Markham,' Germain replied, with as much dignity as he could muster.

Chapter eleven

The last part of the day was the worst time for insects. They seemed to rise out of the still damp earth in droves to torment people who, of necessity, had to remain stationary. The ones that couldn't fly crawled into garments or across bare flesh; ants, beetles and spiders in a quantity that Markham had rarely seen. While the bugs ate them, they fed on hard biscuit, and sipped warm water from the marine bottles. It was also a time for speculation, though no voice was raised to ask the obvious question; why were the French looking so hard just ahead of them? Every ear was tuned to the sound of the French soldiers searching the woods, tensed ready to move as they came closer, easing as the sounds faded. Whispering, Markham had outlined the kind of grid he thought they were working on, and the calculation he had made that they'd never get this far down the hillside before nightfall.

What sunlight they could see was now slanting across the treetops, the colour slipping from pure gold to orange. The road was in near darkness, and Markham waited patiently for the order that must come soon, calling the men in. Once that had happened they could move again, perhaps even using the road to increase their rate of progress. They had planned to be ashore a mere forty-eight hours, and if they delayed too long, then the problems of re-embarking on *Syilphide* would only increase.

Rannoch had set the men in an arc round the rest of the party, who occupied the centre of a thicket so dense that no one would see through it. Markham, de Puy and Germain were on the outer edge, nearest the road, watching the light fade, waiting for the moment when it would be just dark enough to move, but still with some ambient light by which to see any obstructions.

The flare of the torchlight, as well as the smell of fresh-lit pitch, was faint through the undergrowth. But it was unmistakable. He realised, with a sinking feeling, that they were not going to give up, but intended to continue throughout the night. Killing those two soldiers had obviously stung the man who commanded the regiment, and nothing was going to stop him from finding the culprits. He could hear de Puy cursing under his breath, with an unusual degree of passion.

'Our man is determined.'

'He may also be a fool. You do not wander around in these parts with lit torches. That is a very dangerous thing to do. The forest might not be tinder dry as it usually is at this time of year. But one badly handled torch could set the whole area on fire.'

'How dangerous?' asked Germain.

'Put it this way, Captain, I'd rather be caught by the enemy. A fire, once it takes in hold these Provencal forests, can consume a thousand hectares in no time. Neither man nor animal can outrun the flames.'

Markham had eased himself forward to the edge of the trees again, and stuck his head out through a small gap in the hedgerow. The pinpricks of light that dotted the road were, he thought, more numerous than the previous number of guards. Whoever commanded these troops had decided to withdraw them onto the road, spacing them out so that no one could safely cross it. It also put an effective check on movement in the woodlands. It was a hard enough place to traverse in full daylight. At night, even with a moon, it would be near impossible. At the very least it would be extremely noisy.

He watched as a detail came down the road, two men bearing a large metal urn, another two a huge basket of bread. They stopped by each sentinel, dishing out his evening ration. Passing Markham they were no more than ten feet away, and the smell of the stew in that pot wafted across his nostrils to torment him. Behind them came another party, carrying fresh bundles of kindling made up into torches, the odour of the unlit pitch pungent enough to wipe out that of the food. Lastly, there came a trio of officers, who stopped beside each man, no doubt to reinforce whatever orders had already been given.

What Markham did next was risky, but he felt it was necessary. He began to crawl along the ground, on his elbows and knees, determined to get close to the nearest guard so that he could overhear what orders were being dished out. The road was some twenty feet across, if you included the spaces where the hedgerows had been cut back. The guard was no more than a few feet from those, certainly close enough to hear any sound that Markham might make, and with the officers approaching, staring straight ahead as if looking him right in the eye.

But he'd stopped crawling until the scrunch of the boots on the hard-packed roadway covered the noise he made, the final few yards covered quickly, rather than at the previous snail's pace, his progress aided by the spill from the sentry's torch. Markham ended up behind a thick bush, with no actual view of the road, but certain he was within earshot. The sound of boots ceased, to be followed by the sound of a brusque voice, demanding to know the soldier's name.

Whatever it was, it was mumbled and incomprehensible. But the officer, when he spoke, did so clearly.

'It is best to vary any routine, soldier. Do not stand still all the time, but neither should you pace a route at specific intervals. Our quarry will, I think, try to use the road before the moon comes up. He must if he wishes to get clear. Otherwise he will spend a very uncomfortable night in the forest, with little chance of sleep, and we shall find him in the morning.'

'Sir,' said the soldier, this time speaking crisply.

'You will be relieved in two hours.'

The trio moved off. But as the boots passed by his nose, Markham wasn't thinking of what the man had said, he was thinking about the familiarity of the voice which had said it. He couldn't move until the sentry in front of him did so, and was left with plenty of time to speculate. Where had he heard that before? It could be any number of places.

His first real mistress had been French and noble, and she had introduced him to a wide circle of her Parisian acquaintances. There had been French officers in the Russian service, and he had seen duty with them when fighting the Turks. Then there were the *émigrés* who had fled to London at the start of the Revolution.

They were the most numerous. Rich and poor they'd flocked to the entertainment centres of the town, the same places he, seeking opportunity, had frequented. Quite a few were like him, spending more than they could really afford in an attempt to create an attractive illusion, one that might produce some gainful employment. They liked the area around Covent Garden too, for its cheap housing and ready, all-pervasive low life.

The last lodgings he'd had before fleeing the bailiffs had been in Long Acre. And with his many friends in the theatre, he was a constant visitor to Drury Lane, a friend to the Linley family who owned the place, as well as a goodly number of the actors and actresses who performed there. People like Sheridan and Fox were fellow enthusiasts. They were also sympathetic politicians, who could elicit a favour for some particularly hard-up French aristocrat. It was one of their number he'd killed in Finsbury Park, the poor fellow taking great exception to finding George Markham in bed with his wife.

There had been an accent in that voice. Not much of one, but nevertheless something quite distinctive. Then there was the crisp delivery, which was singular. Faces and situations floated through his mind in an endless stream, but try as he did, he could not put a face that voice. The thoughts evaporated as the sentry moved, which allowed him to crawl backwards a few feet, then get onto his hands and knees and turn round. Once clear he had a chance to hit out at the numerous creatures which had been eating him while he lay on the ground.

'Did you find out anything?' whispered Germain.

'I did,' Markham replied.

He was trying to think of another way of saying what he had already stated; they were trapped. De Puy had said that this was a busy road between the coast and Grasse. Yet not a single cart had passed down it while they'd been close. That meant it had been closed. He looked up through the canopy of trees, to the patch of clear sky twinkling with the first hint of stars.

'They will keep those torches lit until the moon is high enough to illuminate the road.'

Germain opened his mouth to say something else, but Markham held up his hand, running over yet again in his head the words the officer had used. Never mind the accent and the familiarity, what was it he had said? He'd mentioned the quarry, but then referred to it in the singular.

'*He* must if *he* wishes to get clear.' Was that just a slip of the tongue?

The shout that split the night air was followed by the crack of a musket, then another, general yelling following on the heels of that. Markham shot forward again, throwing caution to the winds, so that he could see what was happening. He had to pull back quickly as those sentries who'd been down the road rushed past, their torches waving as they made for a group gathered about a hundred yards up the hill. The torches were waving madly until the officers arrived and some sense of order was restored.

Markham could hear one of them yelling like a parade ground sergeant, demanding both quiet and information at the same time.

His voice barely dropped as, having got what he was after, he reported to his superior that the man they were seeking had crossed at the run, and entered the forest on the opposite side. The sentry nearest, who fired off the first shot, was sure that he had winged him, since he heard a cry of pain. The familiar voice raised itself, issuing a string of instructions; that a file of ten men should stay on the spot to seal the road, while the rest should be prepared to march.

'Where is he going to march to?' asked Markham when he'd rejoined the others.

'There is a good wide track along the top of the peaks from the village of Mouans Sartoux, part of an ancient trading route. If he wants to go west he will follow that. It has the advantage of a good view of the terrain below. That, as you can see on the map, is even steeper and narrower than the route we are on. Anyone moving through it will struggle, and he is bound to disturb the wildlife and give away his position.'

'Who is it they are pursuing?' asked Germain.

'I don't care, as long as it's not us,' stated Markham.

In the dark, he could not see any faces. But he did wonder how many showed relief that they had not, as they might have imagined, been betrayed by one of their own number.

'What do we do now? asked Aramon.

'We shall not be comfortable, Monsignor, but I suggest we try and get some sleep.'

It was de Puy's turn to pose a question. 'What plan do we have for the morning, Lieutenant Markham. There are still soldiers on the road.'

'A file of ten men we can take care of, Monsieur le Comte, that is if we have to.'

He wished he could see Germain's face. Was his captain happy or angry that all these questions were being put to him? That was answered by the way Germain suddenly asserted himself.

'Using the road, Monsieur le Comte, how quickly could we get to Notre Dame de Vacluse.'

'Six hours at the most.'

'Then we must do that,' the captain said emphatically. 'Using these tracks through the forest was a grave mistake, especially with the ladies in tow.'

'And if we are seen on the road?' asked Markham.

'We got through the column on the coast road by pretending you were prisoners, we can do the same again.'

'Do we pray for rain so that the men can wear the greatcoats?'

'Why bother,' Germain replied, his voice carrying a degree of authority that had been missing since the failed boarding operation. 'There are ten French uniforms out there, just waiting for us to take them as soon as the sun comes up.'

'Another legitimate *ruse de guerre*, Captain?'

'Yes.'

'Only this time, if we are caught, we will be shot.'

'You really must try to be more positive, Markham. Such pessimism does not become a King's officer.'

The temptation to reply sharply to that was difficult to control, especially to a man who had trouble keeping a grip on his temper. But relations between himself and Germain were bad enough without him making things worse. And given the other potential disputes that might arise, should they succeed, the need for some form of cohesion in the British contingent was paramount. But he had to, for his own sake, say something.

'The acquisition of these uniforms. Do you wish to take personal charge of that, sir?'

'I doubt that will be necessary.'

'We have to do something about them, in any case,' said Markham. 'As long as they are in position we cannot move. We have no idea what their orders are, so they might be still in position tomorrow night.'

'I'm surprised Captain Germain does not want us to form up like infantry and do battle with them.'

'Keep your voice down. He needs no encouragement when it comes to woolly-headed notions of how to fight.'

'It is an even match,' Rannoch responded, in his measured way. His face was nothing more than a ghostly shape in the small amount of moonlight. 'Mind you, if the rest of the soldiers are still on this mountain, we should not be using musket fire.'

'No,' Markham replied.

'It is scarce possible that all of our men will be able to sneak up on the Frenchmen without one giving himself away.'

'Then we must draw them down on us, and deal with them as a group.'

'We cannot be taking prisoners, can we?'

The voice was enough. Markham didn't have to see Rannoch's face. In battle he was a killer of the most ferocious kind. But the prospect of visiting death on his fellow humans was not something that excited him. It was very much the opposite. Useless slaughter was to be avoided on the very good grounds that if you wanted compassion from your enemy, the best way to get it was to be benevolent yourself.

'I will act as a decoy, a single man like the fellow they were pursuing. Let them chase me into the forest at a point of our choosing, and we can take them there.'

'I would fire off a musket as soon as I spotted you.'

'Let's hope none of them are as a good a shot as you then.'

'Even if it didn't kill you, I would have alerted my comrades.'

'I don't see how we can avoid that.'

'As long as we can avoid a fusillade. A single shot could be mistaken for a hunter or an accidental discharge.'

'Sleep,' said Markham. 'Two men to stand sentry, two on, four off. Tell them to use their ears more than their eyes. All except Bellamy, I want him watching those Frenchmen.'

'Then I wish you the joy of finding him. He disappears as soon as the sun goes down.'

'That's why I want him.'

The whispered calls produced no response, forcing Markham to crawl around repeating his name. When the hand touched his shoulder, he was startled, even though he was anticipating it. The voice, mixed with a chuckle, was smooth, deep and right by his ear.

'All colours will agree in the dark, sir, according to Francis Bacon.'

'Damn you, Bellamy.'

'The gods have seen fit to do that already, else I would not be here.'

'You should not have taken quite so readily to the bottle.'

'A weakness of mine, I grant you. That and the fair sex though what I am tempted by is not normally termed fair. Not that is, like the lady you desire.'

To Markham, the man was an enigma. But then he was that to himself as well. Born a slave, he had benefited from a benign employer, who'd educated him. That had acted as both a curse and blessing. It elevated Bellamy above the herd, while condemning him to double the quantity of abuse meted out to men of his colour. The death of his mentor had left him penniless and in Chatham. Drink from a recruiting sergeant had ensured that he woke up one morning as a marine.

Yet still he retained that infuriating self-assurance. Even here, in the dark, encroaching forest, he managed to make his superior feel second rate. Markham knew his Shakespeare, and could hold his own with that. But Bellamy was likely to quote Latin poets in their own vernacular, never mind English men of letters.

'Keep your mind on staying alive. And use what god gave you to stay hidden. If any of those sentinels look like coming anywhere near us I want to know.'

'This is not how I had planned to spend the night.'

'That's the trouble with soldiering, Bellamy. You never get left in peace.'

'According to Renate, it is the same for servants.'

Markham was surprised by the undisguised tone of bitterness in the Negro's voice. When talking about any subject, Bellamy rarely allowed himself anything other than a tone of amused detachment. Perhaps Ghislane Moulins' maid had touched a deeper chord.

Together they crawled to a point from which Bellamy could observe the road, his black face invisible in greenery made dark by moonlight. Moving back into the thicket, Markham tripped over an outstretched foot, falling forward on his hands. The apology was soft and female, his response forgiving, and Aramon's interjection, from no more than a foot away, gruff and unfriendly.

'I think it would be best for all the males to stay on the exterior of this thicket. I have already sent your black man out, who I may say, is paying far too much attention to Renate.'

He didn't bother to tell the cleric that he had nothing to worry about. Let him fret. 'You don't see this injunction as applying to you, Monsignor.'

'I am a priest.'

'Sure, where I come from, that's good ground for a chastity belt and a double lock on the cabinet with the drink in.'

The slight female snigger, hastily suppressed, was worth the growl that such a remark produced from the target of the abuse. Markham reached out a speculative hand, finding an arm, which produced what he sought. The squeeze was as exciting as his first stolen kiss and he lifted Ghislane's hand to his lips, pressing his lips to the back.

'But I think you're right, Monsignor. I will sleep outside.'

Markham didn't go on to say that if he stayed in here, he'd likely get no sleep at all.

He chose the pre-dawn to show himself, that time when objects are still indistinct. It is light, but the sun has not yet risen. The figure might still have failed to draw an eye. But the way Markham staggered was enough, though it wasn't the man closest who spotted him, but another, more alert Frenchman further up the track. That meant no shot from his musket, since with a comrade between him and the target the risk of hitting his own was too great. And as soon as the shout alerted the rest he was gone, stumbling into the thick undergrowth pursued by the thud of ten pairs of boots.

They stopped before plunging after him; a momentary pause while the risk was assessed. Common sense dictated that they split up, with a few continuing the pursuit while the rest stayed on the road. But he was one, seemingly unarmed man, quite possibly wounded, against ten fit muskets. Added to that every man would want any reward that might be going for his actual capture. If they wondered how a single human could leave such a wide trail it didn't surface. Perhaps they were just grateful their progress was so effortless. That is, until they reached the edge of the thicket which had sheltered part of Markham's party the night before.

The French soldier in charge shouted for silence, his head spinning right and left to pick up some trace of their quarry's movements. The loud rustling to their right took every eye, and saw each weapon trained in that direction, so that the men who emerged behind them had a slight period of grace in which to take their designated opponent.

For Rannoch it was clinical; a bayonet on the end of his land pattern musket, plus the extent of his arm, scything into his target right under the heart at a distance of six feet from his own body. Others were less sure of their skill, and sought closer contact. Halsey, Gibbons and Ettrick scored cleanly. Quinlan missed the vital spot and had to grapple with his opponent, who fought for nearly half a minute despite what the blade had done to his insides. Germain slashed with his cutlass, nearly decapitating his man, and such was his desire to kill that he kept on slashing long after it served any other purpose than to ruin the victim's uniform.

Leech and Tully had to wrestle with enemies who were still in a fit state to kill their attacker, the shouts and grunts of all four echoing through the woods. Leech earned a deep gash in his cheek before he overcame his man. Yelland, the youngest Lobster in the unit, used his musket as a club, then skewered the kneeling figure through the neck.

Dornan was slow, as usual, and though he stabbed his man, he failed to follow it through with sufficient venom, and so had to use his weight and strength to subdue his opponent, dropping his musket in the process and finishing the man off by strangulation. Bellamy was nowhere to be seen, leaving one Frenchman to turn and run. Markham and de Puy, who'd sealed off the rear to ensure no one escaped, took care of him. The two officers walked up the line of bodies to check that each man was dead, stopping by Germain, who had his back to the thicket.

'Let's have their uniforms off,' he said. 'Sergeant Rannoch, get out on that road and find where they had their camp.'

Rannoch looked at Markham, who nodded that he should obey. 'I still have reservations about the uniforms, sir.'

'It is my decision, Markham. If it offends you, go with your sergeant.'

To be so publicly rebuked was galling. Germain, it seemed, couldn't make up his mind. He wanted to assert his authority, but only when it was not the time to make any real decisions.

'Fit to be a general,' said Rannoch, softly, clear evidence that he at least understood what was going on.

As they made their way back to the road, they passed Bellamy. There was perspiration on his face, but no blood on his bayonet. The huge dark eyes, made even more prominent by the enormous whites, declined to meet those of Rannoch, but fixed on Markham's. Then they shifted to gaze on the bodies of the French soldiers.

'On horror's head horrors accumulate.'

'What did he say?' asked Rannoch, as they emerged onto the road, now lit by the sun reflecting off the higher trees.

'It's a quote from Shakespeare.'

'Then it is as Dutch to me,' growled Rannoch, as he set off up the road. 'Thank God I have not got his cleverness, for it is of no use to him at all in a fight.'

Passing what remained of the used torches, they found the camp that had been set up the day before, the embers of the fire used to cook still burning. The deep ruts of the coach that had stood on the road were still evident, the bones and bottles around where it had stood an indication that this had probably accommodated the officers. Markham looked up the road, wondering where it had been blocked to stop any traffic coming from the interior. If it were in Grasse itself, they would be all right, since they would turn off the road well before that at the village of Mouans Sartoux. But if they'd barred it before that point they might well walk straight into a fight.

Looking back he saw his own party emerging from the woods. What he observed made him frown, even if his Lobsters, in bloodstained coats, looked better than the others. Ghislane Moulins' dress was in the same state as that of her maid Renate, torn and streaked with filth. Aramon and his servants were little better, the mud that had dried on their dark clothing showing up as pale streaks.

Why did they not change? What was the point in bringing those three square cases if they were not going to use the contents. In all they looked forlorn. Which, much as he hated to admit it, might just be what was required if Germain's plan was to be put into operation. Then it struck him, as he recalled the ease with which Aramon's servants had handled those boxes. It was so obvious he'd been a fool not to see it. They were empty, designed to carry something out, not to take clothes in.

'I will leave you to organise your men, Markham,' Germain called, holding out a coat that, unlike the others was free from blood or any sign of a gash. 'Might I suggest you wear this.'

'Certainly, sir. But if we encounter a superior enemy, I will be obliged to rip it off.'

'Of course.'

He turned abruptly to Rannoch. 'Tell the rest of the men to have their red coats to hand. We'll put Yelland on point, and ensure he rounds each bend well head of us. If there are any more piquets barring the road, I'll dump this coat. The men can escort me to them, as though I'm the fellow they're looking for.'

'Another surprise?'

'Captain Germain's idea.'

'You do not consider we have been lucky thus far?'

'Yes, we have.'

'But that does not persuade you to insist we turn back?'

Markham looked Rannoch straight in the eye. 'God knows I've tried. But if you wish to approach Captain Germain and repeat what I have said, I will not stand in your way.'

The Scotsman was silent for a bit, looking up the road, then at the green-capped mountains that straddled their route. Markham wondered if Rannoch believed him, and was pleased to find out that he did.

'It would do no good. I have never been one for the notion of desertion. And if I was, the middle of enemy territory would be no place to do it.'

'I think it's the only option he would give you. That or, when you got back, a flogging round the fleet.'

'I suppose you are right, him being in dire need of a bit of glory.'

Markham suspected there was a barb aimed at him in that remark. But he didn't respond, because if there was, and he checked Rannoch, he'd only get what was innuendo in plain unadulterated English. That attitude, of careful insubordination, was one of the reasons he appreciated the Highlander. It meant there was someone alongside him who would not indulge in blind obedience; who forced him to think, to look at his actions objectively. In over ten years of fighting George Markham had learned that doubt was a good thing. He'd seen many too many officers, and the men they led, perish for their certainties.

'Let's get them formed up, Sergeant. The quicker we get to this damned church, and load up what Aramon's after, the quicker we can think about getting back to the ship.'

'Amen to that!' Rannoch replied, with feeling.

They marched as they had when they came ashore, so that anyone coming across them by accident, or observing them from a higher part of the road, would see them as prisoners escorted by a file of troops. And Markham set a cracking pace, hoping that the less fit could keep up, constantly consulting de Puy's map, searching for the point at which they could leave the road. Up ahead the two highest peaks never seemed to get any nearer, the only indication of progress the greater definition of the high valley though which the road inland must run. It was a country of brooding dark greens all the way up the summits, oppressive in itself, made more so by the increasing heat.

The sound of a single horseman, cantering, was audible before Yelland signalled. Markham waved for him to withdraw into the .

woods, and hustled his own party to do likewise, and there they stood as the rider went by, glancing neither right nor left. Markham, in the brief time he had, noted that the man was well mounted and equipped, in sharp contrast to his foot-slogging brethren.

As soon as he was out of sight they regained the road. Markham allowed no time for discussion, even ignoring Germain. That rider might be on a duty that would take him all the way to the coast. But that was doubtful. More likely he had either orders for the men they'd killed, or required a report. He might find their bodies, and he might not. But the chances were he'd be back up the route in less than an hour, to tell his commanding officer what he'd seen.

On each side, the forest began to thin, until it was gone completely, cut back to allow for cultivated, steep fields. There was the odd clump of woodland, but basically they were moving out of cover, and approaching the point where the hills peaked on a heavily wooded ridge before dropping in to the next valley. They crossed a tiny wooden bridge over a stream, and, despite the risk from that solitary horseman, he called a brief halt so that everyone could take a cooling drink.

'If we stay on the road we are exposed,' he explained to Germain. 'If we want to remain completely hidden we'll have to retrace our steps and take a longer route through the forest.'

'We don't have the luxury of time, Markham.'

'We don't have the strength to take on a superior force, sir, and might I remind you we are deep in enemy territory. Logic demands that we avoid contact for that reason alone. We have no idea how long it will be before that cavalryman we observed returns.'

Germain raised his voice, his tone deliberately commanding, aware that Aramon and de Puy were approaching, their chins still wet from the water they'd consumed.

'Nor can we be sure he will. We must get to our destination today if we are to have any chance of success.'

Markham knew success meant different things to all present. For him, despite any temptation in the financial line, it had become paramount to get his men safely back to the ship. Aramon and de Puy, he surmised, would consider the recovery of the Avignon treasure as success. But Germain would only be happy when it was safe in his cabin, under lock and key, while he wrote the despatch that told how he'd achieved it.

'Yelland's coming,' said Halsey, softly.

The youngster jogged up, trailing his musket, as usual whistling tunelessly. He reported to Markham, which produced a frown on Germain's face.

'I went on a few hundred yards before I spotted you'd stopped, sir.'

'And?' asked Markham wearily. Yelland was never very exact in his reports. Distance, in this case, since it could be vital, needed to be accurate. But he would not rebuke him in front of the others.

'There are some buildings up ahead, with a square church spire in the middle.'

'That is Mouans Sartoux' said de Puy.

'There's a roadblock at the edge, and a whole heap of wagons and folks behind it.'

'How large is the piquet?'

'Two soldiers, that I could see.'

Germain obviously expected Markham to react immediately, to produce the right solution without thinking. His marine officer refused to oblige him. Instead he remained still, looking at the ground, thinking.

'Well?'

'We have a problem, sir.'

'We have several, Markham, not least the fact, which I have already had occasion to point out to you, that we have scant time for rumination.'

'We can assume that there are more than two men on that roadblock ahead of us. What we don't know is how many. Nor do we know where they are billeted.'

'If we take the two?'

'The others will surely appear when we do,' said de Puy. 'A file of soldiers marching on them is bound to bring them out.'

'Yes. And it was my intention to leave you here and go on as the sole prisoner, in a repeat of the charade I played at dawn.'

'So?'

'Quite possibly we can overwhelm them, Monsignor. But what then?'

'Then I fail to see what the problem is.'

It was de Puy who spoke. 'I think the good lieutenant is wondering what will happen, regardless of the risk from that horseman, when all those people held up in Mouans Sartoux spill down the road towards the coast.'

'That's right, monsieur. What will they say, the officers of that

137

army, when they hear that one body of their own troops attacked another. And can we do it without any of them finding out that we are not French at all?'

'You think they will send men to investigate?' asked Germain.

'I would. Informed that the enemy had a force operating at my rear, I'd detach a couple of regiments to find and neutralise them. At the very least, I'd alert every officer in the area to their presence. That will make it impossible to get back aboard *Syilphide*.'

'So?'

Markham was studying the map again, his finger tracing the route to Notre Dame de Vacluse. 'How much open country is there around the village, Yelland.'

'Plenty your honour. Forest thins out about a mile from the edge. And the its all fields of corn an' that sort of thing.'

'Then that's our route. We have to make our way across those fields and onto the ridge well to the west of Mouans Sartoux.'

'They will see us.'

'Yes,' Markham replied. 'But they won't know who were are. And I am hoping that being ordered to keep the road closed, they will stay with their duty and take no steps to investigate.'

Chapter twelve

It was impossible not to look over their shoulder as they traversed the slope. The cultivation had a feudal appearance, individual strips planted with whatever crop the owner or tenant thought most profitable. Occasionally tall stalks of maize hid them. But when they emerged into plain view again, head and shoulders above the rows of grape-filled vines, or trudging though a strip of purple lavender, every eye was drawn to look at the roadblock outside the village. They knew that they too were under examination. There were a dozen soldiers at the roadblock now, and some had been seen pointing. But none had come in pursuit. Markham had been right. They were not going to disobey their orders. It was therefore just bad luck that the man who'd issued them arrived before the party made it back into the woods.

Not that they knew he was there to start with. It was the firing of a musket that alerted them. That and the sight of the horseman galloping up the road. They looked to the roadblock for a reaction, only to observe that there were many more troopers on duty now than had been there previously. There was also a certain amount of commotion. Markham, with the aid of his field telescope could just make the figure out in the throng, a small officer gesticulating wildly.

The reaction was immediate. Half of the French soldiers, some fifty men, even before the mounted man reported, set off in pursuit. A smaller party was sent down the route from which they'd come. No doubt a messenger was already on his way, calling for reinforcements from the main body further up the Grasse road.

'Captain Germain, I suggest that once we are out of sight again, Monsignor Aramon takes the ladies and his servants away in a line that keeps them hidden.'

'And you?' demanded Aramon, giving Germain no chance to reply.

'We will try to draw the enemy after us. As soon as get we back in to wooded country we will try to lose them and meet you at Vacluse.'

'No. We must stay together.'

'I don't think we are going to have much choice,' said Rannoch.

He was pointing up towards the top of the hill, to the bushes where the open field finished. A unit of cavalry, a dozen in number, had emerged from the woods some five hundred yards ahead of them, the very forest in which Markham had planned to find sanctuary. He looked first at the next patch of maize. He could reach that and take some form of cover in it. But height would give a horse soldier a great advantage in that. Then he examined the rows of thick, heavily laden vines, set to follow the contours of the slope in a way that maximised the sunlight, with a crop on them nearly ready to be picked. The cavalry could not come right at them through those without losing momentum. But given time they could deploy between them, which would give them a clear field in which to charge. It would also present his Lobsters, well trained in musketry, a lane down which to fire at an individual horseman.

Yet they must be confused, unaware that the troops in front of them were not friendly. That wouldn't last long. Even a dimwit, to Markham the natural state of most cavalry officers, would see that they were being pursued, and would react accordingly, at the very least moving to apprehend them. Yet the worst option of all was that they should stay still, and bar access to the safety of the forest.

'Sergeant Rannoch.'

'Sir,' he replied punctiliously, standing as he was next to Captain Germain.

'Let's get out of these damned coats. I would want the enemy to know exactly who it is they are faced with. And let's have a bit of confusion until they are closer.'

'That will only bring them down on us,' said Germain.

'Which is precisely my intention, sir.'

'We would do best to avoid them.'

'That is impossible. They are mounted and we are not.'

The reaction to the sight of a dozen red coats was immediate. The horses, no doubt because of the excitement of their riders, began to prance in circles, and had to be hauled back into line. Then they began to move downhill, trampling whatever crops stood in their way, easy at a walk, less so at high speed. Markham had his eyes on the mounts, trying to assess their condition.

Were they light horse or heavy? Had they been out on patrol for a long time, or were they sleek and fresh? He wanted the latter, since a tired horse was more biddable to its rider than a fresh, oat-fed mount. Being Irish, he'd grown up with the beasts, and had often hunted, or raced them at the local steeplechases. In Russia, he had served alongside Don Cossacks and learned a great deal more about equine lore. Ponies were better in rough country, horses less so. They might not be bright, but they were very selfish. Not many of the creatures, even trained, would plunge at high speed through vegetation. They'd either try to circumvent it, or jump it.

'Monsieur de Puy. Would you take care of the rest of the party?'

The Frenchman looked surprised, but to Markham it was just a way of saving them all from a repeat of the Monsignor's previous insistence that de Puy must be kept safe.

'I would suggest that you make you way into the next patch of maize and continue to ascend towards the woods. You should be able to make it even if we are in difficulties. I would ask you to provide fire if we are withdrawing towards you.'

'And if not?'

'If my men can't hold them there is little point in useless sacrifice. So I would suggest that you show no arms that will bring retribution down on your head. The decision as to what to do next, is one that can only be taken when the circumstances are better known.'

Ghislane Moulins was right behind him, and she met Markham's eyes. Seeing a hint of angry frustration, he favoured her with his most reassuring smile. The Frenchman saw both the smile and, after a swift glance, the look. To Markham's way of thinking, neither did much to please him. He excelled himself with the level of gloom he displayed. Ghislane meanwhile had turned her gaze onto Bellamy, at the same time laying a hand on Renate's wrist, to mouth *bon chance*.

Markham didn't quite know why that annoyed him, but it did. It wasn't competition, since Bellamy was clearly smitten with Renate. Probably it was just the Negro, who had honed annoying people to a fine art.

'If everything works out, Mademoiselle, we might even salvage you a horse to ride, which will at least relieve you of the need to walk.'

That got him her full attention again. 'I think we need you, monsieur, more than I need a horse.'

'Ghislane!' snapped Aramon, who was already chivvying his servants to get them started. 'You are too free with your sentiments!'

'Sure, a pretty woman could never be that.'

Markham grinned so widely that Aramon came near to bursting a blood vessel, then turned to issue orders to his Lobsters. To aim for the men, where possible, not the animals, and if chance presented itself to take the bridle of any horse that was loose. The distance was closing, only four hundred yards now. But Markham was delighted to observe that the French commander was moving crab wise, not straight towards them, an indication that he intended to attack down the vine rows.

'Infantry against cavalry, Lieutenant,' said de Puy, behind his back. 'In what is almost open country that is not wise.'

'I confess to some ignorance,' added Germain, 'but I think the Comte correct.'

Three hundred and fifty yards now, still well beyond musket range. And what would the Frenchmen see, a group of redcoats not yet prepared to receive their charge.

'The way he is deploying is in exactly the fashion I wish,' Markham replied, with a confidence that was part contrived. 'And you have yet to see my men fire their muskets in a disciplined way, gentlemen. Besides, there is no choice. I must draw them away from the woods or no one will have a chance to get clear.'

'That infantry from Mouans Sartoux represents another threat which must be dealt with.'

'True. And if the man commanding the cavalry had any sense he'd wait till they are able to affect the outcome of the action.'

Markham was just about to allude to the endemic stupidity of horse soldiers, when he recalled that de Puy had served in King Louis's cavalry. So he quickly bit back the words.

'No doubt it is his first sight of a red coat, and he wants the glory of taking us for himself.'

'A worthy aim,' de Puy replied, without irony, turning away to muster his charges.

That surprised Markham, busy checking on his men. He'd reckoned de Puy more intelligent than that. But he remembered that if horses could be stupid that was as nothing to what became of some people when they got on their backs.

'Do you wish to stay with us, sir?' Markham asked Germain.

A jolt went through Germain's body. He must have suddenly realised that his marine officer had made at least a dozen decisions without consulting him, and was now asking him what he intended to do. Aramon, his servants and the ladies had followed de Puy towards the clump of maize, leaving the naval officer high and dry.

'I've already told you, Markham, that I'm not sure I approve of your intentions.'

'With the enemy three hundred yards distant, sir, I think it's too late to question them.'

'Since I am in command, I do so nevertheless.'

That finally cracked Markham's self control. Germain was now being stupid as well as obtuse. His voice was harsh, his tone loud enough to be heard by every one of his men.

'Then you won't mind, since no one but a fool would have brought us to this, if I decline to listen.' Germain's jaw moved, but no words emerged. 'You are welcome, sir, to take up a position alongside us. Any one of my men will explain what it is we are about to do. If you follow what they tell you, perhaps you may stay alive.'

Bellamy should not have spoken then. But with his usual lack of timing he did, the cultured tone of his voice, plus its deep reassuring timbre, adding insult to injury. That he did so with a Latin tag compounded the sin tenfold.

'*Medio tutissimus ibis*, sir.'

'What?'

Bellamy completely missed the anger. Nor, smiling broadly, was he aware on his part of the least hint of condescension.

'A paraphrase in translation, sir, I grant you. Not exactly what Ovid wrote in *Metamorphoses*. I merely infer that you'd be safer in the middle.'

Germain, sure he was the butt of a joke, exploded. 'Damn you if your heart isn't as black as your face, you ignorant ape.'

Markham had no time for a shocked response from the Negro, probably more upset by the charge of ignorance than the reference to his skin colour. He shouted at him to get in position. The French cavalry had begun to swing round, in a line directly between the approaching infantry and his Lobsters, each horseman pushing through until he had a row to himself, a clear run at these pitiful, disorganised Englishmen. They had to cover less than two hundred yards, against what looked like a enemy still in the throws of panic, and they felt completely safe until half that distance had been covered.

So when they took the first volley at one hundred and fifty yards, when they'd only broken into a trot, and were still sitting upright in their saddles, it came as a surprise, none greater than the fact that two of their men went down. Their commander had no more than a second to do what was sensible, to rally his men and withdraw until the infantry arrived. But he evidently failed to act, since four of his men immediately charged.

It was the age-old problem with horse soldiers, a complete absence of brains, the intelligence necessary to stop a horse from moving forward and regrouping. In almost every battle in which Markham had taken part, the cavalry had only put in a proper contribution when the action was nearing its end. Launched before that, they were impossible to recall, and were often more of a hindrance than a help.

These men were doubly cursed, trapped in between the vines, and committed to covering a distance that would take them nearly half a minute. That meant they might face at least two more volleys of musket fire, before riding down the bayonets that would be the last line of defence. Standing upright on the left of the line of Lobsters, and excepting the usual ham-fisted pair, Markham was proud of them.

The oncoming horses were ignored as each man went about his reloading procedure. Rammer out, barrel swiped, cartridge torn and powder inserted followed by the ball; rammer re-used then housed, hammer cocked, the last drop of powder emptied into the now exposed pan. Then it was present, to take aim through the sights at two tons of oncoming enemy. No panic-firing, but a certainty of the aim before the heavy trigger was pulled, releasing the lock. The flints struck, the pan flashed and the fire ignited the powder in the barrel, sending a well-fitted ball towards what each man could see of the now crouching cavalrymen.

Despite Markham's plea that they be spared, the horses naturally took the brunt, a couple staggering and falling, though not from the shots Rannoch was firing. Being the fastest man to reload Markham had ever seen he got off a third shot at his horseman with twenty yards to spare. Then Rannoch did what he'd been ordered. He stepped right between the vines to let the animal thunder past, the rider glassy eyed and mortally wounded as something in his brain made him hang onto the reins.

Rannoch ignored that, raising his musket to fire at the man who threatened to ride down Dornan, caught in the midst of reloading. Bellamy, even slower, had only got off one round, and was jabbing at his opponent, who'd been forced to slow down by the realisation that he was one of only four men still upright in the saddle. If the Negro had been any use, he would have probably withdrawn to safety. But faced with those huge eyes, which hinted at terror, and the feeble nature of Bellamy's attack, he came on. He could not know, as he died on Germain's sword, that the man he faced lacked any of the instincts that would have caused him to kill, except those generated by pure chance.

The other three got clear, taking with them two of the horses. They were in a frenzy and had broken though the vine rows. Another animal had bolted past so quickly that it was now too distant a prospect to catch. And with the infantry now jogging towards them rather than marching, there was little time to gather in the other four animals that had participated in the second phase of the attack.

'Packs on as soon as you are reloaded,' shouted Markham.

His eyes were on the approaching infantry, who'd now reached a point equal to that from which the cavalry had started out. Within a few minutes they'd be within range to give them a taste of volley fire. Standing in a row without an assailant, he'd not even had a chance to use his pistol. Without consulting him Rannoch shouted out another order, which had the Lobsters strapping two packs together, then chucking them either side of a horse. Then they began to withdraw straight up the slope.

'A little something I learned in the Americas,' said Rannoch, as together they were dragged by one of the mounts through the small gaps in the vines. 'The Jonathans would steal our pack animals and escape like this, hanging onto the straps, always with the ability to haul up and gift us a volley if we got too close.'

'Let's hope it works for us.'

'We still face odds,' Rannoch replied.

He didn't even attempt to look round for a fresh assessment of the risk. Both men knew that safety lay in cover. Out in the open, even if they could aim better than their opponents, they would be facing odds of five to one, which was too much to contemplate. But the plaintive cry forced them to haul hard and stop the mount.

Germain had got astride one of the horses and was whipping it through the vines with the flat of his sword. Behind him Bellamy and Leech stood with joined packs but nothing to put them on, unsure now what to do. Markham yelled for them to run, then moved along the row to block Germain's passageway. He caught him halfway through the vines and grabbing hold of his bridle, hauled hard so that the animal's head was pulled down.

'What in God's name do you think you're about?'

What he saw was that same face that Germain had worn on the deck of the ship they'd tried to board, the light of battle so strong in the eyes, the face so set, that all sense of objective judgement had fled from the man. The wonder was not that he was riding a horse but that he was heading away from the enemy. His sword was up, and for a split second it was as though he was going to strike down on Markham's unprotected head.

'You've left my men behind.'

That changed the look to one of incomprehension. It was the face of privilege, one he'd seen so often in his youth that it was imprinted in his mind; the look that said Culchies walk and gentlemen ride; that God was a Protestant and don't you forget it, you papist bog-trotter. Germain had committed an act, the wrong of which he was unaware.

'Get off the horse.'

'Leave go that bridle,' yelled Germain, the sword up again.

The shout, the flashing sword and his dark blue navy coat could not fail to attract attention. Neither officer had observed the enemy halt and present their muskets. The fire didn't have to be accurate. Out of anything up to fifty musket balls, one had to strike home. The wonder was that they hit nothing vital. But the ball that took him in the left shoulder propelled Germain forward over the withers, and only Markham hanging on to his other arm stopped him from falling off.

'Discourage them, Sergeant,' he yelled, hauling Germain back till he was more evenly balanced. 'For God's sake man, clap on.'

Bellamy and Leech came dashing through the row of vines. Markham thought Leech wounded till he realised it was the cut he'd received earlier, open again and bleeding. They were dragging their packs between them, a stupid thing to do as they kept snagging in the gnarled branches. Markham grabbed at Bellamy and placed his hand on the horse girth.

'Set your packs across the haunches and secure then. Then get the captain into the woods.'

Bellamy was only too happy to oblige. Despite a volley from Rannoch and the others, the French had moved forward twenty paces and fired again. Suddenly the vinerows were full of flying lead, lopping off the low branches and bunches of grapes as it sought human flesh. Markham heard one of the horses screech in pain, and turned just in time to see the animal give way at the knees and sink to the ground, blood pumping from a great hole in its neck.

Quinlan and Ettrick were dragged down with it, struggling to get their kit free before it was trapped by the great weight of the body. Yet it was silent enough to hear the officer in charge of the Frenchmen steadily calling his orders; to reload, move forward thirty paces and fire. That, if they stood still, could only end one way. And because of what had happened with the captain and one of the horses all their momentum in retreat had been lost.

Never had the towering ability of Rannoch been more important. In a voice that would have single-handedly done for the walls of Jericho, he bellowed out the order to keep falling back. The enemy were no more than seventy yards behind, and with their bodies covered by the vines, they presented no target. In a game of aim and hope, numbers must triumph. It began as a stumble, and ended up in a race. But luck favoured them, since the officer commanding the French, unable to see what had halted the redcoats, had misunderstood and assumed that they meant to stand and fight. The extra yards that gave them were enough to get them into the trees just as the enemy reached the open space between them and the final row of vines.

Now they had the advantage, even with depleted numbers. Markham detailed Bellamy to look after all three horses, plus the wounded captain, with orders to get him to Mademoiselle Moulins for treatment. Once the Negro was gone he joined Rannoch and the rest at the edge of the trees, just as the action was recommenced. The Lobsters took out half-a-dozen Frenchmen with their first volley, aiming at a point just above the tips of the bayonets as they poked through the gnarled branches.

The officer who commanded them was no fool. He saw what was happening and called his men back behind the cover of leaves, grapes, and vines. Markham guessed that there would be reinforcements on the way, or worse, a body of men moving along the wooded ridgeline to cut him off. The enemy could stay there all day. He could not. They would not attack him if they had any sense, and he couldn't bring any force to bear to make them retire. Yet as soon as he left this position they would move forward to engage them in a retreat through the woods.

'There is no choice,' said Rannoch. 'But I will be thinking that fighting in the woods is a game that our boys will be better at than the enemy.'

'How long to reload while moving?'

'Thirty paces.'

'We'll have to wound them to slow them down. We need a gap.'

'Then we stop, let them come on, and deplete their strength every time.' Rannoch gave him a grim smile. 'It will only be a matter of time before they refuse the command to advance.'

The rustling behind them had both men spinning round in a slight panic. But it was de Puy and Aramon's servants, each with a pistol ready to fire.

'We have charged to the sound of the guns,' said de Puy. If it was meant as a joke, it died because of his melancholy countenance. Markham gave him a quick explanation, as well as a warning, aimed more at the servants than at de Puy.

'We will be falling back in a proper formation. If you get behind us you may become a target, to us as well as the enemy. Let us do the work. Only if the French charge should you engage them.'

All four men looked unhappy at that. But it made sense and had to be accepted. 'How is Captain Germain?

'He is losing blood, but Ghislane says that once he is still and some pressure can be applied to the wound, that should ease.'

The use of the given name Ghislane was revealing, and distracted Markham for a moment. He often wondered if there was anything between the pair, and that easy manner with the Christian name hinted at a degree of familiarity. Yet, if that was so, how could they maintain such a degree of aloofness when in company? He was dragged away from that thought, and brought back to the present by Rannoch.

'Ready to move, sir.'

'Right, sergeant. We will run the first fifty yards. I want to draw them deep into the woods.'

'I think, to begin with, they will come without much bidding,' the Highlander replied.

The French voice floated above the vines. 'Messieurs. The position you hold, given your numbers is untenable.'

'It would be expensive to take,' Markham replied.

'I am Lieutenant Andoche Junot of the 78th Regiment of Infantry. To whom am I speaking?'

'Lieutenant George Markham, of His Britannic Majesty's Marines.'

'It is, if I may say so, monsieur, a strange place to encounter you.'

Rannoch was ducking along the front, looking under and over vines to see if the French were using this as a ruse to move men around. Markham held his reply till the Scotsman signalled that the conversation was an honest one.

'We are at war, sir. The marines tend to fight their enemies wherever they find them.'

'Regardless of what odds they face?'

'Don't you know we are mad, we roastbeefs?'

Junot responded with an equally amused tone. 'I had heard so, but did not believe it till now. I shall never doubt it again.'

'And we are men to extract a high price for our own lives.'

'I am requesting that you surrender.'

'No.'

'A pity, monsieur.'

'As much a pity as the fact that I can not sit still and converse with you all day. I must make sure that when I move through the forest, it is not into the arms of the rest of your regiment.'

'One last chance, Lieutenant Markham.'

Markham signalled for his men to move, which they did as he said, 'My apologies, sir.'

The French moved as soon as he was out of sight, a yelling charge to the forest edge with a fine display of brio and sound. Finding no obstacle they plunged on, until they ran straight into Markham's response, nine muskets and a carefully aimed pistol. The advance stopped dead. Markham realised that, despite his request not to do so, Aramon's servants had discharged their pistols. There was a second when he observed them reloading, something they did with remarkable dexterity, given their calling.

'Fall back thirty paces and re-deploy.'

Junot was no fool. He didn't repeat the same mistake, but brought his men forward slowly. It still cost him casualties, but fewer by the sound of the screams. They were still audible when the Lobsters were gone. They took up their next position and waited, but no one came forward. After several minutes, Markham spoke.

'I think our Lieutenant Junot of the 78th Infantry has decided to forgo the chase.'

'Then he shows good sense for an officer,' said Rannoch, aiming a thin smile at Markham. 'That is rare enough in any army.'

'Hold here, Sergeant. We can make no decisions about moving or staying without a look at Captain Germain.'

Rannoch nodded to the front, towards the Frenchman he couldn't see. 'An officer who will not sacrifice his men to no purpose will not harm a wounded man.'

'That I agree with,' Markham replied, well aware of what Rannoch was implying. 'And I have no intention of surrendering us all for the well being of one man. But the extent of his wound will dictate certain things. I must see how bad it is. If he can move we will take him with us on one of the horses.'

Rannoch's voice was full of venom. 'Perhaps the one he stole! The sod nearly got Bellamy and Leech killed.'

'Then justice has been served, Sergeant Rannoch, for he would never have taken the ball in his shoulder had he not been mounted.'

De Puy followed him back, pausing for a second to say something to Aramon's servants. Because of that, Markham reached the small clearing in which Aramon had halted ahead of him. Germain was lying in the centre, with Ghislane Moulins and Renate hovering over him. But their eyes were fixed elsewhere. Aramon stood arms half up and out as though he was saying part of the Mass.

The figure in the tattered, bottle-green coat, edging across in the direction of the tethered horse bemused him. But that evaporated quickly enough when the man, alerted by a jerky glance from Renate, spun round. Markham found himself staring down the twin barrels of a pistol. The way both jaws dropped, as Ghislane later told him, was like a scene from a Moliere farce. But it wasn't funny, it was deadly serious.

'Please do not attempt to raise that pistol, Markham.'

'You know each other?' demanded Aramon.

'It is my misfortune,' Markham replied.

'Doubly so, Markham, since I can shoot you with one barrel and still have a ball left to threaten these people.'

'But can you shoot me as well?' De Puy's voice was hard to place, coming out of the surrounding trees. 'I think, since I have a musket trained on your left eye, that will be difficult.'

The distraction allowed Markham to raise his pistol, and he began to move forward. But he was slow compared to Aramon. The Monsignor leapt forward and swung a fist. If Markham had thought him all flab and piety he was disabused of that notion now. The bunched knuckles took the fellow right on the side of the head with a blow that would have felled an ox.

Ghislane put her hands to her mouth in fright. De Puy stepped out from the trees, pistol in hand. Markham moved forward and looked down into the cruel, thin face.

'Something tells me this is the man these soldiers where searching for.'

'Who is he?' demanded Aramon, his fist still bunched, as though he intended to fetch the comatose figure another blow.

'You are fond of the expression, Monsignor, the spawn of the devil. This is the real thing, not part of your imaginings.'

The man on the ground stirred, feebly trying to raise himself onto his knees. Markham had to resist the temptation to kick the arms away.

'Allow me to introduce to you the Representative on Mission for Provence, from the Committee of Public Safety. This piece of slime is Monsieur Pierre Michel Fouquert.'

Chapter thirteen

'The best thing we can do is just turn him over to the French. They will no doubt mete out to him the same bloody punishment he's seen fit to visit on other people. And I for one, can think of no single person who deserves it more.'

'That will not stop them chasing us,' said Aramon.

'Nothing will stop that now, Monsignor. They know we are here and they are aware we are British. In fact the best thing we could do, to save our skins, is to think about how quickly, and by what route, we can get out of here.'

'But we are much closer to Notre Dame de Vacluse than we are to the coast.'

'The sea represents safety,' Markham replied automatically, not wishing to elaborate on the difficulties of now getting there. 'Somehow I doubt that could be said of your treasure.'

'That is only true if you continue to escort us.'

A perfect solution, thought Markham, giving Aramon the briefest of smiles. Having got you this far, we can draw away your enemy and leave you free to recover what you seek.

But he didn't articulate those thoughts. Instead he looked over at Germain, propped against a tree, his face ashen, and his arm in a sling. The ball that had hit him was still lodged in his back, it being too deep to remove without proper surgeon's probes. Nor did they have any means of cleaning the wound. There was the danger of gangrene from the cloth of his coat and shirt that had been carried into the deep hole the musket ball had created.

'Would they have any medical skills around this Notre Dame de Vacluse?'

It was de Puy who answered. 'There are monks there, and they are of a medicant order.'

Fouquert was by the next tree, with one of the servants holding a pistol at his head. He had to make a decision and it had to be done quickly. The captain could be moved, especially with the aid of a horse. But to where? Marines indicated a ship, so the French would be expecting them to make a dash for the shore. The best way to fool them was to go inland.

'Bellamy, tell Sergeant Rannoch to fall back as quietly as possible to here. Monsieur Le Comte, if you could help me get Captain Germain on to a horse I would be grateful.'

'What is your plan?' demanded Aramon, loudly.

Aware of Fouquert's proximity and what he intended to do, he moved over to the cleric and spoke quietly. 'We go on, Monsignor.'

'Is that occasioned by greed, Lieutenant?'

'No, by necessity. And please keep your voice down. I do it because the captain needs help. It is the last thing the French will expect.'

'They will be very close on our heels.'

'I intend to distract them.'

'How?'

'By leaving, for them to find, the man for whom they were originally searching. I will tie Fouquert to a tree and bid him a heartfelt *adieu*, the only pity being that I will not be present to see him expire on the guillotine.'

'Markham.'

He turned to look at Fouquert, who had pulled himself upright and was leaning back against the trunk of the tree. The face was drawn and haggard, but it still had the look of deep cruelty that he remembered so well. If anything the wear on the features enhanced that. The slightly hooked nose seemed sharper, the face thinner and the black eyes more prominent. And then there was the humourless smile, there even now, that hinted at the man's innate feeling of superiority.

'I need to speak with you.'

'The only word I want to say to you, Fouquert, is goodbye.'

'That will change.'

'I can't see how.'

Rannoch had come into the clearing; although obviously forewarned by Bellamy he still registered a degree of shock at seeing Fouquert. The Frenchman's eyes wandered to him, and he smiled. Rannoch, in a gesture that was uncharacteristic for him, slowly spat.

'I have something valuable,' Fouquert whined, in a desperate tone. 'Something that will force you to reconsider leaving me to my former comrades.'

'How do you know I intend to leave you to them?'

'It is, for you and your men, the sensible thing to do. And you lack the courage to take hold of the pistol this fellow is holding and kill me by your own hand.'

'I was not aware that kind of killing took courage.'

Germain was mounted, and so were Ghislane and Aramon. That was wrong, he'd intended the horse for Renate, with a deep and abiding wish that the pompous cleric should walk. Fouquert had distracted him. The rest of his lobsters were lined up just on the edge of the clearing, still facing the unseen enemy. Unseen but surely approaching. It was time to go; he had no margin to trade words with his capture.

'You must listen.'

'No.'

'Then go, and pass up the best chance you have ever had for honour and glory.'

'I think I know how much you care for my honour.'

'Come here!'

The jerk of the head was insolent, like an irate father demanding the presence of a naughty child. But the act didn't anger Markham, it intrigued him. Fouquert was far from being a fool. He knew how to manipulate people, and that was not the act of a man who had no cards to play.

'Sergeant Rannoch, start to move out as quietly as possible.' When the Highlander was passing him, he whispered so that Fouquert wouldn't hear. 'Go north till you are out of sight of this clearing, then we will be heading due east for a while before turning north again. Ask Captain Germain to read his compass for you.'

'Inland?'

'Yes.' Then he walked over and stood in front of Fouquert, indicating to Aramon's servant that he should rejoin his master. 'Now, what is it you have to tell me?'

Fouquert produced that superior smile again, which made Markham snap. 'You have five seconds before I leave this clearing. So if you have something to tell me, do it now!'

'I have the plans for the invasion of Italy.'

'What!'

'Every detail. Which units and what strength, lines of march, which are feints and which are real.'

'What's to stop me just taking them off you?'

'You can take a list of the units to be deployed. But that won't help you much. The rest of the plans are in my head, with the paperwork giving the details burnt to a cinder. Perhaps you would like to do the same as my former comrades, and remove it.'

There was no time to think. He had to act working on instinct. Fouquert might be bluffing. But Markham, as he ripped at the knots that bound him, knew what he was capable of when it came to treachery. He would listen, then decide. And if that meant throwing this bastard to the wolves on his tail, so be it. He pulled Fouquert's own double-barrelled pistol from his belt.

'Don't even think of trying to run, because I'll put both of these balls through your knees. You don't need feet on the guillotine.'

The shove in the back sent the Frenchman staggering forward. Markham, running behind him, had to resist the temptation to pose questions now. That would have to wait. Paramount was the need to get clear of Junot, and to do that without running smack into the rest of his regiment. They reached the point where Rannoch had turned, leaving Quinlan and Ettrick in wait for him.

'Jesus,' said Quinlan, as the pair appeared, 'he's brought that ball of shite along. I though he was set to leave the bastard for the Crapauds to find.'

'Never know what old Poke em'll do next, mate,' hissed Ettrick, without warmth.

A slightly raised eyebrow was all the two of them would show when Markham got close. To these ex-members of the 65th Foot, a right pair of thieving London villains, their officer was a bit of a queer fish. He could fight and swear with the best of them, and was a dab hand in the caring line. A rich man would have been better, of course, or even better a proper well-connected nob. But if they couldn't have that he, being as how he had clay feet, would do.

Markham had recently fallen slightly from grace. They knew his reputation with the ladies, and had placed bets as soon as Ghislane Moulins had come aboard *Syilphide*. They'd wagered that old 'Poke 'em' would be inside her shift within three days. It did nothing for his standing when the money was lost.

'Give me your coat Fouquert,' Markham snapped, putting the pistol back in his belt.

'Why?'

'Don't argue, just do it.' When the Frenchman obliged, he

ordered Ettrick and Quinlan to take him on and join Sergeant Rannoch. 'I won't be far behind.'

The two men jabbed Fouquert with the tips of their bayonets, clearly relishing the look of fear this produced.

'Don't you be trying fuck all, mate,' growled Quinlan. 'Like making like to run off, or your arse will join up with that slit in your face you call a mouth.'

Markham ordered them to move, then continued straight on for fifty yards. He knew that what he was doing would probably achieve little. But Fouquert's bottle-green coat was one of his trademarks. And the men who'd been chasing him before they came on the scene must have been told to look out for that. To snag it on a tree where they could see it might not delay them for very long. But it might just persuade Junot to divide his forces, giving him the notion that both the chases were within catching distance. Besides, even a couple of minutes in which he stopped to decide would be helpful.

Very faintly, he could hear the French as he ran back to the point at which Rannoch had turned due east. They were moving cautiously, as befitted a unit whose men had already fallen in too great numbers to British muskets.

As he jogged along he thought of the fluke that had brought him face to face again with Fouquert. It seemed as though they were bound by some umbilical cord, and could not be kept apart even in the midst of this war. If it was fortune that brought them together it was not the sort that Markham wanted to foster. God only knew how he'd got here, but judging by the state of his coat and his face he'd had a rough time. They'd had him on the other side of the Grasse road, and Markham had seen someone cross that. Perhaps he'd doubled back in the hours of darkness, timing the moves of the soldiers to slip though. If he had, and thrown off the pursuit in the process, then he'd done them a favour as well. Perhaps Fouquert possessed skills with which Markham would never have credited him.

The forest was thinner here on the ridge, but still thick enough to hide a redcoat at fifty paces. That was reassuring to Markham as he caught up with the rear of the party. Dornan was sweeping with large leafy branches to obscure any evidence of the horses' hooves. It was a sound idea given that the minutes counted, and that as long as the French had no idea of their destination, they'd be forced to cast around a great deal rather just follow a simple trail.

Luck might bring them to a spoor, but in such a dense and large area that was unlikely. Noise was the greatest problem, that and birds like wood pigeons suddenly vacating a nearby tree. But Rannoch had set a slow pace to avoid that, and was calling listening halts to make sure the enemy wasn't close. This gave the forest wildlife plenty of time to get out of the path, or to hide themselves from this alien intrusion. Markham, aware that his sergeant knew what he was about, was happy to leave him to it.

These were obviously things that Rannoch had learned soldiering in North America, to be added to standard drills like the Lobsters falling back in two mutually supporting groups. Markham ached to know what service he'd seen, and most particularly how he had earned that branded M on his thumb. He was also curious to know why the Colonel of the 65th Foot had transferred to naval service someone so competent. Himself he knew about. He was an embarrassment that had come back to haunt them, forced to exercise his dormant commission because it was the only thing of any value he possessed.

But Rannoch was the best NCO Markham had ever come across. He cared for his men and was respected, and his ability with a musket alone made him invaluable. What had he done to so enrage the man who commanded the regiment to get himself sent aboard a ship as a temporary marine? Was it just his hatred of officers, or had something happened that could not be dealt with by a court? Would he, with such a tight-lipped man as Rannoch, ever find out?

He had to stop speculating. There were more important matters to attend to. Quinlan and Ettrick had kept Fouquert away from the main body, nudging him along just in front of the sweeping Dornan, but behind each section making up a rearguard. Coming abreast and producing his pistol again, he ordered the pair to drop away, then, once they were out of earshot, began to question his man.

Fouquert was eager to talk. But he wanted to start at the beginning, to tell his tale of woe; of how the swine in Paris had betrayed the cause, and had undone all the work of patriots such as himself. In his entire story, he was upright and others corrupt, he shrewd, they stupid. Impatient as he was Markham let him burble on, aware that even shrewd creatures like Fouquert can often reveal too much when left to talk. A lot of what he said sounded like maudlin rubbish. There was even a catch in his voice when he mentioned the death of Robespierre, but Markham guessed it to be contrived. A man like this would weep only for his own misfortunes, not those of others, how ever far they'd fallen.

'I was proscribed eventually. My loyalty to the Jacobin cause was too obvious to conceal.'

Markham reckoned that to be rubbish too. Whoever had power now didn't trust Fouquert, which showed a great deal of sense on their part. The man, as company, would embarrass a venomous snake.

'Fortunately, there were a few trusty friends still left. I was warned in good time that the *canaille* were on their way to arrest me. And from my previous position, I still had access to army headquarters. While they ate their dinner, I had a chance to browbeat the guards.'

'And once inside, you stole the plans for the invasion of Italy.'

'I did.'

'Which means, Fouquert, they will now change them. They are therefore useless.'

'They might tinker with them, Markham. But it's too late to overhaul the entire plan, not with the regiments already marching into their positions. To try and change things now would cause chaos. What kind of army are you talking about? Eager, certainly, but the level of training is low. And this is not some open battlefield where a single messenger can change the entire direction of an army. Here, the mountains, and the routes through them, dictate everything.'

There was a parrot-fashion quality to what he was saying, as though he'd heard the words from other lips. That didn't diminish the veracity of what he was explaining, since to Markham it made perfect sense. He'd had experience of this sort of fighting in the Caucasus. Everyone from Hannibal onwards had faced that same problem on this border. There were only so many routes into Italy, and once you'd committed troops to a certain avenue of attack, to call them back would only presage failure. But it was the next word Fouquert said which clinched things.

'If it merely takes a change of plan, why do you think they are searching so hard to find me.'

The place was crawling with troops. Why would they mount

such an effort to find Fouquert if he didn't have something valuable in his possession? As an escaped Jacobin, close to Robespierre, they might want him. But not to the extent of deploying, a few days before a major battle, what looked like a whole regiment to flush him out.

'What do you intend to do with them?'

Fouquert gave Markham a look then, one that almost screamed that he must be a fool. 'I took them in order to pass them over to your allies, the Piedmontese.'

Markham, having listened to his sentimental litany about the Revolution, allied to paeans to the purity of French peasants and their inalienable rights, responded with deep irony.

'You must be very proud of your loyalty to the French cause.'

'My cause is the Revolution. Whatever it needs to bring those swine in Paris down must be done. Barras, Carnot, the Abbe Sieyès, they have betrayed everything. And it's not just the Girondists and *émigrés* who have flocked back to share power. There are men here in the south, who were once proud to call themselves Jacobins. Now they skulk about and suck up to the new masters, begging for a crumb. They should also face the blade.'

'The plans,' said Markham, trying to bring him back to the point.

It only set him off on another furious tack. 'When we return to our rightful place that strutting Corsican peacock Bonaparte will be my first victim.'

The name rang a bell. 'Is that the artillery officer who was at Toulon?'

'Yes!' Fouquert spat. 'He was then a man I thought I could trust.'

Suddenly the voice he'd heard addressing the sentry and the name of the man he'd encountered at the "Battery of men without Fear" combined to bring forward a solution. He should have placed that accent as Corsican, nearer to Italian in sound than correct French. The crispness of that staccato delivery had fooled him. Bonaparte was like that. He was also, the way Markham recollected him, in the military sense, a touch deranged.

'He is the man who is pursuing you?'

'So he should be. They are his plans.'

'To invade Italy?' said Markham, surprised. 'That's a big task for a junior officer.'

'He's no junior officer. He's a Brigadier General.'

Fouquert's voice started to rise, showing even greater passion as he continued, damning the whole tribe as Corsican scum. At the same time Markham was wondering if he was in the right army. Only eight months before, when he met him between the battle lines, Bonaparte had been a mere captain of artillery.

'He is also a turncoat.' Fouquert whined. 'It was Robespierre's brother, through the good offices of Lucien Bonaparte, that saved his neck when he came back, absent without leave, from Corsica. And it was that connection, allied to my influence, that helped the little shit to get the posting at Toulon where he won his spurs. He will tell you it was Paul Barras but that is a lie.'

'I can't say I care, Fouquert. To my way of thinking you're all rats from the same sewer. The only question I have to ask myself is what to do with you.'

'You must, without delay, get me to the commanders of the Piedmontese forces.'

'Must I now?'

'The assault could begin within the next four days.'

'And the Piedmontese army would require time to deploy to meet the threat.'

'Of course.'

Markham was suddenly aware that he was talking to this man as though he was a fellow human being, instead of a genocidal maniac. And he was being sucked in by what he was being told. The thought really annoyed him, and he positively spat at the man.

'You don't even know what a liar you are, Fouquert. But I do. I have no evidence whatsoever that what you say is true. There may be another very good reason why you are being chased, one that has nothing to do with invasion plans.'

The Frenchman opened his shirt and extracted a thick parchment packet. It was damp from the sweat of his body, smelly from the staleness of that which had already soaked it and dried.

'The Order of Battle of the Army of the Bouche de Rhone, now renamed the Army of Italy. The commanding officer is General Sherér. The other senior officers are listed. You will find unit strengths and firepower; artillery and infantry with details of reserves and methods of re-supply. I have memorised how they are to be deployed, the points they are to attack, which movements are feints and which are real. I also know exactly what the Army of Savoy will do to aid them. Remember the time of year. The passes are open over the Alps beyond Chambery, and your allies lack the numbers to be in two places at once. Silence me and they will be in Turin in a month.'

Fouquert was grinning now, with a superior look in his eye that made Markham want to whip him across the face with his pistol. He recalled all the other times he had met this man, and the number of cruelties, include downright betrayal, he'd personally witnessed. His face must have disclosed the depth of his feelings.

'You may not believe me Markham. But the Piedmontese will. And they will be grateful. Who knows what my reward will be for saving their army from certain annihilation? Help me, and some of that gratitude will come your way.'

'Quinlan, do me a service and tie this man's hands.'

'But.'

Fouquert got no time to finish. 'And when you've done that, get something over the bastard's mouth.'

As he made his way forward, Markham heard the voice being muffled. But much as he enjoyed the notion of gagging Fouquert he had a very clear notion of the dilemma this had put him in. Even Germain would acknowledge that Aramon and his treasure paled into insignificance beside what Fouquert might be able to pass on to Admiral Hood. The French had enjoyed military success on every frontier from Flanders to the Alps. The chance to check them, and with full knowledge of their plans, to perhaps even inflict a defeat, was too important to pass up.

The idea of keeping Fouquert alive, never mind taking him through the enemy lines to the people who could make use of his information, was anathema. An even less acceptable picture was the sod standing in Hood's cabin, extracting from the British Admiral some reward for his treachery. It would be useless to plead he should be strung up for what he'd done in Toulon. The needs of war would, as usual, make for the usual flock of strange bedfellows.

And was what he contemplated, given the time available, the best way to proceed? The alternative, to just turn round now and head back for the Franco-Italian border, with a regiment of infantry in the way, was fraught with peril. If the land route was to be used a great many detours would be necessary, using up a lot of time. But the idea of returning to *Syilphide* was not much better. It was too late to attempt anything today. But perhaps, starting at dawn tomorrow, a small party, carrying nothing but weapons, flares and water, moving fast and taking a chance, should get down to the shore in time to signal the cutter.

Alongside Germain, he didn't speak right away, trying first to assess the state of the captain's health. The waxy skin colour, and the way it was drawn tight over his prominent jawbone, was to be expected. The man must be in deep pain. Riding was less strain than walking, but not much. A litter might be better, and there was ample wood around with which to construct one. But that would take time and create noise.

Rannoch called another listening halt, and Markham pulled the horse away from the others so that neither Aramon nor de Puy would hear what he was saying. He spoke slowly, leaving out a great deal about Fouquert, only referring to his background where it demonstrated his previous importance. Germain had closed his eyes tight to hold his pain, but Markham knew he was listening. They screwed up even more when Germain heard what was in prospect.

'Time is of the essence, sir. I favour the option of getting to sea, and setting course for whichever port Mr Booker thinks will put us close to the Piedmontese command. The cutter could be detached with a despatch to inform Admiral Hood of our actions so that he can respond.'

'The person responsible for delivering such information will earn a Gazette to himself.'

Markham knew that Germain wasn't talking about Fouquert. He was thinking that with his wound there was no way he could undertake the task, either by land or sea. And he also knew that it was a mission to be led by an officer, and the only one available was George Markham. The marine was wondering what thoughts were going through the Honourable George Germain's pain-filled brain. Jealousy certainly. Pique probably, plus a general rant against the fates that had seen him wounded at a time like this. He doubted there would be any self-criticism, the notion that the ball that had hit him was his own fault.

'Believe me, sir, it is my earnest wish that you could be well enough to undertake the task.'

Markham wondered if that sounded sincere. It certainly wasn't true. Germain, with his excitable ways, was the very last person to take charge of something as delicate as this. And that had nothing to do with Gazettes. He was merely being tactful in a situation where he could afford the sentiment.

'But even if the ball can be extracted, you will require time to recover.'

'All right, Markham,' Germain hissed. 'Tell me what it is you intend.'

'I think if we can avoid the enemy, then we can make the church of Notre Dame by tonight. There are people there to mend your wound, and care for you.'

'And what about our original task?'

'I will leave you with enough men to impose your wishes on Monsignor Aramon. And when you are better you will be able to complete it as you see fit.'

'You forget, Markham, that with you taking the ship, we will lack the means to get out of here.'

'We can also arrange for that, sir. And who knows, if our allies give the French a bloody enough nose, they may take back that land which is theirs, which will put them within twenty miles of where we stand.'

'I need time to think.'

His marine officer was prepared to leave it at that. There was no choice in the matter and Germain must know it. He was just stalling. Mentally he was wondering who to take and who to leave. He wanted not only men who could move fast, but also those who could think for themselves. He had to anticipate casualties, one of them himself. But could he take Rannoch, the only man he trusted to look after the others, and if necessary stand up to Germain and Aramon? Should be in fact be even be considering the Monsignor and his party?

That was when Markham decided to take all his Lobsters, and leave Germain in the care of the monks. The Monsignor and de Puy would have to fend for themselves. He reassured himself that at least the Bourbon officer, appraised of the facts, would understand.

Chapter fourteen

Compared to those he'd called previously, Rannoch's halt lasted a long time, with the entire party, barring Germain and Markham, listening intently to the sounds of the forest. Initially these were few. But as the wildlife became accustomed to their presence, the level of birdsong rose. The Highlander looked puzzled, and slowly walked over to where Markham stood, requesting that he leave Germain's side so they could talk. The message was simple. If there was anyone close to them, in pursuit and moving through the woods, there should be near silence.

'Either we have fooled them, or there are no longer any soldiers chasing us.'

'Perhaps they too have halted.'

Rannoch was looking up at the treetops, sniffing as if he himself was an animal, able to detect human scent.

'You do not catch people by standing still. And what need have you of too much caution when you are ten times more numerous?'

'I can't believe they've given up. They must have questioned why we are here, and decided on various theories. And even if no solution was forthcoming, they'd hardly leave any enemy patrol to operate unhindered in their own bailiwick.'

Markham's eyes flicked to Fouquert, now on his knees, eyes shut, hands tied and mouth muffled. It was as if he was sleeping. Had that ruse with the coat worked, and redirected the search away from them back on to him? If it had, then that made him more important then every one of them, which was even more evidence that he was telling the truth.

Rannoch had followed the direction of his look. He must be wondering why Markham had brought the murderous sod along. And the Scotsman wouldn't be alone. The rest of his men, having quizzed Quinlan and Ettrick to no avail, must be dying of curiosity.

He'd have to come up with some kind of explanation for

Aramon and de Puy, and that right now seemed like a tall order. There was also some risk in Fouquert coming into close contact with them. They couldn't keep him gagged forever and once free to speak he had no reason to keep his mouth shut. Indeed, in his present mood of whining self-justification, he would probably spill the whole tale to anyone prepared to listen. At this moment, that was not what was wanted. In theory, both the cleric and the Bourbon officer should see where his primary duty lay. But Markham knew that would not happen, certainly in the case of the Monsignor.

'What did that man have to say?' asked Rannoch.

'Nothing that has made our life any easier.'

'Then he is true to his creed as far as we are concerned.'

Rannoch paused, obviously anticipating details. But it was too long a tale to tell. And given his most recent thoughts Markham wanted time to digest it himself before discussing it with his sergeant. But try at he did to appear reassuring, it was impossible to avoid sounding as though he was just being close mouthed, an impression not aided by the way he failed to look the Highlander in the eye.

'We need to know how we stand, right enough. The church of Notre Dame must be close now. We dare not go near if the French can follow us there.'

Rannoch did a poor job of hiding his displeasure, though he tried hard to sound unperturbed. 'We have one or two people who are good in the woods from a life of poaching. I would like to send them back, to see if we are still being hunted.'

'They might be working round to get ahead of us.'

'I thought we had already laid to rest the notion that they know where we are bound.'

Rannoch was now gazing at him, not attempting to hide his resentment, the question unstated but plain; that his officer was behaving as he had from the start of this operation. He was still not telling him the whole truth. Then he looked up at Germain, slumped forward on the horse.

'Besides, it would do some people good to rest.'

Markham was tired himself, and had only begun to realise how much as, having become stationary, a feeling of deep lassitude seemed to creep though his bones. The entire party had been on the move since first light and had covered quite a distance. Though not actually complaining the weariness was evident in the way that no one sought to punctuate the silence. Even Aramon, rarely silent, had now dismounted and was resting his back against a tree.

'Who will you send?'

'I'll take Yelland and Tully.'

'You need rest too, Rannoch.'

The Highlander began to undo his red coat. 'I can do without rest. But I am less happy about being in the dark.'

'It no worse than being in a fog, which is where I am, Sergeant.'

'Is there a risk of that clearing?'

'You'll be the first to know, Rannoch, believe me.'

The Highlander moved away, calling softly to the men he wanted to disrobe and follow him. Markham helped Germain down to the ground and saw him comfortable, then indicated that the other Lobsters should form a tighter perimeter, and that at intervals they should take food and water. Aramon and his party carried their own rations, and Markham took some to feed the captain. He was followed over by Ghislane Moulins, who said she wanted to take a look at the wound.

Germain groaned as Markham pulled him off the tree, exposing his left shoulder. Gently, Ghislane placed her hands on his back, feeling his flesh through the great tear she'd made in his blue uniform coat. She was frowning, deep in concentration, her forehead lined and her eyes half-closed. That gave Markham the chance to once more examine her closely. The shafts of sunlight coming through the trees, allied to the dust which had caked her in crossing those fields, showed the very slight down on her face. Having pushed back her hair, the ear underneath was exposed, a quite perfect *oreille* that fairly begged to be nibbled.

'The flesh is hot around the wound.'

Markham was thinking that Germain wasn't alone in having heated flesh, before he cursed himself for his insensitivity and solicitously enquired whether bathing the wound might help. When she nodded he poured some water from his canteen into her hands.

'We are not over-gifted with the stuff, but some can be spared.'

'Where has your sergeant gone?'

'To look for the enemy. He thinks they have given up the pursuit.'

'Then his departure has nothing to do with your prisoner?'

Markham was suddenly guarded, and she must have realised

that by the way his body stiffened. Ghislane spoke quickly, though she never took her eyes off Germain as she did so, well aware that from across the clearing Aramon was watching her every move.

'The Monsignor is curious. You did say you were going to leave him behind.'

'He was recently a very important man, more powerful than the generals of the French Army. It occurred to me that he might have information that will be of use to us. That is to someone like Admiral Hood.'

'Why don't you just tell her the truth, Markham?' hissed Germain through clenched teeth.

'What, sir,' he replied, trying to sound as light-hearted as he could. Inwardly he was seething, cursing Germain, and convinced that the emotion would be the one showing on his face. Fortunately, she still hadn't looked at him 'Tell this beautiful young lady what I have in mind to do to him.'

That made her look up. Markham held her gaze. 'You have no notion, Mademoiselle, of what crimes I have witnessed that man commit. While I will not do so here in the forest, since it would not do to have his screams overheard, I intend that he should suffer some of the indignities he has visited on other people.'

Germain must have taken the hint, since he remained silent. And the direct nature of Markham's gaze had forced Ghislane to look away again, so he had no idea if he'd been believed. He wasn't sure what prompted him to continue. Was it a wish to deflect her own enquiries that he started on her, or a deep desire to know the truth of her relationship with Aramon?

'Is the Monsignor a relation?'

The emphatic way she replied showed that she understood clearly what a loaded question he was posing. 'No, Lieutenant, he is not.'

'Yet he is your guardian?'

The reply was deliver in a near whisper. 'Yes.'

'A curious estate for a lady of your age, to be travelling unchaperoned with a man who is not your relative.'

She looked up for a second time, the hurt in her eyes plain. The fact that he could flatter her and make her smile, touch her and make her shudder, were two important parts of an increasing intimacy. The final portion was the ability to inflict pain. That he could do so both pleased Markham and at the same time made him feel like a scrub. She stood upright and walked away, leaving him to ease Germain back onto his tree trunk. He was annoyed with himself, not sure if such a direct attack had been necessary to deflect her curiosity about Fouquert. It was the ship's captain who took the brunt of that.

'I would be obliged, sir,' he said with no gentility, 'if you would keep details regarding Fouquert and what he knows to yourself. I am going to have enough trouble with the Monsignor, without that being compounded by loose talk.'

Germain wanted to check him. That was plain in the man's eyes. But he couldn't find the words right away, and Markham, seeing Rannoch, Yelland and Tully return, gave him no time for careful composition. He moved to another tree, well away from everybody else.

'Nothing,' said the Highlander. 'I doubt there is anyone in this forest bar us, within two miles.'

'Get Tully and Yelland fed, then fetch your own rations over here.'

The first words Markham said were delivered in a harsh tone that he didn't really intend. 'You know who the captain's descended from?'

'He carries a name that stinks to every true soldier.'

'Then I will not bother to explain why we are here. But I will tell you what it is we are supposed to be after.'

'You are not certain?'

Markham smiled for the first time. 'Rannoch, nothing is certain.'

The sergeant responded in kind, which went a great way to lightening the atmosphere. 'There was an American once who said that death and taxes were certain.'

Markham jerked his head, Rannoch's eyes following, to light on Bellamy and Renate, deep in conversation, though sat far enough apart to cause no alarm to Monsignor Aramon. 'You're beginning to sound like our Negro.'

'I would not mind his way with words sometimes.'

'Just sometimes?'

'He can charm birds out of trees, that one. He even brings laughter to the young miss you are so set on, gabbling away as he does in French.' Rannoch saw Markham's eyes narrow, a prelude to a futile denial. So the Highlander carried on, in what for him was a quick voice. 'Mind you, Bellamy can also start a row in an empty room.'

'I am not set on Ghislane Moulins.'

Rannoch grinned to take the sting out of his rebuke. 'You're like Bellamy and his insults to those he considers lesser mortals. You cannot aid yourself.'

Rannoch's certainty was galling. It meant that despite all his attempts at being circumspect, here was at least one other person apart from Aramon, who'd noticed the attentions he was paying her. Then the words of Bellamy came to mind, as well as the looks he got from his men every time he went near her. With a sinking feeling Markham realised that very likely everyone in the party knew.

'Shall we stick to the subject?'

'Yes, sir,' the Highlander responded, in a slightly mocking way.

Markham grinned, and the words flowed as he explained the events of the past few days. There was great relief in doing so, almost a confessional quality the like of which he had not felt since his childhood. In the back of his mind was the fact that he was talking to a man he could trust, perhaps the only one, aided by memories of the things that had happened since their first battle. He told him about every doubt and fear he'd had since the mission was first mooted, only reserving to himself any mention of his own complex reasons for agreeing. The light-hearted declaration he'd made earlier would have to suffice.

Rannoch listened in complete silence, looking at the ground for the most part, slowly munching on his ship's biscuit, and washing the crumbs down with sips of water. Only once did he look up, and that was at Fouquert, as if he could not believe that a man like that could have anything in his possession that would stop any decent human being from killing him on sight.

'I have no idea, once we get to this church, what we will face. Aramon clearly has no notion either, and if de Puy has information I think he is keeping it close to his chest. The same can be said for the way he feels about Mademoiselle Moulins, judging by the way that he makes sheep's eyes at her. So there you have it. We have a captain with a name as cursed as my own, who desperately needs to shine, the notion of fabulous treasure and a trio of people whose relationships to each other are obscure, never mind that they don't appear to trust each other.'

'I daresay in the trust stakes the young lady will succeed where others are like to fail.'

Markham ignored that gentle dig and carried on. 'We also have a lying toad like Fouquert who might just have the means to confound two French armies. We must get Germain to a place where he can be treated, get free of Aramon and his need for an escort, then take Fouquert to where his information will be of value, and that will have to be done in the next three days.'

Rannoch responded in his usual slow way, the voice deep and doleful. 'I have heard the men speak often, laying wagers and the like. And what they say about you is true.'

'What's that?' Markham demanded suspiciously, unaware that the Scotsman was indulging in mock gravity.

'That life around you will never be dull. That if you are not in the middle of a fight, then chance will likely find you in the wrong bedchamber, with some cuckold husband trying to shoot off the parts you hold so dear.'

'Is that what they say?' he asked, not sure whether to be pleased or angry.

'It is.'

'Is that your opinion as well?'

'Time to be going I think,' said Rannoch, standing upright and leaving his officer high and dry for an answer. 'I would not want us to arrive outside that church after the light of day has gone.'

'Then we will have to push on,' said Markham, slightly annoyed.

'I think it is safe to do so.'

The church of Notre Dame de Vacluse had been more than just that. It consisted of a number of stone buildings nestling haphazardly in a shallow valley, some made for animals, some for humans, and others for the storage of the products garnered from the surrounding farmlands. The main construct was the church itself, more imposing structures inside stout old-fashioned walls. De Puy described it when it was bustling; carts rumbling in and out of the gates, while inside, in the large courtyard, men toiled to unload and stack what they carried. The spire of the basilica rose above it all, square and Romanesque. But even from the edge of the woods Markham could see, before he passed his small telescope to the Frenchman, that the bells it once contained were gone, the belfry a gaping empty hole.

De Puy observed the same things as Markham. There wasn't a single roof, door or window that had not been burnt away and that included the gates that had once enclosed the courtyard. Aramon was dejected. But allowing for his gloomy nature, once he swept the area with the telescope, de Puy seemed fairly sanguine. Both Markham and the Monsignor had watched him carefully, trying to discern which particular building interested him. But he seemed intent on giving them all equal attention. That was as far as it went. Asked for his opinion as to the merits of proceeding, he declined to give them.

Markham was at a loss as to what to do. Germain could hardly stay upright in his saddle, and the case was the same here as it had been on the coast. Any shelter was better than another night in the forest. But he took no chances, and sent men both ways along the rim of the woods to make sure that no French force was waiting in ambush.

After the protection of the trees, going out into the stubble of the uncultivated fields made him feel naked. He and the two men he'd brought had a quarter of mile of almost totally open country to traverse, through corn stubble or untidy rows of herbs that threw up pungent smells as their boots kicked or crushed the tiny flowers. Even where there were hedgerows or trees they were overlooked by the forest from which they'd just emerged. Despite the reassurances he'd received from his own men he felt certain that there were eyes upon him, perhaps even muskets trained on his back. The hairs on his neck were tingling, and judging by the way Gibbons and Leech kept jerking round, they were feeling the same sensation.

The sun was sinking, creating an angled golden light that turned the corn stalks mellow, and deepened the purple of the strips of lavender. It also threw every standing object into sharp relief. Long shadows stretched across the landscape, shimmering in the heat, creating the illusion of dark moving figures. The time it took to reach the outer wall by the gate seemed like an eternity. Still hot from the sun, the wall towered above them. This was a real medieval setting, and these stones had been raised for defence against invaders. Odd that they'd probably been destroyed by the very people who once worshipped in the church.

Markham went through first, edging round the huge gudgeons which had once held the studded gates to flatten himself against the inner wall, in the deep shadow under the wooden parapet. The courtyard was bare earth running to the steps that led up to the church. There was an arched portico over that, with elaborate carvings that had, up to just above head height, been hacked so that whatever figures of antiquity they represented lacked noses and arms. The entrance to the church itself was just a black hole in the middle of that surmounted by a crucified Christ who had escaped the attention of the ransacking mob.

There was a heavily scented wind, and in the confines of the walls it swirled round, sending up little wisps of dust. There had been wooden structures set against the walls between the doors that led to what looked like monky cells, the outline of the odd lean-to still visible. The sound of banging he heard was too rhythmic to be human; a door or perhaps a shutter that had survived the inferno this must have been. It was easy to imagine the place full of life and prosperity, just as it was depressing to see what it had become, a victim of blind revolutionary prejudice.

'Right, you two, forward down the walls and round to the church door, one each side.'

Markham stayed still, his eyes never wavering from that black hole. Leech and Gibbons stooped at every doorway, to peer through before jumping the gap and turning to see if that produced a reaction, Leech in deep shadow, Gibbons in the last of the bright sun, both with bayoneted muskets out in front of them like feelers on an insect. As soon as they were in position Markham moved, walking right down the middle, up the steps and into the body of the church.

He crossed himself before he called his Lobsters in. Markham wasn't religious, but right now he felt superstitious enough to believe that ignoring the ritual would be madness. All three stood just inside the doorway, staring at the bells that had been burnt out of the belfry, to crash into the stones of the nave. In here it was silence, excepting the odd fluttering as a pigeon changed its perch. Their boots sounded very loud on the stone floor, as they moved past the bells to look at the altar.

They heard him before they saw him, a single kneeling figure, brown robed, the chanted words of his prayer bouncing ever so gently off the barren walls. The discoloration of the stone showed where they had once had paintings or tapestries, the vaulted ceiling a place for singing voices to echo from the now ruined choir stalls. The monk, which was what Markham supposed him to be, remained still as they approached, even though he must have easily heard them. Then, when they were no more than five paces distant, he stood, crossed himself, and turned to face them.

But he had no face to speak of, just twisted, wrinkled and burn-blackened skin with one blue eye staring straight out. There was a patch above that, on a leather thong. The other eye was an empty socket; there was no hair on the head or around the eye and the nose looked like those of the gargoyles outside, a stump. Both marines, even with muskets extended, recoiled from the sight, taking a sharp inward breath and a pace back. Markham felt that familiar stabbing ache pass down through his stomach to his groin when faced with a horrendous wound. No amount of experience could render him immune; it was his imagination transferring the pain and suffering to his own body. And then the monk smiled.

'Welcome to Notre Dame de Vacluse. If you come in peace, the church receives you in peace.'

It was a beautiful voice, deep and masculine, but at the same time tender and truly welcoming, all the more remarkable given the horrible visage of its owner. The face tried to smile, but that made it even more ugly, exposing teeth that only threw the blackness of the skin into prominence. The one eye flicked unblinkingly from bayonet tip to bayonet tip, then to Markham's pistol. Immediately he dropped it, and ordered his men to do likewise.

'You were not alarmed by our approach?'

'No. I saw you come across the fields with such caution that I knew you presaged no danger. Men who kill and burn come in confidence and greater numbers.'

'Are you a monk?' asked Markham.

'Yes.'

'And you were here when this happened.'

The monk raised his arms, to encompass what had once been.

'God has punished us for being too worldly. Our church had wealth in abundance. The friends I had who inhabited this place loved good food and wine more than piety. Other sins of the flesh were commonplace. So is it not fitting that we suffered the fate of Sodom and Gomorrah?'

The hand flicked to the ruined face, stroking the gnarled burnt skin.

'I suffered from too much vanity, cultivated my appearance and spent too much of my time with ladies of quality rather than in prayer. This is what was visited on me. How would those well-born women look on me now.'

There wasn't a trace of self-pity in the explanation, just a matter-of-fact acceptance of his fate.

'Quite a number of them will have lost their heads to the Revolution. It may be that they would envy you.'

'Then I must pray for them on two counts.'

'We require shelter.'

'Would you believe, monsieur, that is what this church was set up to do hundreds of years ago. A place of sanctuary for weary travellers. It is a good thing that it should be returned to the proper function.'

'We have a wounded man. Do any of your monks have knowledge of medicine.'

To see him laugh was alarming in the way it rendered him so ugly, the horror of the face so at odds with the humour of the noise that came from his throat.

'There are no monks other than me here now. Some have returned to the life of the laity, and profess to deny God. The rest have moved to other places, ones that are intact and can still feed them and fill them full of wine.'

'Yet you chose to stay.'

'God chose, not I.'

'Do you have a name?'

'Not one that I wish to share.'

'Are there any soldiers around?'

'There are you three.'

'You are a Frenchman?'

'I am.'

'Then,' Markham said, 'I have to admit that we are the enemies of your country.'

'I was a soldier myself at one time, young man. I know only too well the colour of that coat your wear.' He ran a hand over his face. Perhaps now God has now seen fit to forgive me for the men I killed, both on my own side, and on yours.'

Markham wanted to ask him where he had served, and what actions he had taken part in. But under the gaze of that basilisk, single, unblinking eye, he found any deviation from religion and his purpose in being here impossible. Was the fellow mad or sane? He certainly had the right to be the former. The pain he'd suffered must have been horrendous, enough to turn his wits. Yet he sounded sane enough, if you took away the fact of his solitary existence in this place.

'Leech, signal to Sergeant Rannoch that it is safe to come in.'

There was a pause before the order was obeyed; one caused by the very simple fact that neither marine had the faintest idea what was going on. But once moving, Leech did so quickly, the sound of his crashing boots reverberating off the walls.

'I will leave you to your prayer. I must look at your walls and seek to set up some kind of defence.'

'There is no need for that,' the monk snapped, displaying the first hint of displeasure.

'Rest assured I will not defile any holy place.'

'Indeed you will not,' he hissed.

Markham forced himself to look into that eye, not out of any desire to challenge, more to see if he could discern the workings of the man's brain.

'I must tell you, sir, that a force of French infantry is pursuing us. Should they come upon this place I would be loath to surrender.'

'There will be no fighting, and certainly no killing. And should you choose to ask me why that will be so, I will tell you. It will be my duty to stop it. No one will die within the limits of Notre Dame de Vacluse unless I expire first.'

There was no expression on the face by which to judge the veracity of such words. Nor did the eye, lacking eyebrows, lids and lashes convey truth or bombast. But Markham made no attempt to argue. He would do what he had to and mount a defence, without, if possible upsetting this cruelly deformed monk.

'You said you had a wounded man.'

'He has taken a musket ball in the shoulder. It is still there.'

'Then bring him to my cell, which used to be the vestry by the side of the altar.'

'You can tend to him?'

'With the help of God, yes.'

That, to a man with little in the way of faith, was hardly reassuring. But Markham had little choice. There was no one in his party who could offer Germain any real help. That ball, left where it was, would probably kill him. God's help, through the agency of this solitary monk, was better than nothing.

175

'Gibbons, have a good poke round, but do not go beyond the altar. See if there is any other part of the property that has a sound enough roof to give us a bit of shelter.'

Chapter fifteen

Markham had toured the perimeter by the time the remainder of the party trooped in, their shadows even longer as the last of the light sunk to the very rim of the mountains to the west, the Massif des Maures. The walls were not much use against a modern enemy, having been built centuries before to withstand spears and arrows. Not that he could, anyway, hold it with a dozen men against any type of determined assault. His job was to get out of here as fast as possible.

Germain had finally passed out, and had to be carried to the vestry at the back of the church. The one-eyed monk, as soon as his Lobsters had got over the shock of his appearance, had them lay him face down on his cot, no easy matter in a room into which he crowded everything he had salvaged from the once thriving religious house. There were books, brass candlesticks and cruci-fixes, parts of tapestries and half-burnt altar cloths. A writing stand stood in the way of the cot, surrounded by all the things necessary for illuminating manuscripts. Parts of the choir stalls, heavy craved oak, had been stacked in one corner, in such a way that they looked as though they would topple over. There were horse collars, yokes and leather bits and girths, saddles and the wheels off what had probably been a dog-cart, as well as a mass of unused church candles.

But there was also a whole chest full of proper surgical instruments, saws, cleavers and ampoules for bleeding, including the probes necessary to undertake an extraction. Another con-tained jars of pounded herbs, which the monk assured them would act to help save the captain's life. Men were sent to fetch water from the well house, and a fire was lit in the grate to heat it. The operation took place immediately that was ready, while Germain was still unconscious, watched with morbid fascination by as many of the men who could dodge their duties.

Gibbons wasn't one of them. He had found a couple of cells where the roof could be repaired. Candles were fetched and one was allocated to Ghislane, with the next-door cell for her maid. Another larger room, more open to the elements, contained Aramon and de Puy, plus the three servants.

It was curious to observe the cleric fidget. So close to the prize he sought, he had lost some of his self-assurance. The relationship between him and de Puy now seemed altered, with the latter making it clear that nothing could be achieved in the dark. Clearly the cavalry officer was now in charge. It didn't seem to trouble him, the way he was constrained in his movements by the watchful eyes of the four men who shared his accommodation. If fact, as soon as he could he made up a bed. Then with a determination that could only be explained by his newfound superiority, he lay down and went straight to sleep.

Markham himself found a separate billet for the Lobsters, a former stable close to the exit. He wanted them all in one place, with an easy way out, so that they could depart in the pre-dawn hours without fuss. If anyone wondered why the two horses were in the cell of a monk instead of here, let them do so. Fouquert was placed in a corner, furthest from the doorway, where they could keep an eye on him. Markham tied him to a ring bolt in the wall, removing his gag only when he was secure. That began a long and loud complaint at his treatment, the noise of which threatened to carry to the ears of the other civilians. Markham didn't threaten him personally. He sent Rannoch in to do that. As soon as Fouquert saw the look of hate in the Highlander's eyes, and the way the man was caressing his bayonet, he ceased to moan.

Markham paced the rim of the courtyard, checking each cell and room, while trying to think what to do next. He was dog-tired but had too much on his mind to even contemplate sleep. The whole party had to be fed, and now it was dark that meant consuming more of his rations or asking the monk what he had. Judging by the man's sparse, aesthetic frame that would not amount to much.

He had to get his men ready, and brief them on what he planned, make sure that they took with them only what was needed to ensure that they moved with maximum speed. That meant abandoning some of their kit, which wouldn't please them since regulations stated that replacements had to be paid for out of their pay. Then there was the notion of what they thought they had come here to recover. What were the words Rannoch had used, 'Gold and silver, as well as jewels the size of bird's eggs.' Perhaps, with that in mind, they'd refuse to move at all.

The news that they were leaving would have to be left till later, so that they did not give the game away by loud carping. Then there was the captain. He could hardly go without seeing Germain. He hoped the patient would still be unconscious, so that he could leave him a note rather than proffering a verbal explanation to a man who would probably become a prisoner of the French. All that about arrangement for his ship to pick him up was stuff and nonsense.

And finally he had to consider Aramon and de Puy. Should he write out some kind of explanation for leaving them high and dry, perhaps striking a confident note that the forthcoming battle on the frontier, made successful by his prompt action, would solve the problem for them by opening the road to Rome. Deep down he knew that would be more a missive aimed at Ghislane Moulins that either of the two men. She was the only person to whom he would want to explain his conduct.

Aramon he'd never had much time for. But de Puy had slipped from the respect he'd enjoyed at Calvi to something a great deal less. Whatever reason he had for his secrecy, had it never occurred to him that it potentially jeopardised them all? That once they were ashore in France it would have been better to have been open and honest so that each and everyone of his men could have been sure they were risking their life for some purpose other than Germain's reputation.

Even though sleep was vital, so that his men would be rested and fully fit at dawn, he would have to post piquets on the walls. Really he should put guards out closer to the woods, so as to give ample warning of any incursions. But they were too weary. At the very least he, Rannoch and Halsey would have to split the twelve hours of duty between them so that they each got the maximum amount of rest. Since he would be leading them out in the morning, the last should be his, which meant that he should get his head down right now. Yet he still had to eat, and formulate some plan, as well as a route, from the map he'd failed to return to de Puy. And that should include a talk with Rannoch.

The task of getting back to *Syilphide*, to a fatigued mind, looked insurmountable. He could see in his mind's eye all the things that could go wrong. They had no time to make any errors of judgement, since he'd never know what might hold them up. They could traverse the whole forest only to find some unknown factor that would delay his access to the shoreline. That meant getting there as early as possible, which in turn left little margin on the journey. Any man hurt by a wound or a fall would have to be left behind, and that, in deep forest, could easily be a sentence of death. And it might very well be him.

George Markham was not a pessimist, and was incapable of maintaining such a gloomy state. Confidence soon reasserted itself.

'Food, *boyo*, that's the first thing. Then sleep. You'll feel a different man then.'

At first he thought the scream came from the back of the church, from Germain's pain as the monk, who might be a butcher as well as a healer, probed his wound. It didn't help that it was so loud that it echoed all around the inside of the walls. But then he realised that he could not have heard it from that source, the vestry being buried at the very back of the church. That impression was confirmed by the yelling and shouting now coming from the stables. He ran to the entrance, and saw Rannoch struggling with the one-eyed monk, the brief impression he had of Fouquert showed him cowering in the corner, still attached to his ring bolt.

He was amazed that Rannoch, huge and as strong as an ox, was struggling against such a seemingly feeble foe. He was desperately trying to hold on to a hand that held a surgical cleaver. The single eye of the monk, gazing over the Scotsman's shoulder had no more expression now than it had contained before. But the nature of his movements was frenzied. He was kicking and biting, pulling like a madman to get his arm free, cursing and swearing like the trooper he had once been, a wholly different animal from the tense calm creature Markham had met not two hours before.

The strength of the man was phenomenal, and Markham understood why Rannoch was having such a fight as he tried to assist. The first task was to get that cleaver well away from the Highlander's head, but the grip the monk had taken seemed unbreakable. Markham smashed his hand against the stone of the wall to no avail. It must have caused excruciating pain, but perhaps that was nothing to a man who'd suffered so much. Halsey and Dornan ran in, and it was only the latter's strength, applied solely to bending back the monk's thumb, which persuaded him to let go. It took all four of them to pin him, still spitting incomprehensible abuse, to the wall.

'What in God's name set him off?' demanded Markham, too busy to be aware of the ambiguity.

Rannoch was breathing almost as heavily as the monk. 'Damn me, Lieutenant, I do not know.'

Dornan hit the monk, full force, in the stomach, driving all the air from his lungs and temporarily reducing his struggles. Even though his officer yelled 'belay that', Markham was grateful, since the victim slumped down, a sob breaking from his lips.

'He walked in here looking for you,' Rannoch continued, easing the pressure of his grip. 'He then told me to pass on the message that the musket ball had been removed, and that with God's will the captain would be all right.'

'And then he went berserk?'

'No. He spotted that slug in the corner.'

'Fouquert?'

The name set the monk off again, and having relaxed their grip it took some effort to restrain him.

'He asked who he was and I told him. Then he went to have a look and wanted to know if he could be released. I said no and he departed, with me thinking nothing of it. Two minutes later he came through that door like a bat out of hell, swinging that cleaver and screaming abuse.'

'At you?'

'Not me.'

Markham looked over his shoulder to the cowering Fouquert. He dropped his head so that he could at least partially look in to the monk's face. If he'd been ugly before he was doubly so now. Whatever had been benign had gone completely. The skin was even more gnarled than it had been before and tears were streaming from the ducts of that single eye.

'You know this man?'

The monk must have realised that he could not prevail. His body went limp. The head was nodding slowly, and the screaming and shouting had turned to continuous sobbing.

'Was he here when the church was burnt?' That just brought forth another sob, so Markham released his grip and walked over to gaze down at Fouquert. 'Look at me, damn you.'

The black eyes that fixed on his showed real terror, the kind Markham supposed that Fouquert had seen in the eyes of his victims just before he went to work on them. There was a trickle of saliva running from the corner of his mouth, and he was shaking slightly.

'Were you here when this place was burnt?' The head dropped again. 'Answer me, Fouquert, or as God is my witness I'll walk out of here and leave you alone with that monk and his cleaver.'

'Yes.'

Markham was trying to remember who it was had said to him that Fouquert had the face of a Jesuit. It wouldn't come but the thought remained and it had resonance. You didn't need to know too much about history to realise how much death and destruction the Catholic Church had visited on the world. Priests had condoned, sometimes even carried out, the kind of work of which Fouquert had been so proud. It took no great leap of the imagination to see Monsignor Aramon in the same light. Both he and Fouquert had the certainty of a cause to sustain them, as they spread misery, poverty and death.

The monk was crumpled now, the words he was mouthing prayers rather than curses. Markham indicated that his men should cease to hold him and step back. It was just as well that he was stood between the monk and his intended victim. He didn't actually stop the headlong dive, but he did deflect it, so that the man had only just got his arms round Fouquert's throat before the four of them intervened.

It took several minutes to get him off and back to the far side of the room. Now it was Fouquert who was sobbing, demanding to be released so that he could defend himself. Markham was bent over the monk, repeating over and over again a request to be told what had happened. It came out slowly, in all its horror, loud enough for the perpetrator to hear, mixed with a repeated chant of the monks' sin of vanity, and cries to *le Bon Dieu* to lift the curse it had brought.

Most of the monks and priests had begged for mercy, some had even gone as far as to renounce their god rather than face the violence from the mob Fouquert had brought along. Not this monk! His vanity forced him into outright defiance. Faced with a handsome and proud man, who would not bow the knee to him, Fouquert had taken a torch from one of his men and, full of the wines looted from the cellars, personally burnt the skin off the man's face.

It had been done slowly, piece by piece, the eye that was missing going because the drunken torturer staggered and poked the torch too hard. The screams of pain and anguish only egged him on, The hair was on fire as he left the torch on the nose, so that what had been fine and patrician, ended up as the stump it now was. None of his men could understand a word of the explanation, but they could observe his growing pallor and wonder. And maybe they understood the pleas to God for forgiveness that punctuated the telling.

Markham had to fight back his own feelings. How could he explain to someone who'd suffered so much that he was to be barred from his legitimate revenge? How could he return this man to the level of piety and peace he displayed when they'd arrived? Even if Markham could calm him now, would he stay that way? He couldn't take the chance. They had to keep Fouquert alive, and it was with a voice as heavy as his heart that he ordered his men to tie the monk up.

Only when he said that, did he realise that Aramon was standing at the door. Filthy as he was, he still wore his ecclesiastical robes. And the man had presence. Markham suddenly realised that the monk had no idea that the Monsignor was here. He must have looked, standing in the doorway in the flickering candlelight, like the vengeance of the Lord personified. The one eye settled on that and the monk sank to his knees, begging forgiveness in a pitiful tone.

'Hand him over to me,' Aramon said. 'The man's soul is troubled. He requires the power of prayer, not the bonds of restraint.'

This was a real dilemma. How to explain the paramount need to keep a piece of scum alive; that he could take no risks with his life without even hinting at the information he had in his head, all that without even a hint at his intentions. It was as well that no one else knew them. He had enough difficulty himself in appearing ingenuous.

'If he does murder, it is his soul that will suffer in hell, Lieutenant, you know that.'

Markham had a happy thought then, of both the monk and Fouquert in the eternal flames, with the former still in a position to inflict pain on the latter.

'Might I suggest, Monsignor, that he be left in peace till tomorrow, here in the stable with my men to guard him. In the calming light of day, he may be less disturbed.'

'It has merit,' Aramon replied, moving forward, 'as long as I can confess him.'

'You would do that here?'

'It is obviously not perfect, but if you will not release him what choice do I have?'

'The sanctity of the confessional is too sacred to break. If you give me your word that you will keep him from harming himself or others, then you may take him to a quieter place.'

'Thank you, Lieutenant,' said Aramon, genuinely surprised.

The Monsignor looked at Fouquert, which made Markham's heart jump. But the words he used soothed that.

'I should confess you too, monsieur. But I heard what this poor creature said and understood some of what he suffered. I cannot, in all conscience, deny you the sacrament. But I will risk Our Saviour's wrath by delaying it until tomorrow.'

'I have no need of your superstition.'

'You do my son. If what I have heard here tonight is even half-true, more than anyone else.'

'I burnt God out of that man's head.'

'No!' the monk screamed, the ugly head shaking.

It was now Fouquert's turn to shout, trying to get the words out before Aramon got to him. 'Do not deny it, monk. You denied Our Lord to save what was left of your face. You . . .'

The sentence was never finished. For the second time, mouthing on this occasion some Latin form of eternal damnation, the Monsignor hit Fouquert, this time dashing his head against the stone of the wall. Markham had moved too, and was just in time to save a second blow by grabbing the cleric's arm. As he pulled with all his might, only just managing to stop Aramon, he wondered if all men of the cloth were gifted extra strength by their faith.

'Why do you protect this filth?'

Markham couldn't answer, and for once he could not look Aramon in the eye. The priest violently threw off his restraining hand and turned back towards the doorway. Gently, he raised the monk to his feet and, with an arm around his shoulder, and soft comforting words about the behaviour of St Peter himself, he led him out into the night.

Fouquert was out cold, a long, bleeding gash on his right temple where his head had struck the wall. Markham had to call for water and bandages to bathe and cover the wound. He came round while he was carrying that out, shaking his head and groaning.

'I want them dead.'

'Shut up, Fouquert.'

He repeated himself in a louder voice. 'I want them dead! If you do not help me I will find a way to lose my memory.'

Markham grabbed him by the front of his shirt, nearly raising him bodily off the ground, his voice harsh and uncompromising as he shook him back and forth.

'You parcel of shite. You are going where I take you, and when you get there you will tell them what you know. If you don't the only thing that will stop them from hanging you will be my request to bring you back here, light a big fire, and leave you with that monk.'

Weeping was the last thing he expected. But Fouquert began to cry genuine tears, the fluid streaking down his face, unable to wipe it away because of his tied hands.

'You've no idea how sick you make me, Fouquert,' said Markham sadly, before pushing him roughly back against the wall. 'Sergeant Rannoch, let's get the guard details worked out.'

It was still hot when he woke to take his turn of duty, the sky having clouded over to trap the heat of the earth. He went round with Halsey, changing the piquets on the forward wall, sending the men relieved to sleep, wondering, in the stygian darkness why he'd bothered. Gone was the huge moon that lit the landscape like day. He couldn't see the ground in front of the walls, let alone the edge of the forest.

'No lanterns,' he snapped at Halsey, when the old corporal requested them, a statement he repeated to each man in the last piquet of the night, Yelland, Dornan and Bellamy. 'They will show for miles on a night like this. Stay still, and if you hear anyone moving about the password is Garry Owen.'

'Can we ask for it to be whistled?' asked Yelland, his face no more than an indistinct white blob. It was Markham's favourite air, one he'd marched to as a young man through those Carolina forests.

'Just as long as you don't do it in reply, Yelland. I heard you whistle, and it may sound like a tune to you, but it sounds like music being murdered to me.'

Halsey sniffed. Unable to whistle at all himself, he was taking what he was saying as a continuing rebuke. It wasn't meant like that. Markham felt Halsey himself should have thought of a password, but the old corporal hadn't and there was nothing to be done about it. Perhaps the man they called Daddy was too soft for his own good. He knew himself how difficult it was to stay awake when you could see absolutely nothing, unable even to move around lest you fall of the parapet and into the courtyard.

Markham had to feel his way down the wooden staircase, the old man behind him, then practically feel his way along the walls to get back to the stable. Markham had rigged the half-burnt altar cloth so that when they came to make preparations to leave, they could do so unobserved. But as a screen to block out the light from the stable it did just as well.

'We've gone too far, surely,' he said.

'Lost ain't in it,' growled Halsey.

Markham put out a hand and touched the corporal's shoulder. 'Let's retrace our steps.'

He must have been still smarting from the perceived rebuke, since he, normally the kindest of men, positively barked at his superior. 'Don't see how, as I ain't no blessed cat.'

Holding his shoulder, Markham was able to grip it. The sensation of someone nearby, apart from Halsey, was overwhelming, a kind of slight swishing sound as skin rubbed against skin. But the corporal misunderstood the squeeze, and started to talk in a loud querulous voice.

'It ain't no good you getting on your high horse your honour, and it were ever so.'

'Shut up, man.'

Now Daddy Halsey was hurt. 'And there's little need to go talking like that, your honour.'

Markham squeezed harder. 'Did you hear it?'

'Hear what?'

'Listen!' He did, but indignation had made him breathe with feeling, and if the sound was still there that was enough to smother it. 'I heard someone close to us, I'm sure.'

Now the tone was all vindication, plus a good dose of I would have told you so if only you'd listen. 'Man could walk right by, Frenchie an' all, and you'd never know it, not having the use of a lantern to shine in their heathen face.'

'Let's find the stable, and get you to sleep before you commit a flogging offence.'

That produced the gulping sound of words being swallowed, plus a backward movement. Halsey had been a marine a long time. He'd served under every kind of officer, some of whom would have flogged him senseless for speaking, never mind disagreeing. The way he'd talked to Markham with that type would have seen him broken at the wheel. He could not know, as he fretted his way back to the stable, how much it pleased his officer that he felt free to do so.

They found the stable eventually, led there by the sound of snoring. Once inside, Halsey was quick to get his belt off and his head down, not once looking an amused Markham in the eye. But the old man saw his officer take a lantern, and rig a cloth to shade it, so a sniff of approval was proffered as a peace offering.

'Reveille at five, Halsey,' Markham whispered.

'Christ, your honour, it will still be pitch black.'

'Don't worry, there will be no trumpets. But when you're woken, I want you to be ready to move out in light order before dawn.'

He didn't ask why, or where they were going. Like the good marine he was he just said, 'Right, sir.'

The shaded lantern didn't show much, just the ground in front of his feet and the edge of the wall as he made his way to the entrance to the church. A breeze was springing up, a hot wind from the south that made things worse rather than better. Inside the church it whistled through cracks and crevices, stirring loose objects, that banging he'd heard on first arrival once more audible.

The vestry was well lit by the larger type of church candle, and as he entered Markham was surprised to see Germain sitting up in the cot, a quill in his hand, scribbling away on some of the fine vellum that had in the past been used for manuscripts. The light made him look very pale, and what he had undergone had sharpened his features, so that his visitor felt as though he was being gifted a vision of the older man that Germain would eventually become.

He looked up and stopped writing as Markham entered, greeting him with a weary smile, then pointed the lifted quill to the paper beneath him.

'My despatch, Markham, which I hope you will deliver for me to Admiral Hood.'

'Sir.'

Germain lay back against the tapestry pillows which had been placed to ease any discomfort, his eyes closed. Markham peered then, glad to see that the reason appeared to be fatigue rather than pain.

'You will deliver it for me.'

'If I can, sir.'

'You must,' he replied without much emphasis. 'I am relying on you.'

Markham felt awkward, unwilling to tell a lie but knowing he must. It was with a huge sense of relief that he heard Germain's next words which relieved him of the need.

'You said you intended to leave some of your men with me. I think that would be unwise.'

'Reluctantly, sir, I am forced to agree.'

The eyes opened, and Germain stared at him. 'This was, I perceive, a decision you'd already arrived at?'

'No sir. But it was something I was going to ask you.'

'And if I had not been conscious.'

'Then I would, reluctantly, have had to operate on my own instincts.'

There was a pause while Germain digested this. When he spoke, it was accompanied by a thin smile. 'I am glad they are of the right order, Markham. When do you leave?'

'It is my intention to go before dawn, sir, in about three hours' time. The Monsignor and his party should be asleep.'

'I will, no doubt, have to explain your actions to them.'

'That is something, sir, which I am sure you will do well.'

'Has anything happened about the Avignon treasure?'

'Nothing yet. You will have realised as I have that de Puy holds the key.'

'Indeed.'

With the voice suddenly weakening, Markham was unsure as to whether that was an affirmation or a question. He decided to treat it as agreement. After all, it made no difference now.

'I fear he is playing that advantage for all he's worth. The Monsignor has condescended to him enough to deserve it. He has stated that nothing can be done in the dark, and settled down to get a good night's sleep, with Aramon's servants taking it in turns to watch him.'

'So he intends to recover it tomorrow?'

'I assume so.'

'After you have departed.'

'Yes. What you must do, sir, is try and keep them here until you are well enough to move.'

Germain stiffened then, a flash of pain crossing his thin face. Markham realised he had spoken in too harsh a manner, and sought to soften his tone.

'By then, matters between the French and our allies will have been settled one way or the other.'

'And you will earn a knighthood.'

Markham didn't believe that for a moment, though he was favoured with a vision of himself wearing a red sash across his chest bearing a Bath star. Nor could he tell if that was said matter of factly or in bitterness. He was tempted to point out the dangers, and evaluate the risk of getting killed before garnering glory. But he reckoned that Germain would see that as churlish, so he set out to be as cheerful as he could.

'Why, sir, there will be great credit due to you for getting us this far. And should you succeed in bringing Monsignor Aramon and his Avignon treasure out, I'm sure there will be rewards at home, as well as at St Peter's, to gladden your heart.'

'Please don't try to cheer me up, Markham. Just let me finish this despatch.'

'Sir.'

He pulled himself up, blinking as he opened his eyes. Then he set to with the quill, writing swiftly. Markham's head dropped forward, and he was nearly asleep, that is until the captain reached the point when he signed, this achieved with a great flourish.

'Pass me that wax, Markham?' he asked, as he carefully folded the vellum.

'Of course.'

Germain took the wax, held it to the candle, and then tipped it so that the melted drops hit the point at which the folds met. His ring must have been taken off earlier, because he lifted it from his side and pressed it home, before examining the result and holding it out to his marine lieutenant.

'There you are, Markham. And if you wonder why I have sealed it, that is to save your blushes.'

'My blushes, sir?'

'I assume you are like me, and would not want to see the praises of you that I have sung. I have told them of your exploits, Markham. I would not want you honoured without my personal endorsement.'

189

Markham was embarrassed now, and quite overcome. Their relationship, though short, had not been easy. And what about the man doing the deed? Germain was gauche, rather than malicious, prone to error through enthusiasm not stupidity. Determined to shine because of that burden that he, Markham, knew so well. To think ill of the man was the act of a base creature, and he was not going to be that.

'Thank you, sir. Thank you very much.'

Chapter sixteen

The faint glimmer from the well house caught his eye when he was about halfway across the courtyard. Like the stables that contained his sleeping men a cloth had been hung to contain the light, but the material was thin and ill fitting, which left a bright border round the edge, and the barely discernible shadow of a moving body inside.

He was drawn towards it like a moth to a flame, tiptoeing without realising it. He peered through the gap at the edge, and was gifted with the sight of Ghislane Moulins, stripped to the waist, standing over the rim of the well wearing only her shift, bathing and singing softly to herself.

There was a delicious thrill in watching her unobserved as she raised one hand high to rub the wet cloth over the downy hair of her armpit. The breast he could see was shaped like something off an ancient Greek statue, perfectly formed, firm underneath and smooth on top, though instead of being white it was a warm honey colour, with the aureole of her nipple a dark enticing red. Her young waist was tight, with not an ounce of extra flesh, each rib below her slowly moving hand clear and defined, even in shadow. With the light behind her, her shift was almost see through, and the shape of her thighs and legs were silhouetted, and looked every bit as enticing as what was naked.

The stab of guilt at watching her like this was no more than that, easily submerged under the delight of a healthy man watching a more than beguiling woman. The temptation to throw back the cloth and just walk in was almost unbearable. But he couldn't do it, on the good grounds that if he did she must suspect he'd been there for some time.

The argument in his mind, spoken, would have taken a day. In his imagination it was but a second. She was attached to Aramon by duty, desired by de Puy, yet had made it plain to him that she found him attractive. He examined that for traces of his own vanity, as well as hints of the temptress on her part. It was no great feat to put them to one side. All George Markham's considerable experience with women told him he was right; that Ghislane Moulins was his for the asking, and that despite her youth, she was no stranger to the delights of love-making.

She finished her wash, but instead of taking up the damp dress that was hanging over a broken shutter, she merely wrapped herself in a long shawl and stood over the well, looking down as if trying to see the water below. Now that she was covered, walking in was easy. There was a simple rule that had served George Markham well all his adult life. In any seduction that would eventually prove mutually satisfying, someone had to make the first move. It had been his great gift never to stand upon his dignity on such occasions, accepting that if the humiliation of rejection followed his advances, then that was a price worth paying for the numerous successes he enjoyed. He unshaded his lantern, so that the full light showed, then firmly pulled back the sheet.

'Forgive me, Mademoiselle,' he cried, feeling, as he declaimed the words, like the worst kind of ham actor. 'But I saw the light and came to investigate.'

The sheet had dropped behind him, and the small room, with her long candle and his lantern was full of light. Now it was up to her. She could show outrage and demand he leave her in peace, claim the right of privacy and allude to the idea that he was no new arrival. If she did he would go, not through fear but through a desire to show respect to her right to choose. Too many men, to Markham's thinking, failed in this very moment, advancing too fast as though all the privilege to make decisions were theirs.

'I was hot, Lieutenant Markham, and I could not get to sleep.'

A bit formal, but promising. Time to be bold. He moved forward to the opposite side of the well, feeling the heat of his hands drain into the cool stones.

'I must confess to you I saw the light a good two minutes ago.'

There was no shock in her voice. 'You have been standing outside watching me?'

'I must confess, I have.'

'You confess more than Monsignor Aramon.'

'Would that I had cause.'

Their eyes were locked, and he could see the small hint of movement at the corners of her lips, the hint of humour that was a positive plus. You could never seduce a woman, if you couldn't make her laugh.

'I think, monsieur, that you are a stranger to shame.'

He moved again, not far, but enough to indicate that the circumference of the well was not absolute.

'Sure, Ghislane, I'm Irish, and God save us, we don't know the meaning of the word.'

That made her laugh, her head going back to reveal that beautiful throat, the action pushing those nipples against the shawl. It was at times like these that Markham marvelled at the acuteness of his observation. If he'd had a half an ounce of that on the battlefield, he would be the most successful general in the world.

'Then you admired what you saw.'

No objection to the use of her Christian name. Another important point negotiated. Now it was his turn to laugh, that mixed with words that had to be both flattering and self-deprecating.

'Admired, is it? Why only the stone of this round wall here keeps hidden just how much I admired you. Sure, Ghislane, I'm not certain the rocks, even tied as they are to my mortar, will have the strength to withstand the pressure.'

'There is a bucket of cold water here, Lieutenant.'

'George!'

She dropped her head then, as though that was too much. But she also blushed, which gave the lie to that.

'This bucket of water. Perhaps you could use it. I'm told it is the perfect remedy for too much ardour.'

'Cooling that is the last thing I want to do.'

She bit her lower lip, a bad sign, and he knew why. Ghislane Moulins was tempted, the blood coursing through her veins just as fast as it was racing though his. The risk she ran was something only she could calculate, and only she could overcome. He had no idea the nature of Aramon's hold over her, and what the consequences would be if having succumbed to his advances, she were then found out.

He was leaving before dawn, attempting to do something that might cost him his life. It would be easy to say that if any man had a right to comfort it was he. Nothing would persuade him to plead that case with Ghislane, and that had little to do with subterfuge. He wanted to take her, but not by pleading. If she consented, it would be because she wanted to, not for some specious reason to do with his notion of self-sacrifice.

He moved slightly, just enough to pressure her into a decision, and was both gratified and stimulated by the way, without raising her head, both her arms dropped to her side, letting the shawl fall open, and revealing both of her beautiful breasts. He covered the three paces between them, and had his hands on the flesh of her back, before her head had time to fully come up and meet his eyes.

The real intimacy of lovemaking, especially when it is successful, happens after the event. Talk changes from the guarded, upright and tense, to the languid, horizontal and revealing. Markham, lying on the remains of her clothes and his uniform, found out more about Ghislane in the five minutes after he'd pleasured her, than he had in the previous week. He felt the same as she did, drained. But the words she'd said, just after they climaxed, were to him the real badge of honour achieved.

'No one has ever done that for me before.'

Post-coital languor is no good for personal defences. It is hard to find a subtle and untruthful answer to give to someone who has just surprised you by the depth of your own, newly discovered sensations. Markham asked questions in the same state of both mind and body. She could have lied to him about why she was here and he would never have noticed.

'I am the bargain.'

'In what way?'

'Monsignor Aramon gets the treasures that were once housed at the cathedral of Avignon. Le Comte de Puy gets me, though not as his concubine, but as his wife.'

'Is there a treasure.'

'Oh yes, though not to the value that the Monsignor would have you believe. Certainly there is plate, precious objects and jewels. But they could be old bones to him.'

Markham was thinking of those boxes, and how much Aramon could get in them. 'But valuable?'

'To a man involved in a desperate search for influence, they are very valuable.'

'He resides in Rome now?'

'Yes.'

He hardly needed to be told of the politics and intrigue that surrounded the Holy See. Rome had always been held, even by the faithful, to be nothing more than a cesspit. Into that had come Aramon, a man of influence in the Avignon he had been forced to leave, a nobody amongst the cardinals and other senior clerics that inhabited St Peter's. He needed to draw attention to himself. What better way than to return the stolen treasure of a papal fiefdom to the rightful owner.

'He will be taken into the bosom of the man who has the power to elevate him.'

'And you too are tradable commodity?'

She wasn't offended by that, but replied in a very matter of fact way.

'I am an orphan. Though educated to be accomplished I have no money and no position, nor do I have the aptitude to be a nun.'

Markham ran his hand over her belly, the flat and hard surface of a young woman who'd never had to think of her shape, and had certainly never borne children. But she was not a virgin. But then neither was she really adept at the art of lovemaking. The idea of teaching her was something he found quite appealing.

'If you were a nun, Ghislane, I would be after taking holy orders tomorrow.'

It was, considering the proximity of Aramon, a tactless remark, something he knew as soon as he'd said it. But although she noticed too, she made a joke of it.

'I've had enough of holy orders this last year in Rome.'

'I cannot imagine the Monsignor as a considerate lover.'

'He considers only himself. Luckily, since we arrived in Corsica, I have been spared his more intimate attentions.'

'And de Puy?'

There was an element of sadness in her reply. 'He does nothing but look, Markham.'

'Yet married bliss beckons.'

'He is no beast, nor is he the type to excite a woman. He has estates in this area that were abandoned in '91, and some hope that he may regain them. If a king returns to the French throne, he can look forward to advancement. The Comte worships me, and I am just good enough in my pedigree to make me acceptable.'

'You have a pedigree.'

'I was raised in the Nunnery of Santa Hildegard de Brescia. They are a special order, with a special place for children. Only the unbidden offspring of the best and richest families can gain entry to such an institution.'

'No written evidence of your pedigree then?'

Her finger slipped between his lips. 'Does that disappoint you, Markham?'

'Never in life, girl. If you want to have fun with a horse, a dog, or a woman, choose a mongrel.'

'And in the case of a man?'

'The same. And in my circumstances, the pedigree is perfect. I'm a bastard caught between two nationalities and two religions.'

'Even more of a mongrel than me.'

Markham rolled on top of her, looking down into the deep pools of those large brown eyes. 'And proud of it!'

They should have extinguished the lanterns. But passion drives out common sense, and they made love without thinking that, if Markham had been attracted to the light, so might others. The swish of the sheet being violently pulled back was enough to have both lovers pulling away from each other, seeking in vain to cover their nakedness. Aramon stood there, his bulk and black cassock filling the doorway, a deep frown on his face.

Ghislane was up, kneeling, looking at the ground, the shawl doing a poor job of covering her. Markham realised that he two was in a submissive pose, and deliberately stood up and slipped into his breeches. The Monsignor walked across to the girl, and touched her hair. Markham, expecting some kind of violence, stepped forward to protect her, only to run into his other hand. How much had Aramon seen? Had he stood outside and watched them the way he'd had watched Ghislane. Would a lie help?

'It was all my doing, Monsignor, I forced myself on her. Mademoiselle Moulins is entirely innocent.'

'Come, child,' the priest said, in a surprisingly gentle voice. 'Clothe yourself.'

'Forgive me,' she murmured, in a meek voice.

That tone of abject resignation surprised Markham even more. She had seemed so spirited just a few minutes ago. Yet he had to consider what he had concluded before, that if they were caught he would not pay anything like the price she would pay. This cleric had a hold on her future, and he had no idea how high his costs would be to her, a penniless orphan.

'It may be, in years to come, you will need memories like this to sustain you.' Aramon looked up at Markham, his eyes hardening. 'You on the other hand will, no doubt, forget about this the next time you indulge.'

He wanted to say no, to plead that he would remember every

detail of this night's encounter; her skin, her smell and the delicious pain. But he could not do so, without further compromising Ghislane. Aramon took her under the arm and helped her up, gently arranging the shawl so it served a better purpose, taking up her clothing and leading her out into the night. There was a way with him that the marine officer had never observed before, a tenderness of manner that seemed so out of character. It was almost as if he was the lover, and not George Markham.

Guilt at being caught *in flagrante* was multiplied by his realisation that he had neglected his duties. He should have kept in touch with his sentries, to ensure that they were awake and alive. As soon as he was dressed he grabbed his lantern, rearranging the shading, and went out through the doorway and hurriedly crossed the courtyard. The steps to the parapet were taken two at a time, which at least gave Yelland, if he was asleep, the chance to properly wake before he arrived. He found the youngster leaning over the wall, musket at the ready, massacring his marching tune with his incompetent attempt to whistle.

'Garry Owen,' he said, before the youth challenged him.

'Back to the stables, Yelland.'

'Sir.'

'We will be pulling out shortly, though say nothing till I inform everyone. Just wake Sergeant Rannoch and tell him to get ready. He will know what to do.'

Markham moved onto Dornan, who was still getting to his feet when his officer arrived. The man was incorrigible. But this was no time to chastise him and he sent him after Yelland.

'Bellamy.' There was no reply, so he moved the cloth that covered his lantern just enough to show the stretch of parapet the Negro was supposed to be guarding. His voice was much louder, as seeing nothing, he called out again. 'Bellamy, damn you.'

Still no reply! 'If this is some kind of joke to show the nocturnal superiority of the black man, you sod, I'll have you flogged till your hide is bright red.'

Markham pulled the cloth off completely and, lantern raised, traversed the whole area that Bellamy had been detailed to cover. He examined the wood of the flooring to see if there was any trace of a struggle, or, God forbid a spot of blood. There was no trace of anything. The man had gone to sleep somewhere, like the useless article he was, neglecting his duty in such a blatant manner that Markham would have to severely punish him.

No considerations of like and dislike could be allowed to interfere with that. It was the worst offence in the book, if you took out rogering the Regimental goat. To fall asleep on duty was bad enough; to desert your post was tantamount to going absent permanently. The curses flowed as he made his way back to the stable, in his mind's eye a vision of a bloody-backed Bellamy hanging from the wheel of a gun.

Markham stopped suddenly, realising that if Bellamy had gone to all the trouble of finding somewhere out of sight, he had no way of looking for him. To send out his men to search would only wake up the people they intended to leave behind. He knew he would go regardless, but it would be so much easier to depart without a scene. The last thing he wanted as he crossed that field was Aramon's curses ringing in his ears. Worse than that, knowing it to be the best means of escape, the cleric would probably follow him.

'Bellamy has disappeared,' he told Rannoch quietly. 'Snoring somewhere, I'll wager.'

The Highlander replied in that slow careful way that drove Markham to distraction sometimes. It seemed the more agitated he was the more deliberate became the Scotsman's tardy mode of speech.

'He might be with that Negro girl, Renate, seeing as how they were so very friendly.'

Markham was about to state what an offence that was when he recalled his own adventures. 'I will go and look.'

'Do not go getting caught in her chamber,' said Rannoch, grinning. 'I doubt you would be believed if you tried to explain it away.'

'Just get the men to lighten their packs.'

He spoke loudly, to make Rannoch's job easier, in case anyone was tempted to argue with him.

'And that is an order I have cleared with Captain Germain, who will be staying behind. They may take all the food they have but they must not overload themselves with water. All their spare kit is to be abandoned, shirts, boots and greatcoats. The man who takes the flares and tubes is to spread his equipment out amongst the rest. We will be moving at the run, and anyone who falls behind will be left to die in the forest.'

He pushed out into the night again, stomping across the courtyard until he realised that his own footsteps risked causing the very noise he feared. Slowing down, he dropped his lantern on the ground as he approached the cell into which Dymock had shown Renate. It was dark inside, nothing showing through the same kind of sheet that had covered the well house. He quietened his own breathing, so that he could listen out for others. There was no trace of anyone, so edging the lantern closer, so that it spilled a little light, he fingered the sheet back a fraction and peered inside.

He was loath to go without Bellamy, though if he'd been asked to explain why he would have been at a loss. It was certainly nothing to do with his soldierly qualities, nor indeed his too often displayed erudition. But Markham hated to lose a man, even a useless article. He would have acted the same if it were Dornan.

He could see the makeshift cot the marines had rigged for her, but it appeared to be empty. Cursing Bellamy with real venom he lifted the lantern, pulled the sheet right back and edged in. The place was empty. Not only of Renate, but of Bellamy too. There was no trace of the Negro girl's bundle, which she carried so elegantly on her head. That, he concluded was none of his affair. She could be anywhere. Perhaps she and Bellamy had found another less exposed spot to conjugate.

'Nothing,' he said as he re-entered the stable. His Lobsters were lined up, ready to go, though it was clear they were deeply unhappy about the pile of spare kit that had been piled up in the corner. Rannoch had even untied Fouquert, who, with a white bandage round his cut head looked like a Barbary Pirate.

'No noise as we leave. Stay well clear of anything you might strike your musket against. We will make for the woods and get out of sight before daylight, that way the people we leave here will not know how far we have gone and make no attempt to pursue us. Captain Germain has undertaken to explain to them what I am now about to tell you.'

Their eyes widened when he told them what Fouquert had. Men who had taken wagers on how long it would be before he dangled were now faced with the primary task of keeping him alive.

'It doesn't matter who gets through, one of us or all of us. This man must be taken to where the information he has will be of use.'

'Will they hang him then, your honour?' asked Dornan.

'I doubt it,' Markham replied grimly. 'They will probably make him a Duke, and gift him a huge pension.'

Fouquert, who had very good English, was smiling. But that was wiped off his face by Tully. He had been one of the first men Fouquert had met, outside Toulon, and he no doubt remembered that the then soldier had a penchant for misuse of the bayonet.

'Then why don't we beat everything he knows out of him, sir, and impale the bastard on a stake.'

'He would lie to us, Tully, even in death. He's the type. But I want him roped, so that he is attached to both the man in front and the man behind.'

'That is not necessary. We are on the same side now.'

'Jesus!' exclaimed Markham, 'that will be the day. Tully, search him in case he's acquired something sharp.'

'Pleasure.'

It was a rough handling, with Fouquert seething, as every part of his anatomy was checked for a concealed weapon. Markham meanwhile checked his own kit, throwing out all that was superfluous. The last thing he did was feel inside his shirt, to ensure that the package Fouquert had given him, and Germain's despatch were safe.

'It would be an idea to check the courtyard before we move,' said Rannoch.

Markham nodded and the sergeant went out the doorway, moving with a silence born of long experience. The rest of the men waited, their breathing the only sound to fill the stable, until he returned and pronounced the way out to be clear.

'Single file, lads, and slow on my command. Stay close enough to see the belt on the back of the man in front. If you get lost, you are on your own.'

Rannoch killed the light and they stood for several seconds, adjusting their eyes to the dark. Markham went first, calling softly for them to follow. To him, the noise sounded horrendous, heavy boots scraping on the hard, packed earth. But he reasoned that he was listening for it, and that to anyone asleep, it might register enough to disturb their slumbers, but would be gone by the time they were fully awake.

The compass was, in this light, useless, but the sky to the east had the very faintest tinge of grey at the base, just enough to show Markham his direction. As long as he had that on his left he was heading due south. The ground was still in darkness though, and that caused men to stumble, their muffled curses evidence of their high level of discipline.

He tried to calculate, by his memory of the rise and fall of the ground, how close he was to the woods. He knew that they were at the crest of a hill, and that he would be close to them when that became a steep incline. Yet there was a sense of disorientation in the dark, with no fixed object to give him a point of reference. Even that grey line was deceptive, and he knew that if they were going to get to their target, it would not be in a straight line.

Then the ground became really steep and he knew he was close. He called back to warn Halsey, right behind him, bidding him to pass it on, just as he scrambled up the last of the embankment and felt the first twig of the bushes brush his face.

'Halt ten paces inside, and wait,' he ordered. 'You men on Fouquert, keep a tight hold. Stay still until it is light. If you can see the church buildings retreat further back until you are out of view.'

It seemed to take forever for the light to increase, and much as he was tempted to move, Markham stayed still. To try and negotiate the forest in anything but full daylight would be madness. It wouldn't be easy then, especially moving at the pace he intended to set.

It was an hour before they could see each other clearly, and make out the details of their surroundings. Markham had them eat as soon as they could, insisting that they split their rations with the Frenchman.

'He's no good to us dying of hunger and thirst, lads.'

'Nor am I tied like a hog.'

That was true. They couldn't move fast with Fouquert roped. He would snag on every branch that he passed, also holding up the men detailed to run with him. Markham was going to be forced to trust him, and that was an uncomfortable notion. Yet it had to be acknowledged that much as he hated him, Fouquert's only hope of survival was to stay with them. Last night he'd been tied in the stable to avoid him coming into contact with the others. Now the question had to be asked; was he just roped because of habit?

'Cut him free.'

Markham moved forward slightly, to look back at the buildings. In the grey dawn he could see Aramon standing in the open gateway, his eyes ranging over the shallow hills and towards the forest. A group appeared behind him, de Puy and the Monsignor's three servants. They turned right and the cleric joined them, seemingly heading to an empty part of the hillside with a spare set of trees too far apart even to merit the appellation copse. Yet there was something visible in the midst of the trees, a black dot, not a bush or a tree, that looked out of place.

The telescope brought it into sharp focus, a studded set of double doors, quite wide, set into the steepest part of the hill, and partially screened by trees. That made him smile. He'd anticipated that whatever it was they sought had been buried, and would take a lot of work to recover. One sight of the burned buildings, added to the Frenchman's sanguine response, was enough to tell anyone with half a brain that it was not in any of them. And de Puy had used this very instrument to sweep the valley floor.

But de Puy had been clever. What was it Aramon had said? It had been brought here on the backs of men and could be taken out that way. A burial place would have required men to dig, witnesses to the fact that something valuable was being interred. Even the men who brought the treasure here would not have known its final destination. De Puy could have placed the goods himself, leaving his own men to suspect they were still in the church. And they were as safe as they could be while still above ground, even from the people Fouquert had incited to burn this place down. Who would go into an ice house, even to loot?

The Frenchman had no idea, when Markham turned round, why he was laughing at him. But the idea that this man, who so prided himself on his brainpower, had missed such a prize was amusing. He knew they should leave, there was ample light now, but he swung the glass back in his desire to see the Bourbon officer's triumph. Perhaps Ghislane Moulins would not have such a dull existence after all. A man who could bait Aramon like that, had to have something in his favour apart from innate courtesy.

He was puzzled when the group emerged, with Aramon waving his arms, clearly in dispute with de Puy. Something was wrong. Perhaps he hadn't been so clever after all. But Markham had no time to wait around and speculate. It was full daylight now, and time to go.

'Move out,' he called softy, beginning to jog, 'and take your pace from me. Choose your own path, but do not get out of sight of the men to the right and left of you.'

Chapter seventeen

Progress was good, with his Lobsters moving quickly, unencumbered by the normal heavy packs. The sky had cleared above the top canopy and the light was perfect, dappled shafts of gold streaming through the leaves and branches. Given two dry days the ground underfoot was hard again, the water from the thunderstorms either run off, evaporated, or drained into the soil.

Going downhill was so much easier than climbing up, and not constrained by the need for silence, one or two of his men occasionally laughed as one of their number tripped or slipped. The mule tracks that had been obscured in the ascent seemed strangely obvious now, an avenue they could easily follow, brushing aside the encroaching vegetation.

The manic tinkling of the cowbell was taken as no more than a distraction, with Markham wondering why the animal had come into the woods, away from its natural pasture. But he knew that cows were stupid creatures, the word bovine applied to anyone slow and dense, and their only wish it seemed to be somewhere else, wherever they were at any given moment. Obviously they had scared it into panic flight, so it was no bar to their progress.

It was the single musket shot that made him haul up and slither to a stop, the sound reverberating around the hills, crack after crack as though it was a timed volley. His men halted too, some quicker than others, with only Fouquert jogging on, until a muffled shout stopped him. Markham had an ear cocked, and began to retrace his own steps. He found the cord fifty feet to his rear, stretched between two bushes, no more than six inches off the ground, one end now loose where it had been kicked clear.

A trap laid by a clever man who had worked out that marines must head for the water, to get back to the ship that had brought them here in the first place. Instead of filling the woods with infantry, he'd realised that coverage of all the available avenues was impossible. So he'd marked the obvious trails, assuming that his enemies would use them, and set his troops wide apart, to cover a vast area, the single musket shot a signal to indicate the point at which they should concentrate.

To proceed or fall back? And if the latter, to what? Markham told everyone to rest, and called for Rannoch. He had no time for private thoughts; whatever he extrapolated from the situation needed another mind to sound off against. The Highlander proved his worth before Markham even opened his mouth.

'Quinlan, Ettrick, go straight left. Use your bayonets to mark a route on the trees. There will be another avenue down, another gully where the water has worn the soil away. One go up and the other down. Look for cord or twine or even thread. If you find it don't touch it, but come straight back and let us know. Tully and Yelland do the same to the right.'

'A trap?' said Markham.

'I do not doubt it. And it is clever.'

'They must guess that we have Fouquert.'

'Leaving that coat has backfired. They would not have gone to all this trouble for us.'

'What is going on?' demanded Fouquert.

'Your enemies have laid a snare to catch us,' said Markham, with an almost humorous tone, because he couldn't admit his own chagrin to this man. 'And damn me if they haven't succeeded. They are so keen to get your putrescent head on the block of the guillotine that they are gathering from east and west at this very minute to bring about that happy event.'

'We must run.'

'We must wait,' said Rannoch, without looking at Fouquert. 'And it would do us all good to remain silent.'

That's what they did, kneeling, listening, waiting for the return of the four men Rannoch had sent out, half afraid that they would not do so. The rustling undergrowth had every musket raised, aimed at the source of the sound, until the sight of a red coat took the fingers off the heavy Brown Bess triggers. Tully and Yelland returned first, the youngster carrying a slim piece of twine.

'I cut this right next to the bell, without making a sound. It was an old shell casing for grape, with a stone suspended inside.'

Markham looked at Rannoch. 'How far apart would the sentinels have to be?'

'Not too close with the racket we made.'

'So?'

'They will not rush into the woods.'

'But they will concentrate on the lower slopes.'

'I would!' said Rannoch with a rare display of passion. 'There will be more bells below, and they will funnel us into a dead end well before we reach the flatlands near to the shore.'

'We must go on,' said Fouquert.

'If you want to die keep talking,' snapped Markham. Then he turned back to Rannoch. 'This has told them all they want to know. Even if we could evade them, they will set a watch up to look out for a ship, and with men lining the shore they are bound to observe our signal to *Syilphide's* cutter.'

Rannoch was silent for a moment, and when he responded his voice was grave. 'There is little point then, in continuing to rush downhill.'

'Our only other route is through two armies.'

Rannoch smiled, a rare thing, the whole of his square face changing shape. 'At the very least, one of them will be friendly.'

Fouquert had moved closer, to listen to them conversing. 'This is madness.'

'Born of necessity,' Markham replied.

'It is not your neck on the block.'

Markham gave him a wolfish grin and pointed a languid arm south. 'Feel free, if you wish, to continue on your own.'

'They will be moving across the hill, those men with muskets,' said Rannoch.

'So if we move up the hill?'

'On the same line we took down, that will open the gap.'

Markham was sick of alternatives, craving for once the simple notion of an enemy he could see, and a position he could advance on, with troops to his right and left committed to mutual support. Flags waving, bugles blowing and massed volleys full of flying death suddenly seemed preferable. This situation was too full of imponderables. To split his force, drawing off the French while a small party went east with Fouquert. To stay still, and hide out for a whole day in the woods hoping they would pass by; to try and fight his way through to a beach on which the cutter couldn't land?

'We go back,' he said suddenly.

There was no way of knowing what was the right decision. The only thing available was the lesser of several evils. The old adage about living to fight another day was paramount in his thinking, the notion that, having had a trap set for him, he must somehow contrive to turn the tables on his enemy and set a snare for them.

'At the double?' asked Rannoch.

'Light infantry pace if we are going to get out of this.'

There was no shouting, just a wave of the arm. Markham led the way, trying to spot the route by which they'd come, a task made more difficult by the compound factors of the opposite view of every hedge and bush, allied to the fact of moving uphill instead of down. Behind them, for a long time, there was no sound. Then a bugle blew. Markham suspected that the men who had been waiting to trap him had realised he wasn't coming and had set off in pursuit.

They burst out of the woods right in front of the church building. Aramon, de Puy, Ghislane Moulins and the trio of servants were heading away on a diagonal line that would take them due east to Piedmont. The sight of a dozen Lobsters and Fouquert bursting out of the forest, at first had them spurring the two horses into a gallop. But the red coats soon registered, and they came to a halt.

Markham was met by a string of curses the like of which would keep Aramon in the confessional for a week. De Puy merely greeted him with a look of utter disdain. Not even Ghislane had anything approaching a welcome on her face. Perhaps she felt doubly abandoned.

'You deserted us, you low-life putrescence,' Aramon barked. 'Sneaking out like a thief in the night.'

'Captain Germain surely explained.'

'How could he, in a fever?'

'He was fine last night. In pain certainly. But I spent a lucid hour in his company.'

'Well he is far from it now,' snapped Aramon. 'One must suppose an hour of your company is enough to cause a relapse in a saint. And how can I believe you when you say you spoke with him last night? The poor man is incoherent and near to dying.'

There were drums beating he forest in now, played by men set apart to act as monitors for the line sweeping the woods. Very soon that line of troops would emerge into the open, and when they did, the only hope he would have was to drag Aramon off his horse, mount Fouquert, and send him off at gallop. The less pleasant prospect was that he should go with him, and Ghislane

Moulins was astride the other mount. The only other alternative was to stop the French advance.

'You have deserted the people who were entrusted to you, quit your own superior officer, and it seems the very cause you are commissioned to serve.'

Rannoch poked his musket into Aramon's stomach. His three servants moved immediately to aid him, but the determined look in the Highlander's eye soon stopped them.

'Do be a good gentleman and cap a stopper on your mouth.'

The cleric was shocked, but Rannoch was not fazed by his outrage. He continued as slowly and deliberately as he always did. 'If you have in your head a way twelve men short on powder can confound a regiment of French infantry, the notion would be most welcome. But I suspect you have not, so silence on your part will serve us all.'

'This man has the French army plans for the invasion of Italy.'

He was pointing at Fouquert, who for some reason seemed to shrink from the attention. It was the act of a man who knew everyone present wanted him dead, and who had no idea where the next threat to his life was coming from.

But de Puy had responded to that, his head jerking round, which was the first outward sign of life that Markham had noticed. But he looked away again as their eyes met, a seeming oasis of indifference. Maybe they'd found the treasure after all, and he was now feeling detached, looking forward to the delights that a night with Ghislane Moulins would produce.

'You have proof,' demanded Aramon, brushing the point of Rannoch's musket away.

'I have neither that nor a choice. I must either take your horses and race for the border, or find some method of stopping that infantry.'

'*Garda*,' appealed Aramon, a cry that immediately had his servants drawing their pistols and crowding round their master. If they'd never quite looked like servants before they looked even less the part now.

'Monsieur le Comte,' barked Markham, ignoring them, which was easy since his men had their muskets aimed right at their chests. The sad eyes turned slowly on to him, but de Puy didn't speak. 'You told Captain Germain of the danger hereabouts of a forest fire.'

'I did.'

'Do the conditions still prevail?'

'They are more delicate now than they were immediately after the rains.'

Markham wet a finger and held it up to catch the wind. It was still southerly, still hot, strong enough to rustle the very top branches of the trees, not perfect but then it would just have to do. As he did so his eye caught that of Ghislane Moulins, and he was somewhat thrown by the way she immediately pulled a face and looked elsewhere. What was the matter with the girl? He hadn't promised her anything, had he?

'Flares,' he snapped, in a voice rendered even angrier by her behaviour.

Dornan had them of course, and no one had bothered to relieve him of his own kit. If there was duty going that required no thought and extra effort, then he always got it. The equipment for the blue lights wasn't heavy, but it was awkward, not the sort of thing any trooper with brains would want to transport. Yet for all the ribbing he endured, and all the pranks that were played on him, his good humour rarely slipped, and he never lost the affection of his comrades. That made him think of Eboluh Bellamy.

'Set them up,' he shouted, before posing a question, which had suddenly come to mind, aimed at Ghislane. 'Where is your maid, Mademoiselle?'

'Run off,' answered Aramon, the only one of the trio to show any outrage. 'It seems to be a disease you have introduced, which has contaminated even the most faithful.'

Aramon must have caught the drift of Markham's reasoning. The cleric scanned the faces of his men, and when he didn't spy the very obvious countenance of the Negro, his lips became compressed, and he emitted a loud sniff of conclusion.

Dornan and Gibbons were spreading the tripod and attaching the twin tubes, while Corporal Halsey and Leech were fusing the rockets. If they were curious as to what their officer was up to, it had no effect on their work. And the drums beating in the background, growing louder by the minute seemed to be something they could safely ignore. Halsey, satisfied, nodded to his officer, then slipped the first of the rockets into the tubes.

Fouquert could not wait. The tension and that drumming sound was too much for him. Typical of the bully that he was, he rushed for Ghislane's horse. He moved too quickly for those close to him to interfere, and he was on her, grabbing the folds of her dress in an attempt to haul her from her saddle before they moved. Rannoch switched his musket in his hands, so that the stock was swinging. It caught Fouquert behind one knee, which was enough to dent his balance. Ghislane kicked at the same time, and he was sent flying back to land in a sobbing huddle.

Markham was by the flare tubes, bending down to align them. Designed to fire straight up into the night sky, and to illuminate a target, they were a chancy instrument for what he had in mind. He lowered the elevation as much as he could, so that the assembly was lying at an angle of forty-five degrees, with the waxed paper fuses hanging from the rear.

'Sergeant,' he said.

The Highlander was well ahead of him. He already had out his flints and match. He struck until there was a flame, which was then applied to the fuses. They spluttered into life, burning slowly down until they connected with the main charge of powder. At the critical point they exploded, sending the rockets straight to a point just above the line of trees. Both missiles sped over the top branches, fizzing and spluttering, erratic in their course, the trail they left a crazy whirl of spreading smoke. But Markham knew they would land in the woods, still alight, the phosphorous powder they contained designed to burn bright for several minutes. If that didn't set the forest alight nothing would.

He didn't hang around to find out, instead ordering his men to move out. Aramon immediately began to move off in front of them, and nearly earned himself a sharp rebuke to get out of the Lobster's way. Oddly, de Puy and Ghislane had not stirred, and he saw them exchange a glance that hinted at some form of communication. Then the Frenchman gave the most imperceptible of nods, and Ghislane hauled on her reins. There was a temptation to leave them all behind. But then Markham reckoned that the case for taking the horse had not altered, and if his ploy with the rockets did not produce the desired result, then that would be his final act. That would especially be the case if they faced more cavalry. Abandoning his men would be hard, but he had no choice.

Looking back, he saw the first trace of smoke rising through the treetops. Where had those rockets landed, in front of the French or behind? His aim was the former, so that the spreading flames would set up a wall of fire that they dare not try to cross. The wind would fan the flames until the conflagration reached the edge of the fields. What happened then, he could not tell, but it might be that the entire forest would have to burn before the end. If he was in command of those French troops he would get out of the woods pretty damn quick!

The first sign that they might have done their work was the silencing of the drums. There was a long silence before the trumpet blew again, and Markham was sure that what he was hearing was the sound of the French army being recalled. Now they were all jogging along, Aramon's servants included, two of them hanging on to the straps of the horse, the other its tail. Ahead of them, in the clear morning light, they could see the outline of the hills that rose towards the distant Alps, still capped, no doubt, with snow. That was all they had to get across to be safe.

Markham was working on the theory that whoever was in command of those troops had taken up his position on the southern slopes to catch him. He'd had the impression from the previous day of units which, while much more numerous than his own, had finite resources. Several factors pointed to this; the lack of more cavalry, the way that Lieutenant Andoche Junot had halted his men rather than take heavy casualties, and finally the method used by whoever was in command. He had spread his men thin, using bells rather than sheer manpower to trap them.

If that put them on the other side of that blaze and they like him were on foot, they could not move at a much faster pace than he. And as long as whatever gap he had was maintained, he'd have time to asses the situation when he came up, as he inevitably must, against the fighting troops on the border.

'Fouquert,' he said, his breathing heavy, the map he was trying to read while still moving bouncing before his eyes. 'You know the dispositions of the French forces, which route will take us out with the least risk.'

The Jacobin renegade was reluctant to answer, that was obvious by the guarded expression on his face. And he tried to take immediate advantage of the request by demanding that he be allowed to ride.

'What? Let you on a horse. You'd be off and running before you got a second foot in the stirrups. So stop bleating and answer my question, or we'll never get out of here.'

There was a long silence, if you allowed for the sound of pounding boots, before Fouquert answered. 'The army set to march on Piera Cava through the Gorge de Vesbule is no more than a thin screen.'

'It is a feint then.'

It was like drawing teeth getting an answer, but it came eventually.

'One of them. But that is the obvious route for the Bouche de Rhone army to take if they wish to invest Cuneo, which they must do before they can advance on Turin.'

Markham called a halt, lined his Lobsters up to the rear, and told everyone to take a drink of water. Huge clouds of smoke covered the western horizon, blown north on the wind, evidence that the forest was truly well ablaze. But he put that out of his mind and concentrated on showing Fouquert the map he was using, which ran out just to the east of the Grasse road.

'Point me to where that is.'

Fouquert traced a route with his finger, one that was going due east then hooked up slightly.

'Distance?

'To the point where the armies are facing each other, some three-and-a-half leagues.

Markham translated that into twenty or so miles. A long way for men on foot under a hot sun. 'So the Piedmontese defences there would be relatively heavy?'

'Bonaparte thinks so, and he must have good reason.'

'Spies?'

Fouquert nodded, and Markham presumed that in the placing of those the ex-representative on mission had taken a hand.

'Do you think the forward elements of the French army know of your downfall?'

That stung the man, the word 'downfall', and for a very brief second the cruelty that was his abiding trait evaporated to show something less hideous underneath, something almost human. But Markham wasn't moved to any form of pity by it. If he ever softened on Fouquert, all he had to do was conjure up an image of burning buildings, that scarred, deranged monk, this man, and a torch.

'News spreads fast,' he responded gloomily. 'And there will be a reward if it is known I have escaped.'

Markham was thinking twenty miles and more, of which they had covered perhaps two or three. It was a long way to go. But up ahead the country started to break up, no longer undulating and open, but hilly and wooded. That might add length to their journey, but it would also conceal them from view. All they had to do was to get across the Grasse road without being observed.

'Monsignor, Mademoiselle Moulins, I suggest you dismount and walk the horses. They will be of no use to anyone if they are blown.'

Aramon complied, handing the reins to one of his servants. But she did not, immediately. Again Markham had the impression of a form of silent communication with de Puy, a need to check with him that what was being requested should be obeyed. Watching the pair, he realised that they were a great deal closer to each other than he had supposed. And suddenly Markham had a very good idea where Bellamy might be.

It was the absence of Renate, of course, as well as the Negro marine. The assumption he and Aramon had made was the same. That the pair, attracted to each other in what they perceived to be a hostile world, had taken the chance to desert both unit and mistress. And that interpretation made a great deal of sense. When would either find themselves in a territory when her mistress and his officer could not pursue them? Revolutionary France might be in turmoil, but what better place for two such as they to choose?

'Move out, walking pace, and keep a sharp eye out for anything human. They don't have to be soldiers to tell the men pursuing us where we have gone.'

He took point himself, leaving Fouquert to the tender care of a delighted Tully, who informed the Frenchman that every stumble and he would feel the tip of his bayonet. Markham was half inclined to interfere with that. After all, if they did work a miracle and get through, Fouquert had important information. They would have heard of him, the Piedmontese, but they would take gratefully every scrap of information he had to offer.

And Fouquert would be just as keen to give it to them, that being the only thing that would save his neck from a rope. He might even be in a position to distribute a share of his rewards. But Markham stopped himself from thinking along those lines. The man was just using them. Once he got where he wanted to go they would be dropped like a hot stone, and the swine would hog to himself whatever was going.

'Make it two digs, Tully, one for me and one for you.'

Determined to be watchful while out front, he nevertheless could not help remembering everything that had happened from the day that they'd set out from Corsica. Ahead he saw the first hint of the road, a snaking line that ran between trees, and also disappeared into deep hollows. There was a simile there, since it was hard for him to stop his mind wandering down blind alleys. But he struggled though the maze of conflicting facts, assumptions and impressions, until he felt he had arrived at a logical solution. That didn't make it right, but it made some kind of sense, which was a great deal more than could be said for what seemed like the surface story.

'Coach, your honour,' said Rannoch, who certainly had the best eyes in this complement of Lobsters.

'Where?' asked Markham, angry with himself that he had, despite his best efforts, allowed his mind to wander.

Rannoch was pointing north-east. 'It was coming down that hill, but it has just gone out of sight in a tree-lined valley. I reckon that is the route ahead, by that line of poplars. So we must either go to ground here or find some cover nearer the road.'

'You're sure it was a coach.'

'It might have been a wagon.'

Markham was actually aware that they had a long way to go, and precious little to sustain them on the way. 'With food?'

'I cannot say in truth. But it is possible.'

'We must find out. Take the men on and line them up to intercept from behind the trees.'

'Fouquert?'

'Keep him with you. Just make sure he's not killed.'

He then turned to face the others, addressing his orders to Aramon.

'Please stay here and remain dismounted. We are going forward to intercept some form of horse-drawn conveyance. It may be carrying some kind of food.'

'Then take my servants,' said Aramon.

He and his party had started out with even less than Markham, and the Monsignor was a man fond of the comforts of his belly. Hard tack and water, which is what he'd been on for two-and-a-half days was not much to his liking.

'Will your servants be of any use?'

'They are more than mere retainers, Lieutenant.'

'Are they indeed?'

'They are members of the Pope's Swiss Guard.'

He wasn't surprised. He'd seen them as too fit and alert from the first. And they made the journey without complaint, as befitted the mercenaries with the best soldiering reputation in the world. But his reasons for agreeing were not those of necessity in terms of armed numbers. It was another one of those exchanged secret glances between de Puy and Ghislane.

'They may go on if they wish. Tell them to take up a position beyond my men. If the conveyance gets past, they must make a move to stop it. Since we cannot be too careful, I would also appreciate your presence, Monsieur le Comte.'

'You will forgive me if I decline, Lieutenant. I'm afraid that the idea of killing my fellow countrymen no longer appeals.'

'It's not that, is it, my friend?'

'The ambush?' said Aramon.

'Will be carried out by my sergeant without my help.' Markham said, before turning back to face de Puy, at the same time easing Fouquert's double-barrelled pistol from his belt. 'What I am more concerned about is how I am going to recover the person of Eboluh Bellamy.'

'Who?' asked de Puy, looking confused, as if the name meant nothing to him.

'Tell me Monsignor, when did the count inform you of the location of your treasure?'

The memory clearly revived Aramon's anger, judging by the deep scowl on his face. 'This morning at first light, when he awoke from his interminable slumbers.'

'And had he told you last night, would you have actually waited till daylight?'

De Puy had gone stiff and was deliberately not looking at him.

'Of course not. I would have taken a lantern to the ice house and dug it out.'

'Well, monsieur,' Markham said, his eyes back on the Comte de Puy. The man declined to reply, so he continued. 'Very easy for two Negroes to move around unseen in the dark. All they had to do was disrobe to become near invisible. You had distracted the Monsignor and his men by going to sleep, and such was their mistrust and anxiety that they would not let you out of their sight.'

He turned to Ghislane.

'But Bellamy needed time, so you were sent to distract me. I must say you succeeded beyond the Comte's wildest imaginings.'

Aramon's jaw had dropped. From behind Markham came the sound of shouting, that followed by a shot. He moved sideways, enough to see that the coach was stopped and surrounded by red coats. He waited a moment, but since no further shots ensued, he returned his attention to Ghislane, though careful to keep what was happening on the road on the edge of his vision.

'I hope you mixed business with pleasure, Mademoiselle. I certainly did.'

De Puy was looking at her in a strange way, not willing to believe the import of Markham's words. He would not say anything outright. It was for her to confess rather than for him to reveal. Even having been taken for a fool, he had to admit it had been enjoyable. And with no other information to work on, he had to believe that what she had told him about her situation the previous night was true.

'All I want is my black marine. The treasure I care nothing for. That is a matter for the Monsignor.'

Feet were pounding to one side, with Yelland yelling at the top of his voice. 'Your honour, Fouquert's been shot.'

'Damn!'

'He ain't dead, just winged. It were his own damn fault. Oh! And we've got that dwarf of an officer you had words with at Toulon. He's the one who did it.'

'Bring the horses!' he shouted, then set off at a run.

Chapter eighteen

There was a crowd round the coach, of his men as well as Aramon's servants, with Fouquert lying half in and half out. He recognised Bonaparte immediately, even in his black, gold-trimmed general's uniform, complete with the broad tricolour sash. That sallow skin underneath the large flamboyant hat, the piercing, small black eyes and that air of the fanatic that seemed to surround him.

He was standing with two lieutenants at his side, away from the coach, the trio covered by a pair of muskets in the hands of Quinlan and Ettrick. They were tense, but he looked unconcerned to be so threatened, as if no one would dare to harm him.

Markham pushed through to examine the wounded man, seeing the blood that had stained his chest and spread to cover the front of his shirt, mingling with that which had dripped on to it the night before. Rannoch was to the side of him, pressing a cloth to the wound to stem the flow.

'It is not a wound to kill him. The ball is not lodged, but he will need the services of a surgeon to stitch him properly nonetheless.'

'What happened? How did he come to be in the line of fire? The man's a coward.'

'We stopped the coach without much bother. The men on the seat were not like to be brave faced with a dozen muskets. Then Tully and I went to one door, while the priest's so-called servants took the other. I think the three of them saw the situation as hopeless, right off, for even with their pistols out, they declined to fire.'

How long, thought Markham impatiently, as Rannoch meandered though his tale at his usual slow pace. But he kept the look of interest fixed on his face so as not to offend his sergeant.

'Then they got out. Yon little fellow in the middle was just about to hand over his pistol when that stupid sod Fouquert let out a screaming curse and went for him. The officer raised his pistol once more to defend himself and this is the result.'

'It didn't occur to anyone to shoot him?' asked Markham, jerking his head towards Bonaparte.

'Fouquert was in the way.'

Markham slammed an angry fist against the side of the coach.

'How in the name of Jesus, Joseph and Mary are we going to get him to Piedmont with that kind of wound. He will lose too much blood just moving. Get him off the road and into the coach.'

His eyes went to heaven, before settling on the little Corsican general. Suddenly he smiled. Why take the dancing bear when you could take the handler? It was an entertaining notion. Bonaparte had drawn up the plans for the invasion of Italy. He knew more about them than Fouquert did. There was one obvious drawback! The man wouldn't speak. But perhaps he could get him to confirm that the exit route Fouquert had chosen, through Gorge de Vesuble, was indeed lightly manned.

'See if there is any food in the coach. If there is share it out. And Rannoch, keep an eye on the Comte de Puy and Mademoiselle Moulins. If they try to sneak away, stop them.'

That produced a look of wonder. But if Rannoch expected to be informed why, he was doomed to yet more disappointment. Markham turned away and went over to where the two Londoners were covering the French officers.

'Christ, look at this hamper,' he heard Leech cry. 'There's enough grub in here for a regiment.'

Markham still had his loaded pistol, and he re-cocked it.

'Go and eat, you two, or there will be nothing left. Tell Sergeant Rannoch to post a guard up and down the road. They are to stop any traffic, and take possession of anything they think we might need.'

The pair needed no second bidding. They were gone and Markham was alone with the captives. He nodded his head, in what was meant to be a slight bow.

'General Bonaparte.'

'I know you. We have met.'

'Toulon, monsieur. At a place you called "The Battery for men without fear". That night I tried to destroy it, but you were waiting for me.'

Bonaparte turned half right and left. 'Allow me to name my two aides, Lieutenant Andoche Junot.'

'I think we too might have met,' said Junot. 'Or at least spoken to each other.'

'And this is Lieutenant Auguste Marmont.'

'Sir,' said Markham, returning Marmont's bow.

'Forgive me, Lieutenant, but I cannot recall your name.'

'Markham, sir. George Markham.'

Bonaparte said 'Ah!' Then he looked at the filthy scarlet uniform, and the aiguilettes on the shoulder. 'That is a marine coat, is it not?'

'It is.'

'I recall you as an infantry officer.'

Markham produced a wan smile. '65th Foot, sir, but not much loved by my colonel. I was rewarded with this for my actions at Toulon. Though I am forced to admit you seem to have done very much better out of the siege than I.'

'I was told that there was a party of British marines around. I am forced to enquire why you are so deep inland?'

That was sophistry. He could not know the real reason. But with Fouquert lying there bleeding like a stuck pig, there could be little doubt of what he was up to now, his being in the company of the man who'd stolen his plans.

'That, sir, I cannot tell you,' Markham replied, playing out the game.

'I thought you would have been captured by now.'

'We marines are elusive types.'

Bonaparte waved an arm to the billowing clouds, far off but still visible through the trees. 'You?'

'Yes.'

'Tell me what you did!'

It was like an order not a request, delivered in that staccato voice he remembered, which given their respective situations was damned odd. But then the man was deranged. Markham obliged, not forgetting to acknowledge the clever idea of rigging the cowbells.

'You were lucky to have those flares. What would you have done if you had been without them?'

'Used my imagination, sir.'

Bonaparte was not the type to laugh. The nearest he got was another loud exclamation and a wave of the arms to include his companions.

'There you are gentlemen, spoken like a true soldier. I should have taken charge personally. You would not have eluded me.'

'You are sure, sir?'

'Very. I too have imagination. I would have set fire to those woods as soon as I thought you were in them. Then my troops would have surrounded the area to ensure you could not get out alive.'

Halsey came up behind him, carrying food and a flagon of wine. Markham took it gratefully, and started eating, using the silence to collect his thoughts, before resuming his conversation.

'My task was to get that man to Italy.'

'Fouquert?'

'Who else?'

'I cannot see why.'

'Yes you can, General. He has your plans for the advance on Turin. He stole them. Your men have been chasing him for days through those very woods. If he can be got to Piedmont, you will have to call off your attack. And given the precise location of your troop strength, it wouldn't surprise me if the Piedmontese didn't launch a counter-offensive to push you back to your own French soil.'

Bonaparte positively smirked. 'They would get a bloody nose if they tried.'

'The question is, General, now that I have you, the man who actually wrote the plans, what am I going to do?'

'I suspect you are going to let me go on my way.'

'Sorry. It seems I must take both you and Fouquert through the front lines.'

'You would take that scum to safety?'

'Not through choice. I remember what happened in Toulon. I have also seen some of his handiwork since. Personally, I'd rather string him up to the nearest oak. But I made him a promise, that if he told me the details of your plan, then I would take him to a place where he would be safe.'

'As simple as that.'

'You arranged for a feint in the Gorge de Vesbule did you not, a thin screen of troops to fool your enemies into keeping their own forces there in strength.'

What surprised Markham was the way Bonaparte reacted. He should have tried to look unconcerned, as should his aides. But for him to actually laugh was play-acting of a different order. And Junot and Marmont produced genuine smiles.

'So he did tell you my plans?'

'Every last detail,' Markham lied.

'What a pity they are now of no use to anyone?'

'I admire a man who can bluff, General Bonaparte.'

The little Corsican reached inside his black coat, and pulled out a heavy packet of letters. 'You speak good French. How do you read it?'

'Passably well.'

Bonaparte shuffled through the pack, finally choosing one and offering it, his voice casual and conversational.

'This is the order from Paris, signed by Lazare Carnot, calling off the proposed attack on Italy. This one, also from him, is an instruction for me to proceed to join the Army of the West under General Hoche. He is controlling operations in the Vendee around Nantes.'

'Then you are headed the wrong way, General,' said Markham, taking the letters. He was genuinely stumped by the easy manner of their delivery and the allusion to the route was clutching at straws.

'I shall go via Marseilles to visit my family, then proceed to Paris. There I will take hold of Carnot's nose and twist it for daring to suggest that I serve under a peasant like Hoche.'

Both his aides laughed in a rather sycophantic way, at what was clearly a joke they'd heard before.

'I am not without powerful friends in Paris, Markham.'

The object of that remark didn't care what he had in Paris. He was reading the first letter, which was a copy of an order sent to the Commanding General in the South, Sherér. And it said exactly what Bonaparte had claimed. That the invasion was to be abandoned, and the army to march back to Marseilles to be available for other duties.

'We shall invade Italy one day,' said Bonaparte, his tone bombastic. 'And that is an assault I will lead personally. Then we will not have any of the palpitations that have afflicted that old fool Sherér.'

He couldn't have contrived this, and no amount of wishful thinking on Markham's part could make it so. These letters were official, of that he was certain, just as their meeting on this road was coincidence. Not even the most fertile brain could conjure this one up.

'Sergeant Rannoch?'

'Sir,' he replied punctiliously, in a voice designed to impress these Frenchie officers.

'Is there any luggage on the coach.'

'Plenty, sir. I would say all the kit these three officers need for a long journey.'

'A copy of the plans Fouquert stole are in my writing chest. You can take them if you want. Examine them and you will learn something about higher command, strategy and the movement of large bodies of troops. They are subtle but very, very clever.'

The voice changed to become hard again. 'Carnot is a fool. We could have had Turin like that!' He clicked his fingers loudly. 'Instead of that he wants me to go and do battle with a load of ignorant peasants in a stinking Loire bog.'

'What nonsense,' said Junot and Marmont in unison.

'And what of you, Lieutenant Markham. I doubt you can just walk through the Gorge de Vesbule. But if you stick to the high ground you should be safe. There are no longer any troops on the heights at all.'

'Then the Piedmontese will walk through and attack.'

Bonaparte spoke slowly for once, as if Markham was too dim to perceive the obvious. 'Not with the Army of Savoy to the North. They risk being outflanked. And they are not very good soldiers, you know.'

'And if I invite you and your aides to accompany me?'

'That would be foolish. Right now, no one will stand in your way. Take us and the country will be up in arms. You cannot just make us disappear. But maybe I can do you that favour. Yes, under certain conditions I can see myself letting you go on your road, without hindrance.'

'And what would those conditions be?'

The flippant tone vanished. 'Give me Fouquert.'

'Clever, General, You will take from me the only insurance I have, the man who knows your plans.'

Bonaparte smiled, a thin humourless affair that was not funny. 'But you said he had told them to you. Why do you need him?'

A clever man had trapped him. And he held in his hand letters that told him Fouquert had become superfluous. 'You said you had a copy in your writing case?'

'I do. Junot will fetch it for you.'

Markham nodded and called out to his men to let Junot proceed. It must have been handy, since he didn't even climb into the coach to get it. He just reached in and pulled it out. The case was made of fine polished oak, inlaid with the initial 'B'. Junot held it and Bonaparte opened it, extracting a thick sheaf of parchment tied at the right edge with red ribbon.

Markham took it, called Quinlan and Ettrick back to guard duty, then went back to the coach. Fouquert was lying flat out across one of the padded seats, alternately cursing and moaning, but definitely conscious. Aramon was on the other seat looking at him with disgust.

'Please help me, Monsignor. I want him upright.'

The wounded man cried out as they lifted him, somewhat over enthusiastically, to Markham. He would milk his pain, that was for sure.

'Do you recognise these?' he asked.

Fouquert peered at the sheets, with Markham flicking them so that he could read them. 'You have to tell me if these are the real plans for the Invasion of Italy. If they are, I can shoot those three officers and we can take written proof with us to the Piedmontese.'

Would he have got away with it if Fouquert had not been wounded. It sounded very flimsy to him. But the man had stiffened perceptibly at the notion of shooting Bonaparte, so Markham added the *coup de grace*.

'I'll even let you kill him.'

'That's them,' Fouquert gasped. 'The original of those I stole. Where's that shit Bonaparte.'

'Outside, awaiting his fate.'

'Give me a knife and tie his hands and feet.'

'You are wounded.'

'I will manage,' Fouquert spat. 'I shall cut off his Corsican cock first.'

'Lieutenant!' said Aramon, alarmed.

Markham pushed Fouquert hard, so that he flew backwards, and landed painfully. Then he stood up and leapt down to the ground, to rejoin the three French officers.

'Why do you want him?'

'He has to answer, in France, for more than theft.'

'And I doubt he's alone.' Markham replied, looking Bonaparte right in the eye. 'That is not enough.'

'Junot, Marmont, a moment if you please.' The two aides moved away, and Bonaparte dropped his voice to a whisper. 'I would not have them know that danger threatens. I have friends in Paris, I told you.'

'Yes.'

'No man at a time like this is without enemies. Carnot hates me, and he is a power in the land. Let me have Fouquert as a gift to my friends and I will have many, many more.'

'And I get a safe conduct in return.'

'I don't recall mentioning a safe conduct.'

'Nevertheless, it is what I want. And if I don't get one, I will take you and Fouquert to Italy, and shoot you both as soon as danger threatens on the way.'

At the back of his mind, Markham was examining what he was doing. The notion of handing a man over to certain death was unpleasant, until you accounted for the fact that it was Fouquert. He had killed thousands and would have chopped up every one of Markham's Lobsters for sheer pleasure. What he would do to him didn't bear too close examination. And by the sacrifice of that scum he could save not only his men, but the Monsignor's party as well. It made no difference what de Puy and Ghislane had done. He had to save their lives if he could. The Revolution was well practised at eating its own. One day it would probably eat Bonaparte.

'Very well. It is a bargain. Give me my writing case.'

Markham was so tempted to say 'get the damn thing yourself'. But this was no time for nit picking. 'I want one more favour.'

'What!'

'There is a wounded naval officer at the church of Notre Dame de Vacluse. He took a bullet in his shoulder from one of your infantrymen.'

'And?'

'He will, according to the last report I had, be too ill to move. I would like you to arrange for his safe passage to a point from which an exchange of prisoner cartel has been arranged.'

'Is he a gallant officer?'

'None more so,' replied Markham, truthfully, for if Germain lacked brains he didn't lack *élan*. If anything he had too much of that commodity for his own good.

'Then it will be an honour.'

The parting from Fouquert was noisy and unpleasant. But even if his conscience was pricked there was a feeling of cleanliness about getting away from him. The man contaminated everything he touched with his methods. Markham had never met anyone truly evil until he came across Fouquert. And Bonaparte eased matters by avoiding being vindictive. He obviously hated the ex-Representative as much as anyone. But he insisted in a solicitous voice that he must make himself comfortable and continue to occupy the whole of one seat.

'Never mind that we three are squeezed together, Fouquert. You are wounded, and I am looking forward to delivering you to Citizen Barras whole and ready for whatever pleasure he has in store.'

'May God damn you, Markham,' he shouted, the curse losing a great deal of force by his being in a prone position.

'What you have done is a sin, my son,' said Aramon, gravely.

'Don't call me your son, Monsignor. And just ask yourself whose neck you'd rather have on the chopping block, yours or his. Sergeant Rannoch, call in the piquets and see what we've got. Then prepare to move out on our original line of march.'

'I request a small deviation, Lieutenant,' said Aramon.

'To where?

Aramon looked at de Puy and Ghislane. The gap between them was more spiritual that physical, but it was there nevertheless, a coldness that was almost palpable.

'You told him about the well house.'

'No,' said Aramon. 'He asked and she gave him a truthful answer.'

'Would she have done that I wonder, if I hadn't smoked out what they were up to.'

'We will never know, Lieutenant.'

'Who do you think initiated this?'

'Only God will know for sure. Both were tempted, and that is a ghost that lies within us all, very close to the surface.'

'This detour . . .'

'Is to a hamlet called Coursegoules.'

'And why should I go there?'

'It will take you to your black marine.'

Who had it been outside his berth the night Germain came to see him? Clearly it hadn't been Aramon. That feeling he had the night before, with Halsey, of someone close. Was that Renate, Bellamy or both?

'What will happen to Ghislane?'

'I will take her back to Rome with me. She is a beautiful creature. She will not starve.'

'A beautiful creature who craves freedom.'

224

'Those godless heathens in Paris craved that, and look where it got them.'

Ghislane made a point of edging her mount close to him, in an attempt to engage him in conversation. He was stiff at first, but Markham couldn't sustain it. He understood too much about the need to escape from bonds past and present, and he flattered himself that the girl had gone further than she need to in the well house because of their mutual attraction.

She told him her version; that de Puy, first smitten by her, had been angry at Aramon's bargain. The Comte had suggested that they seek an opportunity to steal the treasure as a way of paying the Monsignor back. He wasn't sure he believed a word of it, but that made no difference. Where would the world be without the odd accomplished deceiver?

Ghislane didn't help her cause by allowing de Puy no good qualities, which made him wonder what would have happened once they had their loot and were clear of danger. If she had any regard for him it was now well submerged, while he was subject to subtle doses of flattery designed to make him feel very superior indeed.

Then the questioning started; about his background; London, Ireland, his relatives and his prospects. 'A soldier's life must be exciting.'

'It's not, girl. It is boring and badly paid.'

'I cannot go back to Rome,' she cried softly and plaintively, 'back to that life.'

'What choice do you have?'

'If you tell the Monsignor that you wish to take me with you. I'm sure he'll agree.'

'He won't.'

'Then don't ask him,' she hissed, excitedly.

George Markham was thinking it was a good idea he was marching and she was riding. If they had been closer, and especially if they been naked in a bed, he knew he would probably have succumbed. Even now, he was thinking of the nights he could spend with her before they parted company, a lubricious waking dream that was beginning to make marching awkward. He didn't know how to deny her, but he knew he must. His life was complex enough without further encumbrances. So he just burst out laughing, and felt truly rotten when she reacted angrily, and pulled the horse away.

'God in heaven, Georgie,' he said quietly to himself. 'She's not smitten with you after all.'

They had to wait outside the hamlet of Coursegoules, till a retiring column of artillery passed through. De Puy was close to Markham now, as gloomy as ever, looking down into the valley that contained the nest of buildings. The ground in between was wooded, with small, colourful, cultivated fields. Some were purple with lavender, others yellow and pink, full of the herbs that had once been used to make perfumed gloves for the high social classes.

De Puy was one of that class. They hadn't exchanged a word since he'd accused him, and that depressed Markham. He was never one to cast stones, and if de Puy had been tempted and fallen, as far as Ghislane Moulins was concerned he probably wouldn't be the last. What was he thinking now? Of her, or the treasure that he had so nearly got away with?

'Why here?' asked Markham.

'My family owned the land round Coursegoules, until we were proscribed as *émigrés*. There is also a small inn at the crossroads that was a tenant's.'

'You may get it back.'

'It has been passed to the people who use to work it on our behalf. It will take a miracle to get it back. You would not know this perhaps, since you can hardly be expected to care. But they asked the late King's brother, the Comte d'Artois, to recognise the rights of the people to elect a parliament on the English model. He demanded all that his brother owned be returned to him as the rightful King of France. He took the best chance we have of peace and threw it back in their faces. Now it will be war till we are all exhausted. And at the end, whoever wins, it will mean poverty for the likes of me.'

Perhaps Ghislane had been telling the truth after all, thought Markham.

'Will Bellamy be looking out for us.'

'Possibly not yet.'

'Sergeant Rannoch. You and I will enter the village alone.'

'But what of me?' said Aramon.

'Unless you think me also a thief you must stay here.' Rannoch had come alongside, and Markham and he discussed the route, using trees, dead ground and an embankment to get in without being observed. 'Make sure your musket is loaded, Rannoch. There might be French soldiers still down there, and if our man tries to run I want him brought down.'

'That's Bellamy.'

'I know,' Markham responded, sadly. 'But I have to take him in if I find him, you know that.'

'Aye,' Rannoch replied, in a rare show of brevity.

They moved as fast as prudence allowed, knowing that if the Negro was watching for them with anything bordering on efficiency, he could not fail to spot their red coats against the mainly lush green background. They reached the first building, a dilapidated barn, and used that to get them as close to the crossroad as possible. Then, taking a tight grip on his weapon, Markham stepped out, the tip of Rannoch's musket following him.

If the enemy was around, this was the moment of maximum danger; a loose shot fired off in fear before he could show them Bonaparte's *laissier passer*. There was not a soul in sight in the noonday heat, not even a dog, just some geese by a half-filled pond. Rannoch joined him when he signalled and together they walked down the road into Coursegoules. The houses were shuttered and silent, but there would be people watching, the locals, too afraid to come out and investigate.

'Is that the Inn?' said Rannoch.

He was pointing to a run-down place by the pond. The only sign that it might be so was the bench outside where weary travellers could, no doubt, remove their boots. They made their way to the door, and ducking under the low lintel, they entered a smoke-blackened room that was suffused with the smell of delicious food.

The woman that came out of the back was small and had once been a beauty. But hard toil and sun had turned her skin loose and leathery. She wiped her hands on her apron, and asked, in very heavy accent, what they required.

'Have you food there for eighteen?'

'There can be, if I am given a half hour.'

'Who is going to pay for it?' asked Rannoch, when Markham told him they were up for a good meal.

'That bloody priest can.'

This was delivered while still smiling at the lady, and he enquired politely if she had other guests. She shook her head, but the rubbing of her hands on her apron denoted a degree of anxiety. Markham came straight out and asked her if she'd seen two Negroes.

What followed was a long voluble explanation, which Rannoch couldn't follow, and Markham struggled to. Cut down to the bone, it meant they had stopped here, but only to eat and write two letters. They left her money, and instructions to pass the letters on to a very beautiful lady, and a tall man that she might recognise as the Comte de Puy. Markham was informed that she would not know the Comte from Adam, and that he was not welcome here in any case, what with him probably wanting back his land and property.

'The letters?' demanded Markham, in a loud voice.

She showed some reluctance so he fingered his pistol. As she turned to go Markham asked Rannoch to signal to the others to come in. By the time they arrived, he and Rannoch were sitting enjoying their second bumper of local red wine, feeling at peace with the world. His men waited outside, but Aramon, de Puy and Ghislane rushed in, to be greeted by Markham holding out two letters, one of them addressed to him.

'I forbore to open mine till you arrived. What intrigues me is that yours seems to be somewhat thicker than mine.'

De Puy opened the one addressed to him and Ghislane slowly, catching the five gold pieces that fell out. When he read it he passed it to Aramon. He in turn went puce as his head dropped down the page.

'They have stolen it and taken it for themselves, and they have the devil's cheek to apologise.'

'They ask that we send that on to you,' said de Puy, clinking the coins, 'by whatever means possible.'

The lady came out of the back of the inn, and having spotted Aramon she sank to her knees and kissed his hand, spouting what sounded like gibberish. He was led into the rear of the building, and no sooner had he disappeared than he was shouting for assistance. His servants rushed in, and they emerged holding fine gold caskets, with crystal glass on each side, inside which lay what looked like piles of old bones.

'The relics. That blessed pair left the relics, with my name and enough money to send a messenger to Rome!'

'This makes you happy I take it.'

'These, Markham, are what I came for.'

The Monsignor reeled off the names of the saints whose bones lay in these caskets, St Gobain, Lazarus of Nimes, speaking so quickly that half of them were lost.

'So you did not come for the gold and silver?'

'The church has much of that, and can when it wants get more.'

'Then I am pleased for you.'

Markham opened his and began to read.

My dear Lieutenant Markham,

You will be angered at my desertion, I am sure. But I beg of you to pause and consider the plight of a creature who carries more natural burdens than most. What could I hope for in His Majesty's service? With you, little in the way of punishment. I fear you are a poor officer, too kindly for the rank you hold. But others are less scrupulous, and it would only be a matter of time before I met a man who loved the lash. You will know, with my tongue, what the consequences of that would be!

So, as this opportunity presented itself, I had to take it. France will serve as a place to live, and if not that then Italy. The treasure Monsignor Aramon sought was not so fabulous, but it will allow Renate and I to live in decent estate, without providing the means to cut a true dash. I have left his relics in the care of the inn so that they can be passed on to him.

As to the lady and gentleman who arranged for us to steal it, I imagine they were sad. But they only have themselves to blame. Renate was easy to engage in conspiracy, but Mademoiselle Moulins' pursuit of me was masterly in its tact and subtlety. Who could not warm to a tale of love denied by circumstance, and be excited by the means to free two troubled hearts?

Yet our star-crossed lovers, even in felony, treated us as servants, never once offering a portion free from entail to the two people they needed most. What were we to do, acquire the means to make them rich, then serve them faithfully there after? What vanity!

Truly it is a strange world where people only see skin colour and not quality. You, it has to be said, were not like that. And for the rest, after we buried our initial animosities we managed to arrange a modus vivendi in which I sought not to annoy them more than necessary. It is my wish that they live and prosper.

That applies of course to you as well. And should chance put

229

you in my way, nothing would give me greater pleasure than to
treat you as an honoured guest.
I am, your most humble ex-servant,
Eboluh Bellamy.

'Jesus, Rannoch,' said Markham with feeling, 'I'm going to miss him.'

Epilogue

Markham stood rigidly to attention before Admiral Sir William Hotham, aware not only of the amount of light streaming into the *Victory*'s cabin, but of the straight white line of the ship's wake. It had taken a month to get from the French side of the Italian border to this place, and in that time Lord Hood had gone home, leaving the man at the desk in charge of the Mediterranean Fleet. He'd heard about Hotham; that he was timid, slow to action, and had let the French slip in and out of Toulon on too many occasions without offering battle.

He didn't look timid now, as he finished reading Markham's report on the events that had taken him from Corsica to France and back again. In fact he looked downright fierce, the eyes unfriendly even when he smiled. Writing it, Markham had been sure that any reader would be impressed. But now that he'd handed it over he was less sanguine. Every fault he perceived seemed to leap up at him from the overfamiliar text. Finally Hotham passed it over his head to his secretary.

'I have here a note from Lord Hood regarding promotion.'

'If I were to be granted that, sir, there is one favour I would very much like to add.'

'So you pleased our allies, Markham,' Hotham said, completely ignoring the inference.

'Yes, sir. They were grateful for the plans, even though they were out of date. A copy was made for our Ambassador, and have I believe been forwarded to Horse Guards.'

'A fine lot of good that will do. Those boneheads think they still use bows and arrows.' Hotham reached out for the other packet. 'And what is this, pray?'

'It is a despatch written by my commanding officer.'

'Young Germain?

'Yes, sir.'

'Know his papa quite well. We hunt together.'

'Is there any news of him?'

'Back in England, trotting around Bath trying to get back the use of his arm. Exchanged at Calais of all places.'

'He wrote that in great pain sir, right after he had been operated on to remove the ball. I fear it will not make easy reading.'

'A game lad, I recall. Always close to the stag.'

Hotham tore Germain's seal and began to read. He hadn't got far before the first 'My God' emerged. That was followed by a couple of 'damn me's'.

At first Markham thought them expressions of happy amazement, which made him wonder just how praiseworthy Germain had been. But when the admiral looked up at his visitor over the vellum, he wasn't so sure. And he was confirmed in that impression when Hotham finally said.

'You're a disgrace, sir, a damned disgrace.'

'Captain Germain assured me he was personally happy with my conduct, sir.'

'He could hardly tell you otherwise you blackguard. If he had, I doubt this would ever have been delivered. I have never read the like. Making arrangements to transport civilians behind his back, including some trollop to entertain you in your cot, undermining his authority with the other officers and interfering daily in the running of the ship.'

'Sir!'

'Silence!' Hotham yelled, the sound echoing off the deckbeams above his head. 'Don't think I don't know your name, Markham. I was anchored at Sandy Hook enough times during the American war to get sick of the sound of it. As for that father of yours . . .'

'My father is not here to defend himself, sir.'

That stopped Hotham for a moment, since the inference was clear. The son was, and any traducing by the admiral might cause more trouble than he could handle. The older man jabbed a finger at the vellum again.

'And what's this about buggering up a boarding party by calling for a retreat when the damn vessel was nearly ours.'

'That is not true, sir.'

'What? You're calling George Germain a liar.'

'I have no choice, sir. And might I be permitted to read what he has said about me so I can rebut the rest.'

'No, you cannot.' Hotham growled. 'I wish his pa were here to witness it. He'd horsewhip you.'

The secretary, who had previously served Lord Hood and had

seen Markham before, leant forward and whispered in the admiral's ear.

'What!' barked Hotham, before adding an angry, 'Oh, very well.'

The vellum slid across the round table, and Markham grabbed at it eagerly. The writing was a trifle spindly, only to be expected from a recently wounded man. But the contents were pure bile. Germain had managed to accuse him of everything but the flood; Fletcher's death during the aborted boarding; of trapping them, against his advice, on a hostile shore in deep forest; venery both sexual and fiscal in the matter of the Avignon treasure; deserting his superior officer despite specific orders not to do so. The only thing that was missing was the regimental goat!

In the background Hotham was muttering. 'Promotion. I'll see you damned, drummed out the service, more like.'

'I demand a court, sir.'

That stopped him. Markham had a right to that. No officer could be denied that.

'I should think you've had enough of courts, Markham. They don't always clear your name.'

That was when he finally cracked, his voice loud enough to match that of Hotham. 'I have always found battle a decent remedy, sir. Might I suggest the next time the French venture out, you try it.'

'Damn you for an insolent pup.'

The secretary leant forward again, and whispered urgently, his first request being for the admiral to lower his voice. There followed an exchange in which Markham only heard the words Hood and personal appointment, that followed by 'an insult to his flag'.

Hood was still the titular commander, and to cross swords with him was something Hotham would do at his peril. He'd already been lacerated by that scorbutic tongue, for the very thing Markham had just accused him of.

'All right, all right,' Hotham finally said, his impatience turning his face bright red. Then he looked at Markham again, in such a way that made plain that whatever pleading had been done in his favour, the admiral had not changed his mind one iota.

'You may have your court as soon as Germain is fit enough to return to duty and the Mediterranean.'

'That could be never, sir.'

'I cannot move mountains, and I have little inclination, I confess, to try. You will hold yourself ready for whatever duty I give you.'

Then he turned to the secretary, and hissed in a bitter tone. 'But don't ever put anything on my desk that even hints at promotion for this scoundrel.'

It was both blue eyes on him now, cold and furious. 'You may well find yourself guarding a prison hulk, Markham, which would be too good for you. Now get out of my sight. You are dismissed.'